$1.08

In a far future where humanity has evolved into a race of Twins who share one body, and the terraformed Moon has fallen toward the Earth so that Earth looms in its skies, Ard and Tared and Ask come to the Moon's harsh surface to seek Atwar, who was the first to arrive there. But Atwar has become something different, something hardly human, and the Moon is a harsh place to establish a family...

In *The Taming*, the poetic and redemptive final volume of an astonishing trilogy, Governor-General's award-winning poet Heather Spears continues the saga of the monocephalic dynasty founded by Tasman in *Moonfall* and continued in *The Children of Atwar*. *The Taming* follows Ard, Tared and Ask to the terraformed Moon. There, trapped in a harsh new world, they must struggle to stay alive during the extremes of the Moon's month-long days.

THE TAMING

BOOKS BY HEATHER SPEARS

novels
Moonfall*
The Children of Atwar*
The Taming*
*published by Tesseract books

poetry
The Danish Portraits
From the Inside
How to Read Faces[†]
The Word for Sand[§]
Human Acts
The Panum Poems
Poems Selected and New

[†]winner of the 1986 Pat Lowther Memorial Award
[§]winner of the 1989 Governor-General's Award for Poetry
and the 1989 Pat Lowther Memorial Award

poetry and drawings
Drawings from the Newborn

drawings
Drawn from the Fire: children of the Intifada
Massacre: drawings from Jerusalem

Heather Spears

THE TAMING

TESSERACT BOOKS
an imprint of
The Books Collective
Edmonton
1996

Copyright © 1996 by Heather Spears

All rights reserved. No part of this book may be reproduced or transmitted in any form or by any means, electronic or mechanical, including photocopying, recording, or by any information storage and retrieval system, without permission in writing from the author and publisher, except by a reviewer or academic who may quote brief passages in a review or critical study.

Thanks to the Canada Council Block Grant programme and Alberta Foundation for the Arts for publishing support. Thanks to Wayne Fitness and Screaming Colour Inc.(a division of Quality Color Press Inc.). Thanks to Daana Downey and Kim Smith at Priority Printing.

Cover art copyright ©1996 by Daniel Goldenberg
Cover design by Gerry Dotto.
Editor for the press: Candas Jane Dorsey.
Editorial assistance: Timothy J. Anderson. Inside design and page set-up by Ike at the Wooden Door, in Toronto and Palm Springs (True-Type Fonts) in Word for Windows 6. Printed at Priority Printing, Edmonton, on 50lb. Offset White with softcovers of Cornwall Cover and hardcovers in buckram with Luna Gloss dustjackets.

Published in Canada by Tesseract Books, an imprint of the Books Collective, 214-21, 10405 Jasper Avenue, Edmonton, Alberta, Canada T5J 3S2. Telephone (403) 448 0590. Tesseract Books are distributed in Canada by H.B.Fenn &Co., 34 Nixon Road, Bolton, Ontario L7E 1W2. Ph. 1-800-267-FENN.

Canadian Cataloguing in Publication Data

Spears, Heather, 1934-
The taming

Sequel to: Moonfall and The children of Atwar
ISBN 1-895836-24-7 (bound). --ISBN 1-895836-23-9 (pbk.)

I. Title
PS8537.P4T3 1996   C813'.54   C95-911248-0
PR9199.3.S63T3 1996

DEDICATION

to Simon

Prologue

*A*t first they appear to be kneeling, their torsos are so long, and the dresses of the two larger ones reach the ground. But the smallest figure has a short dress and look, he has oddly stunted legs showing under it—white as if gloved, or as if there were no flesh on them, and pressed tremblingly close together over large, dark feet. And now you can see that the two others are standing as well, as if painfully, on inturned feet just showing against the flat sward. Three very small figures if you see them from a distance, and their dresses the colour of distance, each with a wide sleeve out of which a single dark head emerges, on a stalklike single neck between unnaturally narrow shoulders. See, there is a streak of white clay down each face from brow to chin, as we traced it in the ceremony, when we gave them over to the journey and to Atwar.

Black, bald faces they have, staring out of the surrounding facehair that stars from their cheeks and brows into the heavier tangle of hair on their heads. And that hair is massy and uncut, the knots undone—only in the central figure is it still drawn back from the face, but the crooked curls have sprung free—it looks as if it had been burnt: this is the hair of her father and Tasman and all the western people who came among us. The other who resembles her has seemlier hair, the undone coil a heavy rope ravelling over one shoulder. They are surely sisters for their faces are identical, but the rope-haired one has a rounder look; her cheeks are more flushed, her mouth muscle redder, her faceskin, if you could see it close by, is like the petals of a black rose. She looks sick.

The third is much smaller, and skinnier. Even one-headed, he has almost the goodly aspect of twins—such a wide, unshapen head and bush of hair. Yet these faces have no narrowed inner cheek, no flattened temple, for they were born alone, without a twin to share that body, no second head to shape and be shaped against, as is the custom among us in the eastern World.

Yet these three faces are intelligent, and it must be

4 ○ HEATHER SPEARS

acknowledged that they have, like Atwar, their own kind of beauty (for we were become used to them in the World, having seen them often, and their father). This one, too, is much like the others; you would see that they are siblings bereft as they are.

Tasman was the first—birthfaulted, one-headed, resembling the Outdead of ancient times, when that race peopled all the World. They seeded the Moon, foresaw Moonfall, died. But their engines remained, small as a second skin, that none but they could have travelled in, until Tasman. Yet it was her crippled son Atwar who went at last, laughing.

And now these his children, born for this purpose, come to join him in the Moon. Ah, their heads we did not shape, but their legs we bound, from birth, that they would be as he was. We carried them ever in the World. But we promised them: You will walk as Atwar in the Moon!

They have bundles bound to their arms, and something that bulges, stitched inside their garments high against the breast. The boy's long fingers touch this burden under his headsleeve carefully, his arms very black against the blue garment. If you were to look into his eyes you would see that they are black with deep blue sclera, and set under an even, unbroken brow, and they dart to and fro–ah, the children are looking about them now, all three.

They stood still at first, when they had climbed down, as if struck silent but now they are restless. If you could see all that is behind them and around them, you too would find it very strange. The sward is not grass as you were led to believe but a hard, hot surface; it looks as if the shore's sand had dried together, with a dried-up tide of green algae to colour it—we have seen this lately in the World. But this green is more green as if it had cooked solid as rock; it is covered with tiny evenly-placed pocks or holes. It is the colour we call growth and there is no growing in it.

The surface is in shade but it must be hot because the children are moving their feet carefully now, lifting them away as if in pain. The boy moves one foot forward and sways—he seems to swim against steady liquid for a moment—and now his hands are splayed on the sward, he *looks as if he is standing on four equal limbs. His body tilts and then pitches slowly forward and slowly he rights himself and stares.*

Look behind them, and over them—there are the Outdead cars we prepared for them in the World, that have brought them here, their branches extending upward from their footbuds—what we saw in the World and called branches are now become as roots, and stand on the surface of the Moon. And the cars, the thickened stems of these dolls of trees, are meshed overhead—three of them, the door of the nearest one visible, an open blackness. For each of the children a car, that left us separately one after the other to merge in the trajectory, to lose its roots in fire, to fall in a webbed embrace into the Moon. There was a fourth.

We could not tell then, which one it was that failed, that did not rise with the others; any one of us could have guessed and been wrong, but that the interval of their going was even, with no pause. Three happy cars rose over us into the sky, with the Sheath's obsidian boiling and collapsing behind them. The surface imploded, the seething wave swept towards us, we ran up into the city. We will never find the body of the child who was left.

But now we would see his absence—Saska, the separate twin of the boy Ask, who is looking about him in vain for his brother. The girls' names are Ard and Tared and they lived.

Ask is moving off now, crouched and awkward, in among the pristine stilts; he goes forward on his four limbs as if he were walking on the bottom of the sea, pushing himself away, almost floating. His body glances off the stilts of the cars—he is foundering among them, his voice has an odd echo, a thinness, he is saying the first human word they have said or heard in the Moon, he is calling his brother.

If you were to look upward, beyond the cars, you would notice first the quality of the light, for it has a thickness, and fills a kind of well. The wall is a grayish shining substance, and rises steep around the peripheries of the sward, a vertical room against which the pale-dark grove presses densely, massy stems going up behind it to a great height, and then the green, a true green, an ardent growing. And that wall— if your eyes were to mount it, you would see that it is not quite transparent, thick and unyielding, like a tough membrane, almost animal. Close up it shines darkly, its swardside marred by long scratches. Near the sward it is black to a certain height, smeared with vegetable rot and decay. You would notice surely its ancient look, how it is stretched and puckered between intermittent black cables that hold it and run up tautly into the sky. Yet it seems to live! it trembles almost imperceptibly, gives off a faint humming.

If you looked over to the east you would see the low houses that crowd against the sward—these you would recognize, for we have watched them all these years on the screens: their flat, mute walls and roofs, their seamless angles, their sign in the True Speech, their one door. Ah—it is opened, but the children have not yet noticed it, they have not yet walked to it as Atwar did then, long ago, across the sward. Instead they are lingering doubtfully all three among the glassy stems of the cars—blue, black, their skinny bodies stumbling and blundering.

Ah, children, do not tarry! you cannot tell how long that door will be open to you, or that air last!

O

Instead, over and over, bewildered they are calling Saska's name. Their voices are like, childish, Ask's not yet broken by adulthood. That name they are calling has whispers in it, a whisper and a rising, a whisper and a desolate fall.

If you could look overhead, far above them and the cars, you would see the sky but it is clouded by a whitish cloud within and past the shining canopy. And the canopy stretches away over the treetops beyond the well you are looking out of—beyond the edges of just visible taut wire, where it seems to swell, with the whitish cloud clearing off against the outer darkness, a jet of dissipation. And that sky past canopy and spurting cloud is blacker than black, and you would be able to see in it the hard points of myriad stars. You would be aware, also, of the hurtful smudge of the sun, through the grove southwest of the well, while here below the sward is darkened in shadow. But the stilts of the cars rise out of the shadow, and their upper surfaces glint and blaze like sparks of fire.

And there is the old car, Atwar's! nestled black and

THE TAMING

derelict beside them, and just west of it, a clearer scape, as if brought sharply into the eye's focus—long gray-white roots and stems rising—you would be looking through a portal opening directly into the grove, the wall rolled down, and the trees pressing at its entrance, crowdingly.

○

And far overhead, ah you would have to be blind, not to be aware of his presence! It is our World, high and steady in the southwest, his waxing bowl whitely embracing the mud-blue ball of his night all dull and pallid against the midnight black of the sky. In that narrow crescent of brilliance you would discern at the cusps his bluish poles, his golden barrens where he swells into the Sheath. You would see the Sheath, the shadow, the crescent like a bright finger, admonishing and beckoning! If you watched for a time, you would see how he turns his face slowly into the light, his inexorable dreaming dawn.

You would have time! because he will hang there forever.

○

What will they see, as our World waxes towards Full, and shows his face to them whole in all his glory, shows his head, turning and turning? Ah, would you not desire as they surely will come to desire, when they have seen him and acknowledged him, some sign in the south?—you would envy the children their field of vision now, for it is Atwar's! they will be able to look for the sign of you southern folk past the Sheath, in whom we believe ardently, having received the gift of the birds in these last days! Whenever the World wanes and shows them his night, the children will see, perhaps, your fires.

They will see our fires in the City, blinking through space between the two worlds. Held in the arms of Atwar, they will look forth confidently, they will see how we watch for Atwar who lives in the Moon. With Atwar they will tend new fires, they will assure us Eating by Eating of this second seeding, this newest City.

○

Scholars of the World's antipodes! if you could be there, would you not long to see all these things come to pass?

I.
The Thickness of Light

Tared

It was a long time ago, this I am telling, and what was wonderful to us then is now familiar and ordinary. But there is no one else who can remember how it was in the beginning. Ard was sick and Ask sick with grief—they could only say, that the time was terrible—and so it was, for them and for me also. But it was also itself, its own time, which we did not tamper with—rather we suffered it, endured it and, as far as our tempers allowed us, wondered at it.

How can I make you see it as it was—everything we saw and touched and tasted? In our minds those first hours, and days of hours in the Moon were stained with the dye of our World's using, and yet, when we went into that grove, we were more stained than staining! If we made some impression, if we changed even then in any smallest way the seeded Moon, what greater changes was he making in us! Against us and in us! We were ignorant—what could we know of how to conform and exist there? What we were knowledgeable in, which was the World and the World's knowledge of the Moon, was of no use to us; so we were ignorant.

Yet everything was as it was. It was we who were the grit in his yeast, the speck in his eye.

○

So I must tell it as it was then, but I cannot help that it was my eyes that saw, with my mind's colour, my mouth that tasted.

We went into the forest. The trees were immeasurably tall, reaching to the very inner surface of that membrane that covered us and every thing. Their whitish stems, swelling out of the high roots that clung to them, were broad and flat—seen through the gate they had looked narrow, but when we came up to them, we saw this was their edges; they were broad as planks. Their skin was a shiny gray, quite smooth and hard, and there were no branches. High overhead, their elongated foliage spread level and floating—leaves, we had to call them but they looked most like flat strips of cloth torn at the weave, laid through and across each other in complex unpatterns of radiant shade and luminosity. No direct sunlight pierced that entanglement; it was a roof haphazardly yet tightly woven.

And everything below, the downward hurl of the stems, ourselves and the ground we stood on, even the thickish air, was washed in a green shadow. The air was very hot though we were in shadow, and humid.

Each tree was secured into the soil by an oval bulge of whitish roots, that seemed to hold it down rather than support it. The roots were like the long fingers of hands, narrowing as if to hold the stem by the fingertips. There was space under them—enough for us to go in between. The soil was very black, slippery and fine, like wetted dust. It clung to our feet as soon as we stepped on it. Squarish crumbled blades of leaf, and blackened lumps we did not recognize, were mixed into it and gave it some purchase.

Inside the forest, the thick air blurred the more distant stems. They were not absolutely straight, but crossed each other vaguely, with the air between them. Here and there rose a black stem, a cable, like those around the sward, so taut and vertical that we knew it to be Outdead-shaped from ancient days. And farther overhead to the west was a big uneven blur of greenish blackness, like an absence; but we did not know then what it was.

The sun's smear stayed past the leaves like a hardening of the light, but from inside the grove we could no longer see the World—ah, we had seen him wordlessly from the sward, as we wandered looking for our brother Saska, not regarding what time had passed. We had turned aside into the forest because the gate was open into its shadows, and we were thirsty, and heard the sound of water.

○

That water was unseen, covered by vapour that filled and spilled from a wide trough—it emerged behind the curve of the sward, and lay like a path of smoke westward through the trees. To look along it was like losing focus at the centre of vision, and we blinked and rubbed our eyes but it did not come clear—it was all softened and blurred as if our eyes had

THE TAMING ○ 13

been harmed by pressure or by staring into the sun. We could not see far along that path; it merged cloth upon cloth into green shadows.

But that noisy trough of mist was the watercourse of our directions, that flowed out of this quadrant towards Fresnel and the Cape. And from its exact curve behind the sward and its sudden straightness, and the seamless bank that showed here and there through an overlay of mud and dead leaf, we knew it was Outdead made.

We knelt at the brink. A familiar light noise of running water rose towards us, not loud, but continuous and pleasant.

○

What do I remember from that time? It was long before any of us would care to remember it, or that place, because of our grief that we left there, in the tiny stuffed cloth of the doll, buried for Saska in the soil. I remember that I thought I must give Ask water, immediately, because I had nothing to give him. I pulled my dress over my shoulders, and lay down naked, loosing it the whole length of my reach down into the mist. It felt weightless; I swung it, listening to the sound of the water.

Close by, the mist had no edge; it was not as bunched or spread cloth, or even as the firm edge of clouds, but gradual, a bright wet dust neither settling nor rising. Yet I could not see into it, or see my dress or even my hand—but I felt the fabric catch at the pull of the water, and drew it up hot and steamy, and squatted back to squeeze water into Ask's mouth, and Ard's, courteously, and no one gave me to drink and I sucked the real water out of its folds.

We were very frightened and thirsty. I do not know how to say how we were, except it seemed as if we had been struck, the way in anger and remorse you might strike yourselves, but with such power, more than any one body could possess, and more remorse, and more anger. Ask and Ard crouched close to me to receive water, leaning together, and I leaned to them. We were already all muddied, smeared with black, wherever we had touched the soil. They lifted their faces to me—that white clay line still traced on them from brow to chin—like dolls they looked, opening their mouths—such a clapping of mouths could clever doll-makers contrive, who had contrived the Doll of Atwar in Fu-en City, so he could take a step forward in the Square. Ah—this shows how stricken I was, to have such snows, such strange pictures pass unwiped aross my eyes! yet they were no stranger than anything else.

I dipped the dress till we had quenched our thirst. Ask was restless again, squirming away, and it was then I saw Ard, for before that I did not; I was most in despair of our brother. Something was the matter with her, the dullness of her face, it looked like a doll, like cloth with its white seam—she shivered, and her eyes turned upward and away.

"Ard, look at-us!" Her eyes in their puffy sockets returned for a moment into my look, and rolled again upwards. Water ran out of the corner of her mouth. A tremble crossed her body. When it was past, her mouth still shook and her teeth clicked against each other. That sound frightened me most.

I thought I would wipe her with water, perhaps it would restore her.

Now I have to say that there is a strangeness of the behavior of water in the Moon, not only in how it changes in the lunar night, but also in the way it moves, which is because of the thickness of the air. We did not know anything about it.

My dress had been lifted by the water and had not snagged, but the sound of the flow was so slight and light that I knew, as if I had seen with my eyes, that it ran shallow in its bed—even how shallow it was. I rolled myself off the brink. But it did not correspond! I foundered and could not touch bottom—it was as the air's strangeness, that upheld us, or the ground's that pushed us away. I had let go of the brim, and fell forward through mist into deep water, and was pushed along before I could right myself, with the deceptive surface lightly, almost too calmly lapping at my face.

I called out, then began to swim—which I could—back against the current. The greenish mist covered me and hid the banks, the water splashed up inordinately around my face, as if I had thrashed at it on purpose, and hung suspended, falling slowly back against my eyes and cheeks and mouth. Ah, I

THE TAMING ○ 15

swam hard! but it was not a strong current and I had come back to the turning.

For Ask, I think my call, and the noise of my splashing, were all he could tell of me. His ears like mine interpreted the water, for we were raised close to water, and knew its ways without thought. It was strange to him I did not stand up, in water that must be as shallow as the wading sea, rippling in its many channels over the sands.

"Tared, come out!"

I let myself sink and pushed upwards—so I was able to come out, for the air lifted me.

For it was very deep. I am telling this as a sign of how it was in the Moon, that corresponded only to the Moon, and that we must teach our bodies gradually.

○

Ard was crouching near the brink. And she made a low sound, almost angry, and her arm struck slowly and roughly at her face, so the line of clay was smudged sideways across one cheek. She picked clay off her mouth where it had caked in bits. She spat. I went to her and she flung herself at me. Her body guessed the distance, and in the Moon's air she fell past me almost into the course. She fell slowly. I caught at her dress. She was chattering.

So I began to take care of her, and did not then know, what was beginning! I embraced her and calmed her, feeling the quick, uneven intake of her breath, trying to slow it, breathing against her breathing just as a real twin will do, if her sister is agitated and afraid. Ah, this was to be my occupation then, and for a long time! and little good it did her, though perhaps in quieting me, it helped me take care of her.

Almost carrying her (and she seemed very light) I moved her gently down into the water, at the curve where the bank was low. I wiped the remnants of the clay from her face and pressed her soaked headsleeve into her mouth, Ask clinging to her dress to steady her: I swam close against her in the mist, to keep her from the current. But she was not comforted. Now when we brought her out, Ask saw her clean face, and mine washed from the course, and said—"Is there a mark on my face still?" He scratched at it, and then carefully pulled off his dress and scrubbed himself with the hem, till the streak was gone. Then he lay down at the brink and dipped his hem and pulled it out clean.

That was the clay we had received from the great scholars, the Ngs', fingers in the ceremony, mixed with our father Betwar's spit and tears. Now, what we had brought with us of our father was in the Moon's watercourse, and carrying west for us to follow, and what was left of the Ng was nothing. For the Ng were not here, and what they had done was gone. What they had done earlier, which was the binding and crippling of us, was undone also for now we could walk, as if we were healed.

I sat holding Ard across my legs, and touching her sticky, cold-hot skin. She moved her head restlessly, and shuddered, and stared without seeing and spoke without meaning.

"Bring your dress to her, Ask—for so much water is squeezing out of her skin, she must thirst."

From habit he pulled himself crawling to the brink to fetch it, and crawled back, laying the hem against Ard's face.

"Walk, Ask."

But instead he got up again on all fours, his crippled legs no broader or longer than his arms, and white and hairless from the binding. He stayed as if held in this posture, then moved one of his feet forward, like a stem, and that hand, and then the other foot and hand, and in his way he walked, head lowered between his shoulders, as if to watch his feet. So he stepped slowly forward along the bank, and around us, on his four limbs, carefully, his hair dragging on the soil and covering his look, his downy back, with its whorled crown high on his spine, his skinny, downy buttocks, his small sex swinging between his poor legs slow as in water.

"Stand up and walk, Ask, if you can."

But he did not answer, and went on with it, to and fro along the rim of the course, and looked not like himself or any being I had ever seen. I watched and wondered.

I was fingering the shape of the bundle tied secretly inside his dress—the bladder he had brought with him, and felt it stirring. So we released the birds, and buried the doll for

Saska's ash.

Ask tipped the bladder to spill gently on the ground. Three small birds slid out, and lay on their sides, their heads stretched as if lifeless. Two were ashy brown and one blue. Then did Ask burst into most bitter tears! Because this was Saska's scheme more than his, to bring them here to Atwar secretly. Ah, I wept also, for it seemed almost that Saska hovered over them now, and spoke to them, and his fingers that had handled them so deftly seemed to appear against their inert bodies, caressing them, touching them to wakening!

Then did the blue one shake itself, and stand unsteadily, and falter sideways and stand again, erect on its tiny hands; it jumped away from Ask, its arms extending to right itself—its jump was long and slow, as if through water. Standing, it made a small noise like a question and, ignoring us, jerked its head as if to nod, and got busily at its feathers. Then, having tidied itself, it looked about alertly, and sprang straight upward among the stems. This confident leap became a tipping, looping, slow-frantic fall, and it landed scrabbling at the strange ground which did not after all meet it as intended. But it stood, and cocked its head and chirped, as if to say, This is the way of it!

So it went looping off again among the stems, sometimes blundering against them, sometimes lost in the mist rising off the course. When it landed, it lifted its feathery arms for balance, and sang out: *Siri-siri, siri-siri*!

Ah, our brother Saska had taught himself to imitate that sound, and speak to the birds, and now—it seemed as if Saska's voice, that whistling and chirping he had practised so endlessly in the World, had been brought into the Moon— that it was Saska who had taught the birds to answer him and sing. If our hearts had turned aside in grief, and refused to continue, it would have been then. But my heart saw Ask and held him, seeing my grief through his—it felt like anger, and the striking of that anger willed him to live, not allowing him to turn aside.

So I think I mourned Saska in Ask, and this kept me, as I kept Ask. Ard grieved later, when she remembered.

The two brown birds also lived, and revived more slowly. They groomed themselves first, and then joined the blue one in that graceless, pointless flight—one plunged straight into a root and fell and lay dazed, but its fall was gentle and soon it rose again.

After they had lifted themselves swimming far into the high leaves, we could still hear their voices for a time, and little showers of water drifted down from where they were disturbing the foliage. The chirping and showering came from farther and farther away along the watercourse, and then it was still again and they were gone.

"They are perhaps eating." Ask said. He stood clinging to a tree root, staring after them. "Or, they are going ahead of us." His voice was thin and dry. I knew from his look that he wanted to follow them.

○

At that time we discovered what else had been secreted in the bladder by the Sanev—those twins who, already adult, had brought the birds to us at the last. It was an adult knife, bound tightly in a strip of white cloth.

"It is Nevi's knife," said Ask wonderingly, when he had unwound it. "Keep it for-us." Not thinking, he still used the dual, speaking for Saska also in his words. He he pushed it quickly across to me, but I drew back.

"No, take it and wrap it up. It is excellent—and you will soon be adult, Ask, and it will be of great use to you here in whatever you are making."

"Saska's body is not yet adult either—" said Ask in a whisper. And he wrapped it, and put it into his arm-pouch as adults do, and felt perhaps a little stronger.

Then I touched the flattened wet stuff that was my doll, sewn into my dress. (We had all received those dolls in the ceremony; this was because the Ng were well deceived, and had not known we would take living birds into the Moon.

I wanted to bury it for Saska' sake, and turned my sleeve out and picked it out of the seam. I laid it on the soil, and took one of Ard's drooping hands, and let her touch it, and told her what I did. Then I scratched some soil over it. Ask watched in silence.

"Keep your doll, Ask; or bury it with Ard's, when she is well."

He stroked the soil over. "But the birds are alive," he said after a pause.

○

Then the heat, which was increasing, overcame me and my brother—not as Ard had been overcome, but even so most heavily, and we slept. So we were used to outsleeping the dayheat in the World, and our bodies were ignorant. It was as if they confidently expected to awaken in a few hours to greet the coolness of evening. We lay down on either side of our sister, not touching her, though my hand kept hold of her dress.

○

Ah—it was at that time, while we were sleeping, that the portal closed. And the door into the house across the sward closed also, and the covering canopy was pulled back into the brim, like a door being drawn away, and also at that time the low humming ceased. It was this new silence that wakened us, a silence in which the running water was the only sound—and even that was lessening in our ears! We looked back, and saw the well-sward filled with a vivid white cloud. And when it was burned away the sward became very clear, and its shadows very black. There was no more air in it, and the sky was open over it and clear black, and full of unblinking stars.

So the sun descended and the World waxed towards half, steady in the high southern sky; he would reach his Half when the sun set, at the passing of the terminator.

But there must pass, before this, as many as three or four days as they are counted in the World.

○

I think in that time we were crazed, for though we slept and woke and drank water, and began to walk westward after a fashion—Ask after his own fashion—we did not concern ourselves with the directions we had so diligently learned on the World, and that were written into our palms, or with the house, or the sward. Even—when we saw the portal closed—

we did not wonder with regret whether we should have entered that house when we could, as Atwar did before he walked into the grove. Atwar had walked into this forest. And we began to wander up the edge of the watercourse, without much purpose except to be moving from the heat which was beginning to seem unbearable. We did not speak reasonably of any thing, or name Saska again, or Atwar. Ask was perhaps looking all the time fervently for a sign of him. I was looking, indeed, if I had any strength to look; it seemed I could hold this as yet a little while—this not greeting him, not being in his protection—but not a great while.

Ard was very sick. She would best have slept that heat out, and she did so but it was no good sleep: she stared and did not answer when we spoke to her, or make any attempt to walk except when we urged her forward. She fell often. I think she was dreaming, and almost we dreamed too. My brother's words were jerky and he said strange things and looked askance, and never answered me so his words corresponded. He spoke as if he were very small, and I thought that now he could not tell whether his lost brother was Saska or Atwar; it seemed as if he could not distinguish between them. Ask said: "*He is expecting his birds to return to him, it is he who tamed them, not me, they are swimming ahead of us to find him.*" And I did not correct him, because I did not know what to say.

I wondered also, that Ask would not walk upright as we had longed to do all our lives, and been promised—that we would walk like Atwar on the Moon. For in spite of our turned feet, Ard and I could walk now without difficulty, and our brother's feet were straighter than ours, having been left alone. But it was the way of him; he walked on all fours, as if he were swimming. Then I remembered how he and Saska had used to say, "We will swim in that air."

○

All the time we were following the watercourse it was drying up, and the air was very thick with water and heavy, and this increased. Sometimes when Ard fell down and shuddered and would sleep, we slept also, because of our lassitude. Large, hot drops fell into our faces from the trees,

THE TAMING 〇 21

and our dresses kept so wet we could squeeze them for a little water to drink, and so we continued.

The sun seemed scarcely to move but it was moving surely and slipping down ahead of us: we saw its effect between the stems on distant leaves. But the World we could not see, except once, when we came past that thing in the sky.

〇

It was only the first of them, but we did not know then that there were many, or what it was, only that the shade increased suddenly and we looked up and saw it among the parting leaves, and it was no other than a great stone.

We were afraid to be under it, and Ask wanted to swim till we were past it, but by then we could not hear any water. He went into the course and found some under the vapours but not much, and it was steaming hot with the bed broken and uneven. But he was easily able to leap out again, as I had done, and walked on as he was used, as quickly as he could, on his feet and the palms of his hands. We would have slept and my sister seemed to sleep even standing, but we were afraid to stay under the hanging stone.

Ah, it was as large as the Square at the top of the City, up there in the World. I supported Ard and so we went forward under it, scared and stumbling, until we were past it. In there the light was all darker, and there came to us in some way— did I notice this then? a taste, an enlargement of our breath, an easing? Surely our bodies took heed if our minds did not, for it was as if we could not hurry; yet we were hurrying as much as we could. I looked up only briefly, and Ask little more—the stone was steep and uneven, all rough, hacked planes of blurry gray; but how high it was, or what it meant, we could not tell. Only we felt that it was lowering over us, that it must surely fall. So we came out again, and that was when we saw the World, for there was an open glade at that place, where the stone was suspended, so the World showed there shining at its edge, at the edge of the leaves.

He was larger, waxing towards half and we could see the Sheath if we squinted: and the crescent was very bright, as looking directly into the sun through haze, and the images swam in my vision afterwards against the trees. It was then we began to understand how difficult it would be, to watch the World, for he was not as the Moon looked, from the World. He was brighter to an unimagined degree, so his sunlit surface boiled away against our eyes. And huge he was, I think twice four-or-eight times the breadth of the Moon seen from the World. The scholars had not said this. And later, when we would have watched, the foliage was so thick, or the climate so dangerous, we had not the opportunity. But then we were ignorant.

Much later, when we had used ourselves to his steady presence and his phases, we watched him intermittently, not as in the World, where it is constant, but as it was possible and that was little indeed. Ah, the scholars chid Atwar in songs for not appearing to them, and believed also that he watched them constantly, but we began to see even then that it was no easy task, to watch the World.

○

We had salt with us in our arm pockets and ate that. I gave some to Ard. Then Ask discovered, sniffing them, that the broken husks in the soil were salty, and he wiped one off and put it in his mouth: he could not break it into food with his teeth, but he licked the salt out of it, and this gave him some ease. My sister's skin felt sticky and cool and I thought that was perhaps a good sign, yet she shuddered as much as before, and breathed shudderingly.

We had yeast also with us, and Ask ate his, and I gave my sister some out of her pocket. I kept mine to farm, because I was not sure any more of what they had taught us, that there was food for us here, or what it was, till Atwar would show us. Therefore I secretly kept it, and doing this made me afraid.

○

We walked with I suppose some idea of purpose, but it would have been as good to sleep, because we could not remember what our purpose was. The heat did not diminish according to the ordained hours of the World's day, for this was not the World. The Moon's day was as long as many days and, as it went forward, hotter and hotter. I let Ard sleep yet I was afraid to let her sleep, in case she would die.

THE TAMING ○ 23

When we were in that glade at the stone, her body's anger made her strike at her face, and pull herself into a fist or knot, and cough and sob, trying for her breath. I could see her legs and feet were very angry: they clenched and would not loosen, and I sat by her and beat and rubbed them till they loosened. Yet our legs had joy of that thick air, which allowed us to walk upright as it was promised us, but they were not strong then, and Ard suffered extreme pain.

○

It was then that the mist boiled off the watercourse and we saw it was dried quite away. We looked a little farther, the stems coming close to the brim and some fallen (but without foliage, and dead) and the ground falling somewhat, and we saw across the course a section of the farther bank broken away, and a spill of black soil into it, as though water had flowed there out of the grove from the north. Some of the stems were half fallen across it and their white roots grew out of it, and some roots were loosened and combed as with the stream, lying on the earth in long ropy strings. The air at this time continued white and thick but more even, so we could see into the course. But our eyes burned.

That secondary course stayed us. It was *place*, like the great stone, something we could mark in our minds, whereas all the scape we had traversed had otherwise been the same since we left the sward. Ask crossed to it, which he could do by throwing himself lightly upward; he found in the bank a hollow under the roots, and crawled inside, and called to us that it was cooler there. So I brought Ard over, and we entered that small place a little under ground.

I do not know if it was cooler, or whether it only seemed so because it was like a house, to sleep in as we were used at home with our father. So we lay there and it gave us some ease. Ah, those were long hours, days of hours, countless! I would not sleep for watching Ard but Ask slept, and I lay breathing slow against Ard, against her noisy breathing that sometimes stopped, till she shuddered; then she breathed again and I saw the pulse in her neck beating very quick and uneven. Her skin gave out a strong smell, Ard's smell but something else souring it that was her sickness. I took salt on my fingers and put it in her mouth, and yeast also. It had swelled in my pocket. Though Ard's eyes stared, she saw nothing, and when I spoke she did not answer.

○

There was water forming big and droopy on the underside of those roots, and I wiped it into my sleeve as it formed, and gave it to Ard as well as I could, and spoke to her. This was our ignorance, that we endured over ground that terrible afternoon of days. For they had told us everything would be prepared for us, so we had not endeavoured to protect ourselves, believing what they believed—that Atwar would greet us. Ah, it was more extreme and dangerous than we had been told, and we endured it without shelter except for those meagre roots and slant of soil. The scholars had doubtless intended us to go under ground, but we did not know the way: after we were cut off from the sward we saw nothing the Outdead had made except the course, and no other sign. So we suffered needlessly and Ard almost died. And all that time the Moon, the great unconscious Mind of solid rock, held his sweet coolness close under the surface and never relinquished it, that he had gathered darkness by darkness over so many uncounted thousands of thousands of years.

○

Why did we not call to Atwar if we were promised to him? It was part of my unreasonableness, for I remember his name was near my lips, and there were times—in particular, when I saw the first great stone—that I could have thought him near. And it corresponded, that we had our idea of him, we grew up with his Doll standing over the city, we heard his name nightly in the streets and ceremonies. The scholars watched for him unceasingly and invoked him, and taught us to invoke him in smallprayer and songs.

Yet what we knew of him was little indeed! To the minds of the scholars and ordinary people, he had great wisdom and power for he had gone alone into the Moon, and made those necessary changes and prevented Moonfall and great catastrophe. All this had occurred before we were born.

He had gone however as a little child, and this was always in some way kept before us as well—that he was a child,

THE TAMING ◯ 25

crippled like us but able to run on the Moon (there were those still among us who had seen him, in Book on the screens), and that he had gone thoughtlessly and gladly for our sakes. Thus we four were promised to him, from our birth, indeed from before, when we grew separated in our mothers' belly two and two. And as we grew towards adulthood (but we were kept small, by the binding) I and my sister learned we were to be bonded to him. That is how they spoke to us, in those last days, when we bled and became adult and our teeth were blackened and they talked all manner of terrible secret things in the rooms, but we deceived them.

Betwar, our father—ah, he never made his brother Atwar into a god of any sort, he never went near the Doll on the hill, and at the last he did not comply with their terrible schemes. I Tared was the child most ardent for Atwar, to follow all his law, but Betwar took me as if between his two hands and turned me at last, and taught me what he had ever known—that Atwar if he lived had no idea of us and, had he known of us, would never have required of us, never countenanced—

It was as Betwar had ever said in the house, when we as small children returned from Book with some new learning he did not like, and he shouted at us and wept, or went out on the strand silently—but I was hardened already against hearing him; it was not till the last that he, with gentleness and absolute authority, convinced me.

He said we would shake off the Ng's terrible persuasions like the dirt that falls back from a thrown stone in its trajectory. And it was so. Saska had dreamed of a City where there was no Doll, and everything was wiped clean. And so it was; we entered the Moon with wiped minds, not knowing what corresponded any more, whether Atwar would greet us, or whether he lived, aware that he had no foreknowledge of how we had been preparing for him, or even of our existence.

For it was twenty-two years before our journey, as they tell years in the World, that Atwar went away, and left his brother Betwar in the World to grow up alone and father us.

◯

I think that Ask, already in his heart's breaking there by the sward, began to confuse his thought of Atwar with his brother Saska. I remember how, in the World, my brothers had chattered sometimes about playing with Atwar on the Moon, as if he would be still a child. Perhaps even on the sward Ask had begun to allow this stain in his mind, that coloured both of them—the image of lost Saska and the image of Atwar—so they slid across one another and somehow became one. For in this way Ask would not die of grief, and would look forward to Saska-in-Atwar, ever looking for his dear brother in the groves. Never have I spoken to him of this, but he lived—surely that staining kept him in life!

And perhaps I did not call out for Atwar because of that new not-knowledge, what our father Betwar said, that Atwar did not know of us, which made me even then a little afraid of what I would find.

○

It is hard to remember now how the Moon first appeared to us. I can describe those aberrations of the climate because they repeat themselves, but they seem less severe now, because we are used to them and protect ourselves and know that they are ordered and will pass. As for the thickness of the air, our bodies took pleasure in it, leaping and bounding, but even this became less strange; we became accustomed, we walked as well as ever but the air gradually ceased to lift us as it did at first, or we lost that ability—for I remember such dizzying jumps, and floatings—we came into ordinary habits, and we swam. There was then a kind of overbalance, a turning in the stomach, when we walked, but swimming was not ever different than it was in the World—when it was temperate the water behaved as in the World, and if it moved more slowly so did we, so that in its embrace we were as we had been. And as for the rest—all that we became used to as well.

But I am anticipating what happened to us, as we lived through that first season, and first felt against our bodies the violence of sunset, the terminator approaching from the east in storm.

○

It was a flood of waters, it was nearly over us when I

understood what the sound meant, a low noise from the east as of agitated voices—ah, it seemed like a multitude of people speaking. I had been half dreaming when I first heard it, and almost it was speech, the crowd on the hill whispering and murmuring in ceremony around the Doll. I had some crazed thought that we were being run towards by a great, frightened crowd. Then it cleared in my mind. It was the sound of water, as of a wave coming forward on a shallow strand, and getting louder. I heard too a crack northeast of us, along the ravine. I shouted to Ask and we climbed outside the roots as fast as we could and pulled at Ard, who was limp and gave us no help—we had to tear her dress from her with all our strength, getting her past the roots. We began to lift her up the side of the ravine, which was slippery, Ask going higher clutching the roots, even holding one fast between his muscular feet.

It was still day, but the sun was very low, his light brownish and slanting so there was a dark, warm stain over the stems and the ground. We saw the first wave of the flood pressed forward out on the watercourse like a foamy wall—it came on high and very, very slowly, and the foam and spray over its brink flowed slowly back; its front was curved somewhat forward and brownish, streaked vertically with foam.

Ah, I have seen that bore-wave almost as many times now as there have been days ending, that comes toward sunset with its welcome and promise! But then we were afraid, for its pace was so slow and heedless; it rolled the course-bed's loose shards ahead of it ponderously, and it carried within it the broken stems of trees.

As it passed, the following water backed less threateningly into the ravine, and filled it up, and left us clinging half submerged against the roots; ah, it was cooler, deliciously cool against our flesh. The current swirled heavily around on itself and a small secondary bore, tempered, approached along its surface from farther up the ravine. Its purpose was to enter the watercourse—we surrendered to it; it took us with it almost gently.

We have ridden that flood often since, but that first unready ride was too strange not to fear; we clung to each other and the secondary bore pushed us out into the current as it dispersed there; we were rubbed against the far bank, and then borne downstream headlong. We swallowed water we needed and did not need, we were rolled about in a slow tumble, and logs bumped against us and sometimes we managed to grasp one—then, we turned with it in a wide, dreamy circle in the bore's slow wake. Long green streamers of leaves rode with us also, that had loosed themselves from fallen stems, and these stroked and touched our legs under the water. They were tough and slippery and I kicked at them and when Ask startled I had to tell him, "It is only the leaves". Sometimes at first our feet touched the bottom briefly, but the course deepened.

It was difficult to hold Ard up and I was not even sure she breathed. Her head was slack on her neck and sunk willingly under water if I did not support it, and the water ran unhindered into and out of her mouth.

So we were carried safe and helpless along the channel, hearing before us the tumbling front of the flood, but ourselves on level water. And it rose as it flowed, nearly filling its banks. My eyes were blinking constantly and closing against the bright, rosy spray and the backward breaking of the small standing waves that rolled on the surface. Ah, the grove was most beautiful to watch, for ahead of us the stems were aligned on their narrow edge, west-east every one, exactly as the course was aligned, yet as we passed them they faced us in their breadth, winking and then widening, and again behind us they all winked away. Almost, they breathed at us. It was as if we were passing down an aisle between innumerable bands of pale cloth hung by the dyers from far overhead, and fixed exactly parallel, in a dyeing-shed so high and immense we could not tell its peripheries. So it was as the sun set and the terminator passed over us, and the brown light into which we rode was instantly gone.

○

It was not truly dark, for the World stood steady overhead.

THE TAMING ○ 29

He was at Half and his whiter light, diffused through the high leaves, filled the spaces between the stems and glanced on the water. Then slowly we came out of the immediate channel into a wide lake, an open place where the flood had risen over the banks at last, and higher, for the roots were submerged now and the stems rose straight out of the water in a circle al around. And over us, what we might have expected—another great shadowy stone was hanging in the sky.

When we moved under it, the World was eclipsed, and we were carried less and less urgently, till the water became still around us, and we floated in the white silence of nightfall, just under the belly of the stone.

We came later to call that time the *time of distance*, for we saw best in that cool blueish light, and farthest.

○

Rain is rare in the World, though we knew it and when it fell we played that the World had been pierced through, where the puddles lay revealing another World of houses and sky. The housecloth would stretch then, holding a taut little pool of water—waking near nightfall I would watch it from the mat—a darkening where the dirty leaves gathered, its shapes sometimes like faces. It rained with no sign to anticipate it, out of clear sky, and very lightly, though Betwar said it rained more in the North.

But here, like the flood, it took us by surprise that first time—the Moon's rain.

○

The pool was dark under the stone, and very still, with the stems around it dry at its curled lip as if the water had risen to the very trembling brink of its being. Ah, the air rapidly cooled—already it was temperate, no different than a hot day in the World. And that was such rich joy to our bodies, to our lungs breathing in air that no longer slaked and scorched us, to our limbs moving freely in the water! Ask brought a broken stem, and we rolled Ard over it, because it was broad enough—she was still droopy and asleep, but I thought looking into her face that she breathed more easily. Her dress was lost, and her naked body was wound about with slick leaf, that with its broad bands made a kind of garment. Her skin was puffy on her bald face and her hair all unknotted and tangled, with green leaf under it—I unwound that from her chin and neck, with some difficulty, for I could not break it across, even with my teeth, though it parted easily enough on the weft, in stringy shreds. Ask too was pulling the leaf from his body; he did not like the feel of it.

The rock overhead still scared us, though as I stared at it I could admit it was steady and not lowering. But how could it stay there suspended without falling? Dark gray it was, on its underside, and uneven, broken as if by quarriers; but towards the rim its colour turned into a very cold, distant red, of many shades, as if it were flushed over with unstirred dye or covered with a thick, unevenly dyed cloth—at the lighted edge it was made blurry by this covering. We could not see all the edge, because the belly of it hung down.

And to be close to the stone was very good for us, though we did not acknowledge it then.

○

We swam away from it, still as we thought westward, breathing very deep and happy in our bodies' alleviation. We were looking out for land, I suppose, but there was no land as far as we could see among the stems. Then the wind was upon us, and very soon after that it rained hard.

The Moon's wind in the Moon is not what is called the Moon's wind in the World, that in the time of Moonfall ran ahead of moonrise—we had learned from Book, how it refreshed the people, but later (as Moonfall was imminent) became violent, and how it was dangerous to be out in it; those were the times in the World of earthquake and terrible waves. But after the Moon was stayed, there were no more great winds in the World. So we grew up not knowing how fiercely air could move—but we knew there was Moon's wind in the Moon.

It came like the floods out of the east, following the terminator, a gushing of cooler air. The water ruffled as it passed over, and whispered, forming very short, high waves that stood almost still, so slowly they moved, as if they were digging in their heels, resisting the air's push. They broke

THE TAMING ◯ 31

nearly before they had peaked, the drops of spray carried ahead of them. The water clucked at the plank, and we drifted over against the first ring of trees. Among the stems there were fewer waves. We could hear the leaves soughing, and looked up to see them waving as strips of cloth would wave in water. The World's light wavered on the stems, diffused and whiteish, and the stems leaned, all together, and righted themselves, and leaned again, and rocked in harmony.

The heavy vapour that had surrounded us was now was gathered high up against the leaves; now it thickened as we watched, till they were hidden in it. The stone's belly bulged gray under closing mist.

This rain appeared around us rather than fell; it wet our faces when we turned into the wind. It was small and cool and unhurried; it fell sidelong drifting in the wind in shimmering, wavering bands across the water. Then greater drops reached us from overhead, that had gathered on the leaves and were shaking off, and embraced the small rain as they fell. Ah, so cool it was after the terrible days of the afternoon. Ask opened his mouth and let the rain enter it, and then I did also—it had an untaste, which pleased us better than the course-water full of churn and soil. I turned Ard's head, and soon she began to coughed and swallow, and scratch at her neck; she said some words—this was when I knew she would recover. The large, slow-falling drops splashed on the surface of the water, so it was all covered with interweaving rings.

So we drifted, and drank, while the rain and wind lasted, and our bodies were comforted. We began to feel hunger.

◯

Everything is provided for him, they had taught us of Atwar, and they taught us that we would also eat what the Outdead had prepared for us in the Moon—having to make and keep no farms, but receiving freely as in a market, or as children receive, and the old. And so it was after all! because as the rain and wind subsided, there was a drift out of the trees, not only of leaves, but also of fruit. It was those husks Ask had tasted, and these were not dry, but soft and edible.

The loosened leaves floated down in long, looping bands,

clogging the water, and their fruit pelted after them, so we could gather it. But some slipped immediately between the leaves and sank. Because Ask had licked the husks for salt, we were sure that the flesh would be good also. We ate it at once, biting through the hairy outer membrane that was a dark, grayish red, and somewhat green at the neck where it had grown. This outer husk we could not chew. But inside was a thick, dark pulp—it was sweetish, and at first we coughed at it and spat, yet it seemed acceptable to our mouths. Only the husks were salt, on their inner sides, and for this we kept them, stuffing them into our sleeves. We kept the whole fruit also, as much as we could store in our pockets.

This first windfall scared us, for we did not know how much it would increase in strength or how long it would last. But it did not harm us; even the pelting of the fruit was slow and soft. If it struck us we were not hurt, and it made soft plops all around us in the water. As for the leaves, they angered Ask, who wrestled with them when they fell over him, so he got even more entangled. Ard was afraid as she wakened fully—she stared about and then squinted her eyes shut, and held out her hands, so we had to put the fruit into them as if she were blind. Ah, ignorant we were then, lying in the water, garlanded with loops of leaf and eating greedily in that heady fall!

I told Ask then to undo his doll, so he could carry food instead, and he did so carelessly, laying it aside on a thick float of leaves. It was flat and wet but still dyed the bright blue that Saska had first worn on his dress, before any other.

That was the third and last doll we abandoned: one I buried beside the sward, and one was lost with Ard's dress near the first stone. We did not think then, that we were marking our way, making little new marks in the Moon—to bury one was a small finishing for Saska, and the second was left by accident, and the third so we could store food.

Ard came to herself, her body allowing her mind to see us and understand. Her body would eat though her mind was not yet hungry, and she took food and licked the salt. And she dared now and then to open her eyes and see us. We told her of the time she had been sick, how we had brought her with

THE TAMING ○ 33

us through the heat along the dry watercourse, and slept beside her under ground, how near sunset the flood had carried us away, and the air cooled and rained and moved with the Moon's wind blowing.

She looked both well and sick, her face very black and, about the eyes, bruised and swollen, but her gaze, if she held it towards my face, clear enough. She spoke more, and more steadily, asking us about what had happened. She asked after Saska, as if she had forgotten. Then she said, "Is Atwar there? Where is Atwar?" glancing into the grove fearfully and closing her eyes again, and I told her, "We are going to him—" and she took hold of my dress between her fingers, squinting and frowning—she said "Sanev—" in a low voice. I was not sure what she had understood.

The wind and the small waves had driven several broken stems up against the rim of trees, and Ask steered the most useful of them to us—these were long enough to lie on outstretched, and they floated level, the broad side over the water. We cleared them of leaf and pushed them close together. Here the trees grew close and we could not see any channel. So we pushed ourselves between the stems with our hands, Ask first and then Ard and I following, gathering as much fruit as we could. The mist had disappeared with the rain, and the air was very clear.

○

Ah, the Moon did not seem in any way to correspond to those directions we had learned! certainly not to the maps projected in Book, in the World. Here, we could not see our way. Of the regular system of grids and watercourses, the circular vales, the seeded groves and highlands, nothing was clear to us within the grove, with water flooding everywhere. And what we did see we could not understand, for it did not answer any expectation; we could recognize nothing.

○

Our first direction was along that course westward, towards Hadley and the Cape, because this was the way Atwar had gone when he was last seen. And some scholars had told of faint lights in the Sea of Vapours and in the Lake of Death, though others said they had watched and seen nothing. So it was towards the narrow dale between the great *maria* Serinitatis and Imbrium that we had set forth. The mark of that watercourse we believed we were following was written into our palms.

But it was a fading mark, and meant nothing. We could not tell how far we had gone, or what this wide lake among the trees signified, or in looking about understand how wide it was or how far it extended. The area was low and flat without boundaries, and the leaves closed in around us.

We could not even see the horizon, though the air was clear now far in among the stems. There was something most strange: indeed, in the World, objects present themselves on the surface of the eyes, according to their distance, and the eyes understand. But here in the Moon, our eyes were ignorant and told us otherwise; they said: the farther trees are smaller, and the roof of the forest is pulled down around about, and it will crush in upon us if we continue. That was the nearness of the Moon's horizon, as it was apparent to us.

We did not reason then, how any of these differences appeared to us—the harsh green taste of the air, which even when it was not wet was somewhat abrasive in our throats, the sweetening of the air in the barrens and near the great stones, the ponderous behavior of water—in all this we felt a general discomfort, because it did not correspond to what we were used to in the World. And our bodies were set out of balance in having to heed it: we registered everything in our bodies, not only the lifting air that enabled us to walk, or the burgeoning World so much too bright and large in the sky, but also every subtler fault—the sunlight that held for days, the seasons we could not catch the rhythm of—ah, it was worst for Ard but in all our bodies this lack of correspondence insinuated itself, weakening and undermining their certainty. In trust, our patient bodies waited for ordinary daylight and darkness and desired to wake and sleep—our blood moved blindly with the tides of the World, our cells circled to that circling—and there was no way to make them understand.

Later we called it *learning the turns*, because Ask and Saska had longed to tumble and do the *heads-over-heels* like

THE TAMING ○ 35

other children in the ceremonies around the Doll. And now we had to learn to tumble, and the turns were utterly strange to us! But we would learn them.

○

There followed a new season for us, and one that changed little for many hours—for four-or-eight days as they would be counted in the World. Even Ard who felt the changes most was nearly well at that time, and our bellies were full of food. And my mind was cleared.

We were intent for Atwar, even Ard when she dared; if she kept her eyes shut or squinted downward, her fingers caught at me, and I thought she was saying, "Seek for him among the stems! Tell me if you see him!" It was an easy season with space in it, but we did not know how long it would last.

We saw the level mark on the stems left by the receding water—but the fall was slow—everywhere around us the surface of the flood still stretched among the stems. We found the open course where it led on out beyond the stone; it was not as even at its boundaries here, and the trees grew sometimes thick and sometimes sparsely, though the leafy roof extended as before—behind it were those small glints and glimpses of the World, and he was brightening.

We followed the course. It seemed to have no discernible movement, but there was perhaps a slight current to help us. So we pushed or rode our planks, and ate what we needed of the fruit, and gave each other of the water, which cleared as the sediment settled.

○

The air was very transparent in that season, and it became quite dry and cool. At the time, we thought such a chill was extreme—and this was another strange thing for us, that what was our comfort and delight would become a surfeit, and then a source of harm.

For the people of the World avoid the heat of day. Coolness is their desire; they love the coolness that comes each night, and most with Kaamos at the end of Darkening, when the sun stays almost continuously below the horizon, only showing himself for a few hours at mid-day. In the World, it is never so cool that any would say, Enough. So this greater coolness was very strange.

The water and the trees, when we touched them, remained warm. Once Ask, though he shuddered at the touch of the leaves under water, dove to the base of the trees, feeling his way down by clinging to the roots, for the water was as yet too murky to see into, and brought up fruit and soil in his hands and it was warm also.

So our bodies delighted as they ought in that air, but we also stayed more and more in the water, and we learned that coolness is not always good—ah, we would learn that lesson soon enough, and in earnest!

O

We saw the roots emerge as the flood waters fell, and now there was a push in the water, as if it were gathering itself together; and so we rode the planks, or followed clinging to them, and the smell of the air was very tight and clear. Ah, when we breathed it in, it pricked and chilled our bodies inside. Ard sometimes shivered; she began to say that she did not like to breathe it. But we came out into a glade under another stone, where the air was easier, and there to one side where the tree cover was drawn back, we saw the World.

O

He was waxing. He was what we came to call *Twelwerd*, that is to say, he had the look of a Twel head with the right temple shaped by binding, as they bind twin infants in the City, so their heads are flattened on the inner side: this they call beautiful in Fu-en, in the World. Also, the waning World we call *Twarwerd*—shaped like a Twar.

He was bigger now than half and shed much light and we could see him almost in his entirety. He hung a little on his side, as if considering, so that the Sheath's band crossed at an angle, lower in the light side. Ah, how wide it was! it seemed from this viewpoint to cover the most of the World! But its edge in the south was almost completely hidden by the curve of the World. We could not see any coast that resembled Fu-en, as that part of the World was turned away from us. What we could see was dull blue, as of trees, and looked uneven and broken: we thought there was also water there, entering a great bay.

THE TAMING ○ 37

"Now, the scholars are not watching for Atwar," said Ask, "for they are on the other side of the World."

○

Indeed, from here the World stands ever steady, and turns himself—even as he shows us the home land, he is withdrawing Fu-en and its coasts, and the tawny fastland rolls forward along the Sheath's featureless gray with its sunflash blazing. Much later, we learned to tell Tasman's birthplace in Scandinavia, small in the north, and that sea, and another fastland, and we discerned in the south many things, and studied how to interpret them. This took a long time, because it was so seldom we could look at him.

○

For those who watch in the World, how easy it is to glance up at the Moon, to see him steadfastly! For them, it is the Moon that laboriously journeys around the World, and appears to set; then, those nights we called moonless, and we would wait for what we called moonrise impatiently.

We had been taught that the World and the Moon are two worlds, twins eager for conversation, as the Outdead had intended from ancient times. But from here we understand their unlikeness—and I cannot think even now they are twins. The Moon is at best a bereft twin—as the child Atwar, or as Ask. Then, the World is another bereft twin—a fathering Betwar, older and greater according to his generation.

○

We stayed for a time just at the boundary of the third stone, where the World's white light poured into the flooded clearing against its deep shadow. We could let the World lean wide from the stone's edge, and eclipse him again—so, it was easier to see him. Even his air was visible, a soft skin of light, circling him.

In there under the stone it was very dark. That stone was very large—Ask thought it as wide as the City. Upturned, it could have held all the Fu-en houses, right down to the shore, and the Square and the Doll—"Then, the Doll's head would hang down to us so we could nearly touch it," whispered Ask.

But there is no City in the Moon—and no Doll, just as Saska foretold in his dream, and the stone was very black and silent overhead, with its worldlit edges glowing.

○

We thought we heard a sound then, and that it was the birds—we all heard it—from a distance a lifting note, and then another and perhaps another, the same unspeech—and afterwards it seemed we could hear it again in our minds where it had written itself. But we did not see the birds at any time in that season. We left the stone and went on through the opening among the stems.

○

Why did we continue westward, when Atwar could have lived as easily close to the sward where he was last seen, near the old Outdead habitations? We did not reason it; we followed the watercourse and made those marks in our minds, as we had begun to mark on our circadian bodies these new diurnal seasons—ah, when we should come through one entire lunar night and day, that would be the beginning of understanding! For now it was so new and difficult, this gush against our senses, that to continue forward was perhaps our bodies' choice and intelligence, so that we would not stand still to be overwhelmed by that wake of amazement and grief.

Yet I was well, as I had never felt in the World, until the last. It was our father Betwar who had sewed up that tear in my life—which was my refusal to hear him, my fierce trust, believing the scholars utterly and so thinking myself strong. But it did not correspond! their faith was blind and dangerous, they drew me out to the sharpest edge. There our father found me and restored me. His love restored me, I carried it with the Moon's air, at every breath pulled into my breast that made a space for it without difficulty. In this way the strangeness and newness of the Moon was never harmful to me, or great with seeming purpose and heavy meaning—but instead, even at its most beautiful, rather flat and meaningless and clean. Ah, it was not Book or the diligent scholars who had prepared me after all, but Betwar, who gave me the gift of this innocence, this simplicity.

I bled in that time, and longer than would be ordinary in the World, which was perhaps the Moon's influence, or my

THE TAMING ◯ 39

body's immaturity. Ard had bled before me in the World, and gone to the initiation before me. But I thought, if she bled now, it was into the water; I did not see it, or speak of it—that time in the World had been terrible for us, when we were almost persuaded by the scholars' words—I say, to forgive myself, almost, but I was wholly persuaded! Yet it was not me. It was the not-me they had made, like a doll, to stand in me. It is gone. Betwar delivered me, delivered us.

Ah, how I drag in the telling of this—yet so much happened to us at first within our bodies, as well as in what we saw and did, and it is necessary that you understand. But I must tell you what happened outwardly.

◯

The course deepened. The force of the water was like the mbrace of strong arms and drew into itself all those tributaries and smaller channels of the flood, so that we felt on our bodies its hold strengthening. We were moved more purposefully, and again could watch the slow winking of the stems as we passed between the two banks—Ard saw for the first time how they widened and seemed to stare at us, and again narrowed. She did not look more than once! The water had a very surly push, it advanced with that same unnatural slowness, its surface again somewhat murky.

Small circles and curlings appeared on the surface, and then sleek hillocks, and standing waves that broke unhurriedly over themselves, and we passed across and among them, as though the course were shallow; but it was deep. Now the trees' roots showed again, and then the ground on either side, here and there, the waters flowing towards the course in torn sheets and after that in ropes and threads. And at last we were floating down a bounded channel, with land on either side.

We were at some distance from any stone, passing as always under the thick roof of leaves, with the World's light dispersed through them. They were whitish and bright gray in that light, yet even so far overhead their detail, their long, layered warp and weft, was infinitely sharp in the chill air.

The temperate water still comforted us, but the air we drew into our lungs had a more and more piercing sharpness. Ard gasped at it, putting her face under water as much as she could. The air that dried the splashes on our skin, especially on our bald faces, was almost painful—I could not see any change on Ask's face or Ard's, but it felt to me as if the World's white light was hardening into a second, tighter skin over my skin, in some way burning me. It is strange to describe such coolness as burning, but my body comprehended it in this manner, not having any adequate memory. We came to call that season *Svalbrand*, the cool burning—to say that, as the World came into Full, the air was cooking us—this was because we had no better word for it.

O

At this time there was a change in the current. The water on the surface seemed to stand still, almost to back up, while deeper down it dragged us resolutely forward. This pull revealed itself on the course ahead in close-packed standing waves, the first unbroken but farther along steeper and foamy white. There in the distance the course looked all white, with a cloud of spray hanging over it, and we could hear its noise. Ah, we need not have feared it so much; we could have ridden those broken waters, reassured—as we had already learned with our reason—that they were without haste, and did not mark a dangerous bed. But our bodies did not believe this, and were scared, and before we came to those rapids we came up out of the water's pull and lay over the planks, and steered them into the southern bank.

The roots warmed us, where our hands held them, but they seemed to burn when we first touched them. We stepped out, and beached our goodly planks and for a time walked along the brink. The soil oozed warm and our feet touched into it gladly. Yet here and there it had a new, glassy surface that splintered when we stepped in it. The fallen leaves were also glassy where they lay exposed; here and there they were wound about the roots like bandages.

Ah, it was the influence of that air that frightened our bodies and made them tremble. It hurt to breathe and our mouths dried and cracked at the edges, and our eyes burned—it was hard to blink them. Now we began to feel anger in our hands and feet, and Ard most—her body was

THE TAMING ○ 41

almost recovered, and now it returned to sickness.

○

We continued for some time, with the white water close by doing its slow heads-over-heels. For all its seeming danger, it claimed us from that coolness and again we swam; we were rolled about but not harmed. At last we came to a place on the southside where the bank was broken—and again it seemed a marking place, a refuge.

This one was narrower, and very deep, the slick soil of its banks scored with the branchy traces of rivulets. A great tree rose directly out of it, facing us with its system of white, exposed roots swelling out of a mass of tangled leaf and dreck—they bulged like fingers cupped for holding—they pinched and held up the stem. It stood with its wide side facing us—a faceless face, a stare but not unfriendly.

Below the outlet was a spit, and within its arm a space of still, dark water. The foamy waves were prevented; outside, the loud course tumbled and rolled. Quiet water was backed right under the roots of the tree. Ask slid down into it at once to warm himself, and we followed.

This place, under this tree, was where we stayed over that first mid-night, and on through the terrible hours of days before morning.

○

The water warmed us for some time, and when the World waxed Full, its fair light alleviated the coolness, but afterwards, towards dawn—ah, that was worst, and I do not know how we lived through it. We were near to killing ourselves from carelessness and ignorance.

○

I remember yet how I stared forth at that widening light. How bright it was with the World at Full! yet there was no green—as if the leaves had swallowed their colour, the cells cringing so as not to be burnt away. The light through them spread and fell among the stems, and caught at the wall of spray in the course, that hung almost suspended, lifting and drooping over the standing waves; they were caught in a turmoil that fed itself and did not change, while we lay in the backwater in the stillness.

Here the water was lowering, leaving its traces in a glassy skin, and that skin spread from the roots also, but we broke it with our hands. When the World was at its Full that skin ran like dye running in a vat, but afterwards it formed again, and in earnest.

At that time two of the planks appeared, riding in their own calm measure, and Ask saw them and had good time to leap to the spit's tip and turn them, and pull them inside. The third plank we did not see.

As the hours passed, the water cooled also, till it was just as cool as the air. Its surface glassed over and dropped away. We squirmed deeper into the mud—we wore it like clothing. We clothed ourselves roughly, when there was no more water, in thick clots and bindings of leaf and mud. The mud made our hands as clumsy as if they were thrust into footgloves; but it was not just the mud—our palms whitened, our thumbs and fingers going very pale, and they ached, and it was worse with our feet though we did not know this, for they ceased to ache; we could not feel them at all. The soil hardened. There was less noise from the course, and the Moon was held tighter and tighter in coolness and silence. Then there was a loud crack! from deep in the grove, as if a tree had snapped over—and this cracking or snapping sounded from time to time in the growing silence—near and far, with no pattern in it, so that each time we started up in fear.

And Ard's body was very angry. She shuddered most, though we all shuddered—it was like being shaken hard, like cloth shaken fiercely out and then loosened, but for Ard it was continuous. We ate, more than our eyes wanted; it was our bellies asking for warmth. Ah, it was their desire then— to be a little warmed!

O

Then Ask made a fire with his oil. His hands had none of their deftness and he wasted the whole bladderful spilling it into the earth, when its purpose was those fires we should make as a sign to the World. He burned it in a depression in one of the roots, right inside the fingers of the tree. We fed it with bits of root. The fallen leaf also caught and burned, with a terrible odour, and some kind of blackish oil boiled out of it, and burned on in the pit, the flame dark red and spitting.

But there was scarcely any warmth from our poor fire—the air ate its heat, as fast as it could. And Ard we had to hold back. So we were at that time—not attentive to what we were about, not thoughtful or careful or considering what would be best for us, Ask crying with the coolness and uselessly feeding the flame and me holding my sister, so she would not fall forward into the fire. Her arms would jerk out and I held them also, close against her body. Her trembling ran through her like the beating against her of many hands—this was good if I had known it, because she became from it warmer than me. But at the time I tried to quench it.

Drops of the lit oil kept falling into the ground, and catching in little gloomy flames. I felt the hardness of Ard's hair—if I turned my head, my own hair struck like wood at my face and shoulders. I looked across into Ask's squinting look—he was now very strange to see! with his hair sticking out from his head all filmed with that glassy skin; the whiteness stuck in the down of his brows and on his eyelashes, and around his mouth also.

"What shall we do?" Even, it was hard for my mouth to form words. And Ask's mouth, too, slurred when he answered me.

"A house," he said.

Indeed it was a house our bodies required; and somehow we made one, using for its walls the roots of the living tree. We laid Ard down on the ground, pulled the mud out of the floor, deeper where it had not hardened, and banked it up with the junk of leaves in all the spaces between the roots. There were some broken roots outside, where much had piled up in the flood, and Ask fetched them. He strove much, though he was ever stumbling and crying. Then we dragged our two goodly planks inside the tree—one we used to fill a great gap on the east side but the other we laid on the floor, and put Ard on it. Ask shook the fruit he had gathered out on the ground, and pushed his dress under her.

Westward, the roots were deep in the ravine wall, with little space to fill. We dug with our blunted hands and then with pieces of root and Ask with the knife, to reach the soft mud. Yet as we strove, our blood was warmed with the effort, and the house also became warmer.

○

What a house that was! full of smoke and bad smell from the leaf, with bits of oil flaring here and there on the floor—and then the root that held the fire burning though, and the whole fire falling down, setting the floor ablaze! Ard's arm, flung out, was singed of its hair, and that unseemly smell joined with the other.

The fire on the floor burned well, and the one side of the broken root went on burning—it threatened to reach its flametips up into the dry recesses of the tree. But we damped it with soil, and when that was not enough I pulled off my dress and pressed it around the stump to extinguish it. As I strove, I could hear the down on my arms crackling, so warm it was; yet the heat comforted me—it was strange, to be at the same time harmed and comforted!

Eventually the fire obeyed us, though leaves spat and ignited, and burned us here and there like teeth biting, so even Ard started up, when a bit of this oil struck her. We burned those roots and broken planks Ask had dragged in, and after that, we burned the good plank which had been Ard's bed. It warmed us slow and well. We ate of the pulpy fruit and I squeezed its juice into Ard's mouth. I held her again, as well as I could, and we crouched very close together all three, with the two dresses across us, in a kind of waking sleep, starting up at every crack in the forest and at every snap of the oil, and ever staring into the red fire.

○

Had it been one night, as they are in the World, it would have been as a Tale, a brave undertaking and fit for singing about afterwards. But that night after Full was as long as four-or-eight days as they are counted in the World, and after about half that time had passed, when we thought it was as cool as it would get, it became very much cooler.

○

Ah, how dangerous it was—one small, careful lamp would have kept us alive, had we been under ground! and even here

THE TAMING 45

we would have been safe enough, had we understood. There was no more cracking among the trees—and no sound from the watercourse, for by then the whole of the night surface of the Moon was covered as with glass. And here within the tree we heard only the spitting of the fire. The red light came and went on the roots, and Ard shuddered. We must have slept, all of us, because there was a sudden, immense crash!—the smouldering root had fallen, and the inside of the tree was afire.

We heard that rather than saw it, for the smoke came rolling and pouring down out of the hollow, pushing to find an opening. The fire on the floor was mostly out—but the rootfire must have run upward, and ignited the tree. There was a creaking over our heads, in the splintery sound of the fire, as if something were about to break.

Then the whole south wall of our hazardous house burst into flames, and the rush of its spitting heat touched us, for the room was very narrow. Ask was pulling at the plank in the east wall and crying for me to help, and when I did it fell outward; and thus we escaped, dragging Ard. That plank was even a bridge, for it fell across the slant of the bank. Ask jumped, but I was carrying my sister and I walked on it, and we drew it after us and crouched on it, for it was dry and at first warm.

So we were left at the ravine's edge in that worst hour, staring at the tree that had sheltered us, the heat of its wound radiating outward into that terrible coolness, granting us what we in our ignorance seemed to have taken from it, which was life.

O

The root's fingers held a great bloom of fire, and narrowed and blackened against it as we watched, and ropes of smoke streamed out between them, filling the air. Ah, it was well that the ground had that skin, for the leaves near the tree would have ignited, had they not been covered, and the fire run farther, and other trees would have died.

We watched and hardly heeded our bodies, though indeed they were wretchedly angry, at the same time scorched and chilled, and our lungs in pain from breathing the smoke. Yet we watched, and saw the roots burned up at last—we thought then, that the tree would come falling down. The stem hung steaming, with the last flames licking its glassy throat, and the curling strings of the burnt roots hanging under it desolately, no longer touching the ground. But it did not fall.

○

Who had seen that fire? watchers in the World? perhaps from the other fastland, or south-folk we had dreamed? Had Atwar here seen it, was he hereabouts? Then, we did not consider these questions; we were too miserable, the coolness falling now on us with terrible force and press. Ard was asleep or worse, and when I looked at her and my brother they were so scorched and whitened they were almost unrecognizable —and I was surely as the same. On Ard's head were big patches where her hair was burnt quite away— and the down on our bodies was burnt also. When I brushed my hand across my breast, hair like crumpled grasses fell away. My feet and hands had begun to ache again, whether from the new coolness or from touching the fire I knew not— and my skin burned, and my lungs from that chill air, more desperately for all the smoke that had seared them. Our brows and eyes were so clotted that we saw as out of tangled white bush, and it was difficult to move our mouths. Yet our bodies feared the chill-burn more than the fire.

I began to crawl across the plank—but it slowly broke away at the other side and I slid into the ravine and the ashes. Ask helped me, and we helped our sister, and returned to the blackened site of the house, and crouched there under the dangling roots, finding the heat of the fire still hidden in the soil. We burrowed our arms down into the ashes, and covered Ard, and were burnt by hidden embers and did not care.

This was the only place in that dim, dawning scape that was not white—the ravine, the higher ground, the stems and far overhead the roof of leaves—everything was covered as with clouded glass. And the water—ah, when we first turned to look on the surface of the course—it was absolutely still. It looked like the Sheath except in colour—water is indeed the Moon's Sheath in this season, for it closes over and hides away everything it contains, and all its slippery cells grasp

THE TAMING ○ 47

one another and become as stone. Inside the spit it was as sleek as the Sheath also, and almost as dark, but in the main stream bright and broken; it resembled a wild field of white boulders. It was silent. The Moon was utterly silent. I looked up into the tree's heart—there, the last of the fire glowed in little squarish pits, and seemed as I half-slept to be the City seen from a great distance, from the bluffs or the far strand, all the patched houses with their friendly lamps shining behind the cloth walls.

That the tree held, though it was surely dead, was no stranger than any other thing, and we did not fear to lie under it. Ask broke off a bit of the nearest root, which he could just reach, and ate it in mourning, and pressed it into my mouth and Ard's, for we dared not eat the ash; we had some understanding that the leaves were not good for us.

We slept in some fashion, and then in that rosy change before the sun rose, Ask and I crept out and broke away bits of hardened leaf, and roused the last of the fire in the ashes, and kept close to it. The leaf spat as its whiteness changed into water—that was the first we saw, of the way *water returned to itself*, into the likeness of water. And on our bodies also the white returned into wetness, when we were near the fire. We pulled the last plank close, and it caught at its blackened edge, and the goodly flames spurted and climbed. I remember Ask said as he poked about, "Now we are World-children", for in the World we had envied those children who chose not to go to Book, and who played much with fire along the beaches.

"Moon-children," he corrected himself, coughing. "Or, you-are not, for you-are adult—but we-are—"

Ah, he spoke using the dual yet, referring to himself and Saska as he was used.

○

The moonscape had been bluish-white and dusky, lit by the World now waned to half, and the sun's light seemed in contrast very warm and near. We could see where he was rising, a smudge of ruddy brightness over the ravine, and the glassy ground and all the stems reddened. It was a most red sunrise through the dust of smoke, still spread about from the fire. So we lived into the first dawn, and it seemed to me surely, because we lived, Atwar lived as well, and would find us in that dawning.

All this I Tared have told, as well as I remember.

○

Is this the bond of Atwar? her body covered with soot, her headhair burnt short and uneven with its edges all jagged and crumpled, wide red sores on her skin, that is scratched and scorched and in places bare of down? her body squatting like the body of babes on her bald, thin legs all smeared with ash and blood? Is this his bond, staring with reddened eyes into the fire? She is naked, she holds the remnant of her dress across her sister's unconscious body—that dress was once bright blue and now is burnt and mostly black. The fire lights her unevenly; she is stroking her sister. She stares past the flames where her brother is crouching forward to push the burning plank farther into its embers. Is this the bond of Atwar who was prepared for him, clean and marked with her father's clay? Now it is light, it is the Moon's morning and the chill will draw back, the sun will restore the vegetable Moon. But she shivers and presses the ashes over her limbs, and keeps so close to the flames that she cannot avoid being scorched further. Is this his bond, baring blackened teeth to chew the husks among the ashes, her breath harsh, the skin of her mouth sore and cracked open? She is lifting her sister's arm and turning it clumsily in front of the flame. With the heel of her hand, she is beating at the cloth of her dress where it is smouldering. The smoke smells of their flesh. Whiteness forms in the pit of her hunched shoulders. Behind her the watercourse blazes in terrible whiteness.

Ask

This is the tale of how we entered the Moon's day for the first time, which was for us the second day in the Moon. When the sun rose the air began to warm again, and we knew that we had survived that night, and we began to recover.

As for the night, it was terrible for us, without at first any protection, and Ard sick. Tared had taken care of Ard in all that time, while I made us a house as well as I could, and kept the fire. When the tree burned up, we ran out of it, but we returned and hid in the ashes—we burned the last good plank then, as was necessary. Ah—we were ashamed, yet we burned only one tree, and that was by mistake. It stayed standing among the others, held up as we supposed by its leaves, woven into the other leaves overhead.

○

The sun's light warmed the air. First the leaves overhead shed their glassy surface; that ran and steamed and made the air unclear around them. Now we understand the behaviour of water and are not impatient when day comes, for we know there will go as long as four-or-eight days, as they are counted in the World, before it all has returned to itself and flows freely. In the World the water is ever temperate, so we did not understand how it can be made hard by the Moon's climate.

That morning I walked on top of the water inside the ravine. I fell on the surface, which was as slippery as the Sheath. Gradually, it was returning to itself; at first by clothing itself with a slick of runny water. The channel outside the spit was all pointed and rough, and later I climbed about on it.

At first we were too sick to do more than rest, and gladly breathe that warming air. I kept the fire, going off a little farther away each time in pursuit of wood. I began to see how the Moon must harm the trees by the violence of his floods, for in places the stems were torn away and lay broken. And what we had done was perhaps also a necessary violence. I am not sure, now, whether I began to understand this then, or whether in looking back I dye it with my knowledge, and pretend I understood. Yet if we had not burnt the tree, how could we have survived? That was however the only night we did such harm, and it was because we were ignorant and had no proper house to protect us.

I broke much wood out of its mess of whitened, blackened leaf where it lay. Then, I hated the leaf, though later I learned its good properties.

○

Tared has told how I strove, but she was not out among the stems with me foraging; she had not felt what I felt. Ah, my hands and feet were as wood, as if that deadness in the skin of my legs, which we ever knew from the binding, had spread in my body even to my hands and my living feet. The Moon's air supported me, or I could not have managed. Some roots I slung through my dress, though they burnt my sex and my belly with their coolness. The leaves I threw across my back, and spoke angrily at them as if they were not dead but conscious, headstrong and disobedient. I fell much, but softly, and took all that I could.

Who was abroad in that whiteness and silence? I heard no sound except of my own making—and four-or-eight times a crack among the stems overhead—that was sometimes, when I looked up, the sign of a glassy shard broken off and falling—its own tightness split it away. Once, I heard a whole space of the forest crackle; it sounded like catching flames; and far among the stems a white cloud of glassy bits showered down. Ah, so it is in the night of the Moon, strange in silence with great cracks and sudden white showerings, but we are wiser now and not out in it!

I went on, wrestling with the loosened ends of roots as if they were the arms of stubborn playfellows—so we had rolled about with the Sanev on the floor, in their house, and been scolded by their dull mothers! Thus I took hold of a root as if it were my twin's body under me and walked, and he burnt me and was indeed dead—ah, Saska, in those roots, in that silence, I brought you back for your burning! but I said nothing of this to my sisters then or later—indeed I was only that child, going after that necessary wood, so the fire could keep us alive till morning. Tared has told you what happened, and how we thought we had killed the tree.

○

Tared was earnest to clothe us—we had two dresses between us only, and hers was so full of holes that much of it came apart in her hands. My dress was less burnt but small. We unpicked the headsleeves that in the World are not useful, except to the Fu-en people if they go out in daylight, because they tie back their hair that would otherwise shelter them. Our hands were then very unsteady and our fingers blunted. It was better however when they were angry: when that anger left them, they were as dead—like the flesh of our legs where they had been bound.

There was plenty of cloth in the sleeves when we spread them out, for they were sewn wide after the fashion, as for twins. We dressed Ard in them, and together they covered her body. We put on our dresses again as they were. There was no heat in them except in our minds' desire for it. As for the pockets on our arms, mine held but an empty oil bladder and the knife. Ard's held a tiny bladder of oil, which Tared said we must keep to make a sign to the World, and Tared had still some yeast, dried up and crumbled like black dust in the seam. We thought it could not be good any more. Tared would keep it however. She smelled of it. And we did not lose that harvest because, as she later said, "I am a farm"— some was kept living in the folds of her body.

We ate the runny fruit in the ashes under the fire. I pushed in more of the husks that had gone hard, and their fruit also softened—even inside a husk that was shrivelled and burnt black, there was a little left for us. It seemed too sweetish to like, then. Our bellies liked it, however, and our mouths have come to like it since.

○

Now the sun had been up about as long as a World's morning, though still very low in the sky, and the air had quickly warmed in that time—enough that the soil had lost its toughness, and became black and wet. I went out on the course and it was hard indeed, under a runny surface that formed into pools between the solid waves. Tared gave me a piece of her dress for a drinking cloth, and we drank that good water from then on, squeezing it into Ard's mouth also.

Ard was awake, and cried much with the pain in her legs. Tared had ever been speaking with her, and now she answered, and talked rapidly, and took much food and water from us. Except for her head her sores were less desperate than ours, because Tared had taken care of her.

○

The morning brought the Moon's wind, this time very gentle and wet, and with it came a more gradual warming and thickening of the air. But we were too sick yet to be much comforted. Ard's mind healed as soon as the air relented—yet it was still painful for all of us to breathe because our throats were scorched by the smoke. Even to drink the water hurt us, though it was clean and good.

Ard and Tared lay for many hours in the ashy ground, moving only to ease their bodies. But the oily ash was healing us, and the warmer air. I kept the fire burning for some time; eventually we had no need of it.

Ah, the scholars had done no good thing to my sisters, in the binding of their feet! Their toes had been broken and turned under, and one foot bound across the other so its arch was very curved and high. That first terrible night harmed their feet so they have never really healed. But our hands healed. We suffered much anger from our bodies in that Moon's morning, and it is well, because we needed to hear and heed them, and never again provoke them in ignorance as on that first day. Thus as we lay healing we spoke earnestly together about how we could protect ourselves, both from the terrible coolness of the lunar night and from the heat that would surely come in the long afternoon ahead. And, because he had not yet helped us, we began speaking openly of Atwar—ah, we were very afraid to begin.

○

We did not then know whether the scape ahead of us would continue in forest or become open land. Or whether we might find some natural opening, as in mountains, or an Outdead house from ancient times. We had ever been taught that the Outdead had provided for us, from that seeding of the Moon they began those three thousands of years ago. They all died, leaving many marvellous devices our race was slow to understand. Yet we have the benefit of them; we are the inheritors. The Outdead anticipated Moonfall and in the Tales it seems they longed, as now we do, for that conversation, that goodly twinning between the two worlds. Some scholars hold that they would have prevented us this harvest if they could, for they hated us, the race of one-bodied twins who outlived them to inherit the World.

Other scholars deemed the Outdead more kind—for was not Tasman, born late in time, like them one-headed? and her children Atwar and Betwar, and we her children's children? But Betwar said ever that the Outdead could not have foreseen us, to make provision for us—he had it from his fathers the Sorud: their Twel was the greatest of scholars— and not like the eastern ones, for he was neither stupid nor cruel. He had ever said, *"Do not prophesy."*

The Outdead are gone and with them their reasons. And indeed that seeding they began in the Moon had thriven: the air we found in the Moon was good, and there was healthy vegetation, and food of a sort, and water. Surely there would be shelter too, whether Atwar helped us or not. But shelter we had not yet found.

○

"In four-or-eight days the air will be very hot again, as it became before," Tared said.

"And then again very cool. I think that when the Moon endures these greatest changes, Atwar is under ground, not ranging as we have been."

"Ah—if we had gone over the sward, when we could!"

"That was not his house," said Ard, looking downward, picking at her wounded hands. "He walked away into the forest." She held up her twelhand then and spread the palm, and licked the ash from it and spat. They she looked closely into it, where was written the line of the watercourse, and the marks of the mountains that almost closed the space between the *mare* Serinitatis and the *mare* Imbrium, with that narrow channel between them, the place of the first seeding. She extended her hand so the splayed fingers pointed west and pushed her twarfinger west across her palm. "This burn is the tree. That way, Atwar lives."

"Look there, to where Atwar lives," she repeated slowly, looking across her hand and then squinting her eyes shut. We looked at her request, seeing beyond it only the course and the grove. Ard would look then only look at her own body, or sometimes at us, directly into our faces. I glanced across her at Tared.

"We must light that fire then," Tared said without expression. "That they are watching for in the World, unless he greets us." She spoke as if she were thinking.

"Even the tree burning, they would not have seen," I said. For it must be a great fire indeed, to see it up in the World. The tree, such a conflagration it seemed to us! but it had not even burned into its leaves, only at the ground.

Tared said, "There are barren mountains farther west, and the Lake of Death where some scholars say his fire was seen."

But we knew that others had looked and seen nothing.

○

We had no real idea of the distance we had travelled. There was as yet no change in the vegetation or the level ground, no sign of the narrow Cape or the mountains. Yet we wanted to be going. Ard had suffered too much here—another such night she could not bear.

"Atwar will take us under ground," she said and Tared stroked her with an ashy hand and told her gently, "We will indeed be under ground, Ard, before that time that sickens us."

"Atwar will bring us into his house!"

Ah, we had all of us some idea that in the course of this day we must find him. The slow, extreme seasons were fixed and measured, and had an ordained pace. Already we accepted them, because we must, even Ard who had been so ill. If we did not find him, what we had endured we must surely endure again.

○

I was stronger and more restless than my sisters. I desired to go on immediately—and I had not that need for their embrace that they assumed. I could feel their pull at me, when I foraged, and when I was out on the course—like a braid dragging me back to them. It was their sister-braid, extended to hold me. But against it the whitened course, stretching westwards, exerted a stronger pull—it desired me to go forward, towards Atwar, towards those birds' notes we had faintly heard. The fire had seared me all night and distance seared me now when I looked away west; the front of my body felt naked and wanting to leap ahead, to close that open nakedness.

Tared told me later that she thought it was Saska my body was looking for, but this does not correspond. I was never so deranged in my mind that I pretended him here. Ah, my body did at first, ignorantly. But I had mourned him in that night, and burned him within that tree. I could not have said it then but the pull was his absence, my loss of him.

So I was careless and restless, and would go, but my sisters were as yet too weak, and slept heavily.

◯

The Moon's morning was not warm, though the sun's smear climbed behind the leaves. The air was as a cool night in Darkening in the World. Or even more cool! it refreshed us—this season is indeed ever the most pleasant in the Moon, and continues so almost to New World at the sun's height, at mid-day. We wasted much of it in sleep and doing nothing.

I was walking on the course, some way downstream, when its surface first began to move under me. There was a loud crack and I thought a tree had fallen—the tree we had burned—and I stared, but it hung firm. It was the breaking of the water. The hard surface would eventually collapse and change and be carried away. I heard Tared call out, and went easily back to the ash-house, and there we watched the course through its changing.

What sounds it made! Tared said it was like the breaking of stones, like quarriers working. The surfaces changed shape, some blocks forced under and some turned up on their points. Deep cracks appeared and widened, broken walls showed transparent green. Everything was trying to push its way downstream at once, and there was not space for it, because some part of it refused to behave as water and run where it would.

Later, the course flowed indeed, and within it the last freed, jagged islands, some rolling past heavily (for it flowed as slow as ever in its bed) turning over and over, some floating flat and raft-like. Our backwater held a smooth, loosened slab in its midst, and this I stepped out on as it pushed against the spit. When I stepped, its edge sunk under—the water was still cool, but no longer hurtfully.

It was a raft as large as the earth floor of our house in Fuen, and thick also. My desire to ride it was very great!

The air was now temperate, but growing heavier in its taste; it had the greenish stink of the leaves in it, that recalled the worst of the lunar afternoon. We knew nothing then about the benefit of the great stones—but we were far from any stone, and our bodies may already have yearned and understood. And the water, when my sisters waded over to me, was temperate also. So we agreed, and took what fruit we had left, and rode that strange raft downstream.

It tilted and dipped among the other blocks and pieces, and rubbed among them with loud complaints and scourings, but it was as yet sturdy, and we learned how to crouch on it, in the centre and a little back, so it would carry us safely. The water rising and splashing gently back against us was pleasant, and we must ever strive and lean in the changing current. Over the whole course hung a steam of whitened water drops.

The air was warming. Again Tared watched the stems; and she made a little mind's image of it, that we call in our language a *snow*: saying that the trees widened their long eyes at us and then closed them as we passed. But I stared after any other thing, an Outdead house—a sign—

O

Ard slept between us; then when she wakened she clung to me while Tared slept. And then I slept. I woke with their hands clutching at me, just as we were tipped over into the water.

For a moment I was under the breaking raft, my hands striking against glimmering green. Then I climbed out, downstream than my sisters, who were already pulling themselves over the bank. We sat down.

There were no big islands in the water any more. We had lost the last of the fruit. Our mouths, hearing this, persistently desired to eat, as in the saying.

My sisters rubbed leaf mud on our sores, though Ard would still not allow her head to be touched where it was burned. The air was now warm and wet but the taste of it easier, somewhat lighter and more delicate. The grove was the same. The water gushed, and the last small lumps nodded along in it, almost submerged. The sun's smear was at its highest. The long morning was over.

○

We began to walk along the bank, not speaking to each other, pushing, almost floating, between the roots. For me, it has ever been easiest to walk swimming, on my hands also, but my sisters walked upright from the beginning. Tared was ahead of me and Ard after. I could see in Tared's shoulders her concentration—not to lurch into a root, to step exactly, to use the roots carefully to push off from. Her bad limp was a pausing and beginning again, over and over. My sisters have never learned to walk evenly, yet that walk, which they both have, has become harmonious after its fashion.

Now Tared stopped and gestured past her—we stopped also to look and listen. Nothing seemed different except for a deeper note from the channel ahead.

"Something is changing."

We continued more eagerly, looking ahead and hearing the noise louder, but as yet seeing no change in the grove. Tared said, "Look, the trees are leaning." And ahead of us, where the grove seemed to lower into the ground, we could see a small round of darkness—not a stone—for the quality of this darkness was otherwise. As we came closer it grew larger in our sight; it contained stars.

Indeed all the stems we passed among were leaning forward now, as if listening with us attentively, and the noise grew gradually louder than the noise of the channel. We walked, unable to take long leaps for the many roots. Here they all bent forward with us as well, yet higher overhead they rose straight again, high into the leaves. We came out of the trees.

○

We saw a wide, flat scape, grayish and flooded, covered with huge, random stains of darkness. I know now that it was not anything wonderful, yet it seemed to us so. At our feet the water rolled slowly forward over the brink, with the roots of the last trees stretching down. It was no great drop, hardly our father's height, but our eyes had no measure for it. The light was so strong it made us breathless and giddy, this, and everything we saw there.

The sun blazed through the canopy, not to be looked directly into, and the World close to him was at New. In our sight's confusion he looked as if he had drawn away from us—this was his smaller aspect clear of the stems, in the open sky. He was still very big, brownish and murky, almost invisible, the sun too near, so we could not look at him.

Ahead of us, two rows of cables stood stood out of the water as if they marked the channel, invisible except against the flood. Ah, we have learned to discern them overhead, and the sections of the grid, by the winking of the stars, but they are very faint there even to the eyes of children, as my eyes then were. At the other side of the vale the trees closed on it again—as it seemed a shorter growth, with some smooth, low, reddish mounds just visible behind them.

What frightened us was our bodies' fear, being unable to interpret what we saw and so, almost, being unable to see it. There was not any great drop, yet we felt it to be great—the vale, the cables, the grove and hills sank away too soon. That was the effect of the near horizon—so the whole scape seemed to be pulled downhill, to roll right off over the limb into space.

The stains were shadows. Overhead, they were repeated in holes of starlessness, unevenly edged with light—which were the great stones.

○

That basin we crossed at mid-day, with the heat building.

THE TAMING ○ 59

The water was shallow and cool. Tared would have lingered at the fall, but there were trees ahead of us also, and past them those reddish, beckoning barrens—it was our first sight of the rising ground. Having seen them, we desired indeed to go to them.

Within the broad bounds of the cables was the deeper channel—the course. The rest of the flood was very shallow. And the ground under water was soft with a kind of tough grass, with uneven rills in it that led in towards the channel. This great cloth of water moved hardly at all; its sunlit surface was an oily, whitish blue. Easiest for us was to look down into it, into the reddish grasses underfoot. I looked also for food, my hands among the grasses, but I could not find any thing.

So followed the cables, south of them in the shallows, and came near the nearest of the stones. The air was indeed goodly there, less green and heavy. Though it still seemed that such a great stone must fall, we were enticed under it out of the harsh sun. The shadowy water, when we disturbed it, ran with slips of reddish light cast from the edge of the stone.

This stone was even larger and more irregular than those among the trees. But we could not tell its size with any accuracy; it hung there with nothing to tell us even how high. And so this looking was not pleasant despite the shadows, being strange—indeed it frightened Ard so much that she would not look at all.

The water was very shallow and we could leap easily—liking to walk upright, my sisters stood to their thighs and soared, dark bodies over that pale surface, holding the ragged hems of their dresses between their teeth, their black hair lifting. Tared took Ard's hand; almost, they floated, the water lifting in slow white splashes around them, the dark image of their bodies looping under them on the water.

Coming out from the stone I turned over on my back, and looked upward into the World. The World and the sun were very near. But if I stayed where the sun was hid by the stone I could gaze for a short time.

New, he was all darkened, but not so black as the sky around him, and his edge softly gleamed, with a rim of haze around him, very thin and faint, like the slenderest thread. At such distance what is seen is indeed seen, yet it cannot be sure of itself. The eye strives, and the distance defeats it, the mind will not acknowledge what is wordlessly given. Ah, that ball of the World at New was downy and trembly, and what was there refused to reveal itself! Most of the visible World is Sheath or water, yet I could not differentiate even these. The habitable World was turned back, away from my eyes, at the poles. There in the north lived the people, our father was there and the Sanev our friends, and all the scholars in Book with their stupid, complicated talk and ways. There somewhere was the City with all its lamplit houses, and the Doll. Saska and I had speculated, whether we would be able to see the great Doll from the Moon. But nothing was as we had thought. I could not discover how to look for any thing—it all merged and blurred in that brownish bowl. And in the south—those folk we had so often talked about, where everything was heads-over-heels! Was it possible that I could see their fires, and my mind deny what I had seen?

Now there was a dulling, a reddish shadowing of the light, and I swam a little outside the stone and saw that the sun, who had been nudging at the World, was pressed close against him—a little eclipsed by him. Only a glance and my eyes burned and I turned away. But that redness remained for some time, though the sun did not then completely hide himself. Later we grew used to this redness at noon—almost always it came, a ruddy darkening that would last four-or-eight hours, from its first tinge to its clearing off.

I had drifted outside the stone and when I tried to look again, the threads of sun cut sharp between my fingers. I rolled over in the water, and leaped to catch up to my sisters.

○

By the time we had crossed the basin, the sun was out clear, his light again harsh, and the twar limb of the World was glowing more strongly. He would wax now. In the space of two days, as they are counted in the World, he would become that great crescent that we had first seen, and we would have lived in the Moon a whole lunar day.

○

At the farther side were again the same trees, growing out of the higher ground, with their exposed roots reaching over into the water, and circled by a thread of dark, drying wet—that showed how the water was falling. We swam among those roots in their shadows, and pulled ourselves north through their skirts to where the cables entered the trees. But we found no watercourse, only a gray Outdead bank partly stacked and covered with broken roots and drying ruck—that was a sign.

The grove was the same as ever, the aligned planks of the stems, the soaring roots, the green roof and greenish taste and shadow—but silent; there was no sound of water. My sisters climbed out.

Behind us was the basin we had crossed. Reddish bars were appearing on each side of the channel as the water receded. How the brightness bleached our sight! The forest we had left behind was a pale, strange green against the black sky and lay low, too low at the eastern horizon. The soundless course emerging was so distant it stood still in its fall. Overhead, the stars gleamed between the stone-darknesses, and here near the edge of foliage, the terrible sun sought us still, out of black sky. But we had crossed, and we could hide from him—the World was hidden from us already. It would be good to turn away, to enter the welcome shade.

I was in the channel where it met the bank, and saw that it was deep. I could not touch bottom, and turned over, and dove. At first the bank was by me, slippery and cool, Outdead smooth. But lower, in the broken, underwater light I could see my hands reach for it and meet instead an absence. I felt perhaps the smallest drag forward along my fingers. Here was the course! under ground.

A door under ground was a good marking—such a passage might serve as a house against the heat, for later it would be dry. I thought then also that perhaps it hid the entrance to proper shelter, even to Atwar's mansions. So we argued, but we could not safely swim into it yet; the water filled it. So we walked into the grove, intending to follow it over ground, and find another opening.

First we slept in the shade, and when we woke it was

already much hotter. I think it was then, that we marked without marking it the passing of our first whole lunar day.

○

So we walked westward, searching for the channel, using the sides of the stems and the sun's smear to guide us, and finding after a time another cable—from cable to cable we took our directions. Sometimes we found one to the north of us, and must turn; sometimes to the south. But the tree's alignment we trusted. We passed four-or-eight cables and as yet no visible water, and no stone.

It was easy to walk, but not easy, for we were very tired from the increasing heat, and the thickening air, and from thirst and hunger. I had those four husks in my pocket and we licked them again for their salt, and ate Tared's yeast. It was very little, and she dared not let us eat all of it.

"I think, if I am its farm, it is eating me," she said. Indeed, she was much thinner now than Ard, whose skin was tight and shiny and who looked by contrast somewhat swollen.

Soon Ard sat down. She was beginning to breath fast again, and her body was returning into that sickness, that anger.

"Do not go away from us, into your mind!" Tared said to her urgently.

"No, I will not, if I can help it, but my body is remembering!—"

It was not yet so hot, the air not yet so thick, that she should stop, but she remembered and was afraid. Later, she was within her sickness and remembered nothing.

Tared argued with her about the good course under ground, and that we would soon find it, and for a time we persuaded her to walk with us. There were more husks in the soil, with good salt in them, but without water they did not comfort us.

The air thickened quickly now. The foliage was misted over and the stems blurred, and it was no longer possible to stare ahead after the next cable. But the stems we could make out, and the sun's position overhead, and so we kept on, wanting to sleep but not daring. The World's gleam showed through the weave of leaves; he must have swelled to a goodly crescent. Him we had confidence in already, for we had done nothing else in the Moon but travel westward, and he stood ever constant in the sky. Now, our bodies recognize his place—we can tell our whereabouts without thinking. And such familiarity was beginning already: the seasons would violently change, and we would journey in many narrow paths, but he was steadfast.

I was the searcher, for Tared was busy caring for Ard. She was again very sick and dreamy, and her skin was hot-cool and slicked with sweat. She spoke aloud of Atwar in no clear way, using the dual—perhaps it was of the Sanev she spoke. It was not as if she complained—and that was strange, for looking back, all the World's words to Atwar, all the songs and prayers, had been a kind of plaint. Rather she spoke small, personal things, that were better said to her sister, that Atwar would never have understood. And when Tared interrupted her she did not hear. It was thus if I remember it, her voice going on rather fast and harsh, as Tared urged her forward.

"Be careful when you braid my hair into your hair, because my head is burned. Hold me carefully, because my body is burnt with your oil. My dress is a colour you have never seen, pressed close against your face, it is the colour of the most distant mountains. I will clothe you, I have clothed you in distance, I have clothed you in sapphire."

"Come Ard, and do not play thus, do not lie down!"

"Look into my bald palms, and into the bald surface of my mouth, and the bald inner sides of my fingers. Can you read the directions written into my palms? In the right there is a mark from the wrist to the centre finger and that is your path to-us, walk across it with your tongue, walk across it with your finger. In the left is Chmedes, circle it with your finger, and the Cape begins at the heel, and Hadley here, at the thumb."

"Give me that foolish hand and come! Listen—help-us to listen for the water."

"When you press my left hand together, the deep watercourse runs into the Sea of Rains. The marks of your oil are your directions on my skin. I will read you in them. My face is Chmedes also and my head is the broken Sea."

"Ard, cover your breasts, let me lift you. Come forward, come to the house that is waiting for us."

"I am raining out of the cells of my body. Do not cover my head with ashes, it is harmed. No one shall cover it! My breasts are angry, they pain me, my body is angry. I am raining into your garment of distance. When I squat over the pit, spread there your braid and your bright blue cloth!"

This I have recorded because, though we counted it for nothing, there was some reason in it that we later understood.

○

By then Ard would not walk, or could not. Tared lifted her up, and laid her arms and sinking head across my back, and held her there—so between us we carried her forward. So tired we were! we would gladly have lain down to sleep then and there. Tared had a determination past her strength. But she would soon have fallen despite herself. The roots gave us little space, and the air was so thick we could scarcely take our direction from tree to tree. Then I noticed a change in the soil—the old trace of a rivulet, that we stepped across, and then another. I began to look more closely at the roots where they emerged, and saw evidence of the passing of water; some dead leaf trailed broken around them. Then we came to a whole, broken tree, a plank rotted and cracked over where it lay, with its roots torn loose long ago from the ground. They hung softened and broken, and the tree's stem lay ahead of us on its edge, then broken and lying on its plank-side partly covered with soil, like a descending path.

We walked there beside it, till we had followed its length, and saw how its high leaves had fallen with it—mostly they were gone, swept or rotted away. Yet we saw there for the first time how they are attached to the stem, at the top, by two rows of whitish buds like stumpy fingers. From some, a dead twig still protruded, with its remnant of blackened leaf. As for the fruit, we could see how it must grow under each leaf, there where it widened, but none was left, only four-or-eight thickened bits of membrane, and whitish discolorations where the fruit had pressed.

The last of the blackened leaves lay combed out towards the north and forward of us.

THE TAMING ◯ 65

"Tared, if we follow these signs in the soil—see how they are leading in one direction—surely we will come to the course!"

What we had found gave my sister new courage and she strove, her breath hissing through her teeth. I think then that I carried Ard myself, but Tared would not release her hold. We fell often, but gently, as it would be to fall forward in water. Ard was then deeply asleep, and when she shuddered she coughed and ceased breathing for a moment—all this I could feel from her body lying across my back.

But now we saw numerous goodly signs—much black leaf caught against the trees, and the soil broken with the small tree-images of tiny confluent streams. Ah, it was no ignorant thing that my body chose to walk on four limbs, for I saw all these things clearly! The tree-images—they are not as lunar trees, but as World-trees, seemly and spreading, with innumerable branches. That water should pattern itself in the soil to correspond to the way trees grow in the World is ever a wonder to me! Yet it does so by running as it were backwards, into the stem from the branches. Even now do these intricate mind-trees continue to give me great joy; my eyes have pleasure in them, remembering the trees in the Fu-en marshes, where I played with Saska in the World.

◯

Thus we came to the course somewhat west of where it emerged from the ground. It had been close to us for some time, but contained so little water that we did not hear it, or see it through the mists. It was as good as empty. We lifted Ard down, and gave each other what water we found there. I wiped and filled my empty oil bladder, and the bird bladder as well, turning it inside out because it stank, and tying it with its string of human hair. That was the Ludh hair, I remembered how the Sanev cut it from their mothers' heads carelessly—and the Ludh let them. It was tough gray hair and well-lasting.

We turned back, and saw the opening. It was the shape of an overturned bowl. The last water flowed unhurriedly across its lip in a short, rounded fall about as wide as my arm.

Ah, this was indeed Outdead made, with a gray, seamless

wall. Inside, the air steamed and the floor was sticky and blackish under my hands and feet. But the space was high enough that I could stand upright, and wider than I could touch with outstretched hands.

I went in, as far as I could go and still see the gleam of water under me and the pallor of my dress. Our eyes are very wise in darkness, and I went some distance, till Tared's and Ard's shapes at the bright entrance were very small. Indeed it was cooler here, and I called out to them—what a loud, round noise my voice made! so I jumped with surprise at it. Tared came in with Ard, holding her by the sleeves, pulling her along over the floor.

"Ah, it is cooler here! It is dark."

"Come farther—it will be cooler still—"

Tared gave a little laugh. "This is our Darkening, then."

"Or our Defile." I was thinking of our father Betwar's Tale, how he and Atwar as children had hidden in the Defile from the snake, in the distant mountains in the World.

But we dared not go so far that we could not see the entrance, because of the coming flood.

"When we hear it behind us," Tared said, "there will be time to escape from it. It is strong but it moves slowly."

"It will push us out."

We lay down on the floor immediately and slept.

○

I wakened well before sunset, thirsty and very hungry. Tared was up, giving Ard water, and Ard was again sick. Tared had given her yeast, but Ard could not or would not swallow it. Yeast and water ran out of her mouth.

The air was very hot, and the steam from outside had entered the passage so we could see nothing of the entrance except a blurry light. That light had a brownish colour to it, however, that we remembered, and Tared said, "I am listening carefully for the flood wave. Perhaps we ought to go out." But we lingered, because of what it would be like outside.

"Drink, Ask," she said. "There will soon be water enough."

We undid the bladder and soaked the cloth, and drank the last of the water.

THE TAMING ○ 67

I said, "There will soon be fruit also."

She gave me yeast on a bony finger, but so little it saddened my belly instead of comforting it.

"Ask, we will gather this day such a harvest! We were very ignorant, that we did not take enough, and then lost what was left."

"They gave Atwar food with him."

"They gave us also, a little—"

We were silent then, thinking of Atwar, that he had not yet helped us.

○

That extreme hunger did not anger our bodies, but grieved them in a very quiet fashion. It did not feel like hunger but like a turning aside, a carelessness—which was dangerous. When I thought of the fruit, almost I could not remember it as good, and the thought of the taste of yeast was unpleasant, as if I were licking it out of some fold in Tared's body I would not like to see. My belly ached dully. It was difficult to move, easier to lie still, to be almost asleep. If the flood found us, would it not surely take us with it out of the passage unharmed? The water would be cool, and the air easier to breathe.

We did not see how the bore entered the lowered lands or how it spread there to fill them. But its height was dispersed and its force broken, and what reached us was almost noiseless. Suddenly we lay in water, that was quickly rising. It was indeed cooler, and brought me and Tared well awake, chattering and scrambling. We grabbed Ard's sleeves and arms and half-walked, half swam towards the opening.

So fast the water rose that only a narrow slit of reddish air was left at the top of the passage. Then that filled also. We emerged in a tumble.

○

Again the sun took with it the bright reddish light, and everything was suddenly twilit and gray-white in the light of the Half World. This happened sooner than we had thought. The filling of the basin had delayed this flood, precipitated us into night.

The course was now only a treeless space, with the water

brimming everywhere. Swiftly the Moon's wind came, swaying the trees, and then the cloths of driven rain and the drops that ringed the water. And again when wind and rain subsided, the good fruit fell.

○

Here we settled in at that time, and this place provided for us—or, we forced it into providence! It was a grove as wide as two cities, and lay between the vale we had crossed and the open barrens. These barrens I saw later that long morning. I will tell you how I persuaded my sisters to let me go.

After we had eaten I foraged, leaving my sisters to gather fruit, and brought back planks and roots. The great bands of leaf that had fallen lay all around us in the water. I still did not like them, but I went bravely among them—to be angry with them made them even more stubborn. I had to part them courteously, and patiently unwind them, and duck under them when they tried to catch about my neck. I had that knife but ah, I was as children still; indeed I had cut at the soil for the tree, but unwillingly.

Ard and Tared had many fruits, and we made slings of the leaves, tying them up with their long fibres. We wove fibres across their breadth as well, which was four-or-eight leaves wide. They were primitive, for we did not have the knack of it. But Ard climbed into one and it held, though she said the cross-strings were too tight. There she sat half-submerged, with the fibres straining; she rocked, and pulled at the tangles in her hair, and picked at her healed sores, and smoothed and arranged the two sleeves that were her only dress—"I am most ugly, if I am half as ugly as you, Tared!"

We were glad to see her returned to herself.

And the cool light was pleasant for our eyes, and to be able to see so far among the stems. It seemed to me I could sniff a great stone, and I said this to my sisters.

Ah, to go away from them, my restlessness, to make haste across absence, to close that emptiness as if to close my grief! At that time I began as well, to make myself to speak myself alone, to say no longer "We-are going," as is seemly, but instead to receive that aloneness into myself and acknowledge it in speech, as our father Betwar did. And the very words seared my mouth, and I stammered much, but I did it.

○

They let me swim as far as the stone. It hung over the course, and west of it the spaces between stems were all empty, like a row of high, straightened doors. I could see out into a halved scape—bright barrens and black sky.

I swam immediately back and told my sisters. Tared looked at me tiredly as she stood to her neck in the water, still harvesting, and Ard stared stubborn from her sling—ah, they were not much like twins now! Tared was all bones—even her black teeth were more visible, and seemed sharper, her lips pulled back from them and her cheeks sunken. Her hair curled like a bush around her narrow face and shoulders, matted with filth and old leaf, its ends grayed from the fire. Even the healed burns on her skin were thin—long marks like writing, whereas Ard's were broader—all of Ard was broader, stretched and shiny. Ard had braided her hair after a fashion, and it hung down her back and her face was very round, the newly picked scars bright pink on it like splashes of dye.

"I would have gone and looked," I said slowly, refusing the we-form, stammering. "It is not dangerous. But see how courteously I have first returned to tell you."

So they let me go and I went leaping, pushing through tangles of sunk leaves, then swimming free above them under the stone. I could feel the current's steady westward push, and it increased. I heard also the noise of the fall.

○

The water was flowing over a shallow brink at the edge of the grove, and below gathering itself, filling four-or-eight meandering courses that continued out over the barrens.

So much there was to see, a great wash of scape across my eyes! the World hanging at more than Half overhead, and here the big brownish spread of the open land, the mountains! the same narrowing grid of cables rising out of the valley, the same shadows of great stones, marking the convolutions of the ground like dark cloths. I saw Hadley! but I did not know it was that mountain, so smooth it was and low. What I saw seemed only an absence, a falling away of the near horizon which still made me a little dizzy and scared. There was another grove there, set against the mountains—I could discern it across the clear air, a bluish darkening, and the course led my eyes towards it by many shining strands.

Here, the water pushed past me calmly, unhurried, almost as if pausing at the brink. Its spray hung against the bright scape and its sound was low and constant. Below me, it gushed fuller, as over an outcropping, but I did not then understand what it was.

I lifted my eyes to the World. He stood tilting, the waxing *Twarwerd* who would be Full at the mid-night of the Moon, and his face was already too bright to recognize. I looked towards the northern edge of the Sheath, right at the terminator, trying to guess our fastland, whether I could discern our coast in its early dawn. My eyes teared. Then, it was as if something black crossed there suddenly.

I turned back, which was harder against the push of the current, and the leaves trailing towards the brink. The surface water eased under the stone, and I eased in my stroke as well. I called loudly, carefully to my sisters, "Wait for me now, I-am returning!"

But in that ease there was an unluck—a band of leaf, heading me off—and when I stood to steady myself I felt for a moment a hard edge; then my feet slipped. Ah, I must have disappeared from the surface without a sound. I was under, skidding harshly downward against a smooth wall I could not catch at, then tumbled suddenly over and drawn into choking darkness! Had it been quick it would have been better, but it was very slow, and yet I could not prevent it. The last I saw behind me were the leaves streaming after me, against a patch of wavering light the shape of an overturned bowl.

Ard

And yet they have not told how we first, immediately, walked on the Moon. Immediately walked—and we had never walked before—of all the promises they made us, this one came to pass. I remember most the stretch and tallness of my body, when we stood out of the cars. And the lightness—that was the air's lift. It was not as in the World. If we were stood upright by the scholars and they did not support us—there, we were heavy, we crumpled into our ordinary crouch.

We were crippled in the World.

But in the Moon we walked from the very first.

It was the same as being lifted up to be carried—that first swoop of lightness, before I was settled between the scholars' shoulders, or in our father Betwar's arms. Then the Sanev lifted me so—

But in the Moon it was not passing; it was enduring, and that changed it. Indeed any good thing, if it endures, becomes ungood—as the coolness, that we welcome, and then we hate it.

What I remember of those first hours on the sward—almost nothing, except the lifting, that did not settle, did not return into rest. The walking, the good turning to ungood. Ah, it was all ungood, in the beginning in the Moon!

○

When Ask went off Tared was afraid, and began to count like children. "Now he is at the pool under the smaller stone, now he is nearing the trees again, now he is looking at the scape. Now he is turning back as he promised—" and she would not be easy or stop counting, till we heard his glad call.

Then when he did not appear she said nothing, but set off swimming towards the channel. She did not even say to me "Come," but I followed. Was Ask playing with us? We knew that he was not.

Ah, there was the glade he had told us of, with the stone's dark shadow on it, and no sign of our brother! We circled, looking in among all the roots and ever calling. Tared said, "He has seen—something else, and gone there."

"We heard him calling."

"What he said was something other than we heard, and he has gone somewhere else—"

"Tared, he said, *I-am returning*."

She kept staring about with her teeth bared—ah, she was bone thin, and her look very sharp and wild. I did not think it then, but later I thought it, she was afraid he had seen Atwar, and followed him.

"Returning—to what he saw, then—look, there is the edge of the grove—he is surely there." She almost laughed, then struck herself. This I had never seen her do before. She was repenting having let him go.

Tared made me look over. He was lying on his face in one of the streams, with something black running out from him into the water, and a mash of leaf around his neck. I had to squint for the light, and hold tight to my sister but I saw him, and standing bold on his shoulder was the blue bird. I think too we heard the other birds, singing. That one looked at us, and flew away.

○

We lived at that time in a house, which we made with great effort inside the first culvert, and that kept us from harm through the lunar night. Ask is deft in many things, a maker, clever with his hands. So he was then also, but his hands were harmed, and Tared and I had to make the house by ourselves—but his mind contrived it, and he told us what to do.

○

Ah, we had brought him with great difficulty back to the slings! but there was less leaf in mid-water by then and we were two, and I was also strong. The water had fallen a little and he lay over water, but the air being now cool I got in with him; so we lay deeper. He wakened, and told us chattering what had happened, and called the leaves cruel—though they are but leaves. His head's wound was not serious, but he had bled much from it. We laid the drinking cloth over it carefully. His right arm angered him, and his hands also.

THE TAMING ○ 73

Tared tied up his arm—she took one of the sleeves and tore a great strip from it. I said, we should bind his hands with leaf, but he shouted he would not have leaf near him any more, since it had nearly killed him. His fingers were scraped; two on his twelhand he could not move.

After he had shouted, he cried. Tared told him about the bird, and we said we had heard perhaps all three singing. He smiled at this, and cried, and after that went to sleep.

Then Tared bound his crooked fingers straight with the drinking cloth, for his head did not need it, having stopped bleeding. Ah, we cried over him in pity, then! His bald knees stuck out of the water, and his skinny arms, one tied up in a soaking rag, one covered with pink scars. His hair was stuck with dirt and dried blood. How could we heal him?

"The qualities of the leaf were good for our burns," she said doubtfully. "The scholars had done better to put us in Medical Book and teach us to heal, and given us some of their grasses."

I said, "They believe Atwar has grasses."

"Whatever fails us, it is the scholars' fault, whatever is wrong, Atwar will right it when he chooses," said Tared half laughing. "This is the way it is for us in the Moon." When she laughed it was ugly, because her mouth was already pulled away from her teeth in a kind of grin.

I said, "You ought to feed your body, Tared, it has become very thin."

She was leaning over the sling, her eyes sunken but clear over that false smile. "I am eating all I can. I have a full belly. I think it is hard on me, this farming. We will see how it is, when the night season is over." She had an idea we could make a well, that would produce yeast before the next flood.

This was the time when the air began to burn in coolness, the water receding, keeping itself warm over warm soil. I was yet comfortable because my belly was full, though it made me sick to gaze up into the stems, and I was afraid of what would come. We were glad when Ask wakened and we could talk with him.

○

I helped with that house, though Tared quarrelled with me that I did not. I think I helped in a kind of desperation—until it was finished, there was no where to take myself.

When the water abated, and we could enter the culvert, we planked up the two walls like dikes, against which the water could lean and harden. For it cannot be shaped as it is hardening, only afterwards, and we had no knowledge of it.

And I did not sleep, or quite turn away into my sickness, Tared and Ask persuading me. Tared told me many times to remember that this present coolness was as great heat, compared with what was to come. She also said, "If you will move, you will be warmed." And: "Do not cry like that, or your eyes will cover over with a skin." But I held my eyes almost shut, always.

O

Ask kept to the bank, but Tared and I strove much. As soon as the water was lower than the entrance, we built the first wall, a little farther in than the width of a small house. We had to tilt our heads to breathe, so little room there was. A small push of air came through the passage above the water, and lay on our wet faces and hurt with coolness. Ah, we were forced to fill our lungs with it, to go under water. Tared's legs tangled with mine and sometimes she kicked at me and pushed me out of the way. When she emerged she said it was easier to do it herself, but if I waited she was also angry. Ask said our round shouts from the culvert scared him—they scared us, also.

Then we were glad that it stood fast. We stuffed the gaps with leaves, till we had blocked the passage entirely.

O

Meanwhile Ask, overhead, made a lamp out of the husks of fruit. The husks liked to break into two bowls, no deeper than a cupped hand. Ask's lamp was a husk not fully parted, but opened in a slit. He had broken many in the trying. He shouted at his hands and grimaced.

"Ah, these fingers will not obey me. The scholars -" he began.

"*Ought-to-have-given-us* a lamp", finished Tared with her strange grin, and I quickly added: "*Atwar-will-provide-for-us*

THE TAMING ○ 75

a lamp."

And when Ask wondered, we laughed and told him, speaking together, "*This is the way it is for-us in the Moon.*" It was ever a proverb with us after that.

He blew into it to dry it, and rubbed the stem off, and scoured it so it sat. We watched him light it—he put in it a little of my World's oil. Ah, we were unsure whether it would spit, and we drew back! But it burned low and steady, and when I put my hand over it, I felt its warmth in my palm.

○

Ask could not yet move about, so we helped him get down into the soft mud of the ground, and crept also under the soil, as close to the lamp as we could, to eat and rest.

Then Ask made a fire there in the ground, using the spitting leaf, and they let me sleep a little in that soil it warmed, but Tared complained, and began the second wall. It was built crosswise this time, so we could go to and fro over it; but by then I could not help her much.

○

And our house was as yet full of water! and the water still behaving just as it liked, and except on its surface going where it liked. Yet we had stopped it from the east.

Now the air burned our throats, and everything was whitening over with that skin—soil, roots, stems, our bodies as well. We must still fill the house with what we needed—leaves, wood, a bladder of dry earth, a sling of fruit. Tared was very weary, and this made her complain, and Ask cried, because he could not help us, but she said—"It is not you—Ard could if she would." But I could not.

This is what our house was like, when we entered it, not habitable! filled with water over the brim, with bits of wood floating on top, and thick with leaves and muck. Its floor was deep in slippery leaf and mud, and the burst sling, the fruit bumping. Had I not been so tired, I would have seen how desperate and pitiful it was! The fire we left to burn itself out. So we went into the house.

Ask brought the lamp in himself, floating it before him, going forward cautiously with his hair spread out on the water. Inside the culvert, the light glowed suddenly forth, happy and rosy through its base, and brighter from its lip, showing us the roof and more dimly our farther wall rising. Little slips of red light ran like oil on the agitated surface of the water; we saw them dance across each other's faces. Tared slid inside, and we helped Ask easily—it was I who had trouble, my body not being so thin.

"Do not lose that last garment," Tared scolded as I clambered over. "Oh, oh, oh—" Ask hooted in the rounded air, and Tared and I hooted also, "Ah, ah, ah!" We listened to our foolish voices.

○

The water stood still now just over the highest plank, about three hands' breadth from the roof. Since we had begun to build, there was gone as much as three days, as they are counted in the World. Out on the channel, and wherever we had not recently broken it, the surface was grown over with a slippery skin.

Tared filled up the wall with pieces of root we had left, Ask directing her very minutely, and looking about at what we had made, and telling us how it could have been better done. But he was unable to help us because of his arm. He kept the lamp, protecting it with his hand.

When the frame was higher than the water, we began to empty it. Perhaps already it was warmer, perhaps the house itself, the containment of it, warmed my mind, for I was able to strive also, without anger.

We had no bowls—saying to each other, *"The Scholars ought—"* and used our hands, scooping and scooping across the uppermost root. All that time we could not be sure we would succeed—whether the walls were adequately sealed. Yet the level of the water inside the house was falling.

When I rested I immediately slept—and there was no where to sleep, and Ask could not support me. He kept crying out, cautioning us about the lamp and the walls.

"Ask, you are angry at your body which will not allow you to help us," said Tared, gasping.

"Strike me then, as you are used," he answered.

It was a strange striving, if any one had seen it! if the Sanev had seen what we were doing! but twice that house, they could have built in the space of a World's morning! The water resisted our haste, falling slowly away from our hands. But at last I could lie down—I lay in the deep mud. Indeed, our house was filled with air, and that air was warm!

I woke more comfortable. I could see my sister and brother standing, and Ask crouched over me turned away—their bodies were thick with mud; the lamp glowed behind Ask steadily. I lay warm and listened to their voices; Tared was working at the leaking walls. They had made a mortar, the earth in the bladder being dry. Mud fell against my face and I flung up my arm.

"Ard is wakening." Ask nudged me with his knee. "Ard!"

"Let her sleep—she will wake, when the house is completed." Yet it was good for them that I had slept well, for I could later watch the lamp.

"Ah!" Tared sighed and stretched herself, her voice harsh with tiredness but glad also. "Let us wash the bladder, and fetch in clean water. Look at our sling—so filthy—is this indeed the sling?" She had crouched down, and was pulling it out of the mud. The last fruit bumped over me. "Ard, we know you are awake!"

The surface of the water cracked when she leaned out and struck at it, and the sling came back spraying chilly water over me, when she threw it down! Ask gave her the drinking cloth from his hand. He said, "My fingers are stout, like Ard's! but straighter now than they were."

Tared washed the cloth, and the bladder, and gave him water out of it, and me—then I must waken indeed, for she pried my mouth open with her fingers! But they were smiling.

○

The walls were firm. This is how it was—the water outside was going hard. It would seal the house.

We set the sling up then, tying it into the walls; but we dared not sit in it, or set any thing at all in it, for fear of pulling the house in on us.

We ate then, sitting in the mud, and were warm and comfortable. Tared slept suddenly, sitting with her head back against the west wall and her mouth open. Ask's eyes kept closing, and he fell asleep cautioning me much about the lamp. Tared in her sleep slid sideways, and started up—she said rapidly, looking around—"We must hang the leaf across the sling to dry, for burning!" So we roused ourselves, and took what was lying in the mud and hung it up. Then, I was well from that warmth, and though I slept it was a good sleep—and when Tared woke me saying "You must watch now, I cannot keep awake any longer," looking down at me with her deep, hungered eyes, I was immediately ready to get up, and take care of the lamp and the house, and let her sleep beside Ask.

O

It was very good for me to be under ground where I did not see the Moon—to look about me up there ever sickened me. Whether it was mostly through looking I cannot tell, but it seemed that if I looked, I fell forward inwardly. My belly was out of balance, and my body received everything I saw outside as ungood. I know Tared and Ask noticed this a little also, for we have talked of it since, but it did not sicken them, so they could not understand. To be so sick—it was worse even than the pain of the terrible coolness, or the seizing up of my limbs in that hot season, and it continued for a long time. Even now, I am not so used! And sometimes it seems to me I would be well again only if I could return up into the World, though there I could not walk or stand. So I have ever liked to be under ground, to think of the weight of an Outdead roof over me, or the hardened water pressing, and nothing to look at but familiar faces and lamplit walls.

So it was I who best endured that second night—my purpose already was to hide, not only from the violence of the climate, but also from that scape which my eyes did not understand. Ask and Tared did not know this, and their expectation of me then was surely more argument, more trouble. They were comfortable enough, but for them that night was very long, and they grew restless from inactivity. There was nothing to strive against: the lamp was our only necessary care.

The sling kept well, its greens paling—and we learned that it was the coolness outdoors that blackened and rotted the dead leaves. So we lay in it all three, and it held—there was also enough to eat. Ask managed to fix the lamp into the wall, and we put bits of leaf in it—that oil burned with its darker, sputtering flame, and its stink was bearable.

I spent hours combing my hair with my fingers, and after it was sleek I combed theirs also. I did not tire, and though sometimes the strands were so tangled that they cried out, they permitted me, and I think my patience, my stubbornness in unknotting all those matted, ashy strands, calmed them. From that time Tared ceased trying to press her hair flat, as she had in the World—she let it curl where it would.

When Ask was plaintive and did not sleep he would weep, till we persuaded him to play with the knife. He was well tempted, and he made more lamps and small bowls, and worked bits of wood, and did not cut himself. His fingers were healing. The Sanev used knives before they were adult.

"They did not receive them," he said doubtfully. "They took them in the north."

"But this knife they meant for you and Saska."

I said to him: "Nevi and Nevar would think you foolish if you do not use it now."

Ask grinned when I said that. He knew how the Sanev would have scoffed at his doubts.

We were very dirty. We did not have enough clean water even to drink, but Ask found he could cut the water outside with his knife, standing in the sling as we held him steady, and reaching through the smoke hole with his skinny arm. These bits and shards we laid in our ragged cloth until they had entered it, then squeezed that water into each others' mouths, as we have ever done. Ah, we could have put them directly on each others' tongues, but we did not think of it then.

Ask held one up, and stared at the lamp through it till it ran into his hands; he said it broke the light. We looked also—that was the first time we played thus with it.

That night, also, Tared tried to make a yeast well in the floor, but what she put in did not thrive. Nor did it die, and this was another beginning—that it could survive the lunar night away from her body. Then, she began to complain and chafe to clean herself, and talked with us about making farms.

We worked at the leaf, for Ask could cut across the thinnest fibres. Then, we did not think to scrape it, and it stank, and was tough and unwieldy. But we patched our dresses, and Ask made pockets for his thighs, as men wear, and as Atwar wore when first he went into the Moon. Thus we occupied ourselves in those hours, those days of hours. Ask and Tared looked out ever, and were eager for the day, but I was comfortable.

That Moon's night passed. When Ask first fetched down the water shards, the World had already begun to wane and the worst coolness was setting in. But we had no harm from it in our house, lying close together with full bellies. And finally, when he looked out, he saw at the opening the rosy light of morning.

○

Ah Atwar, where were you when they wandered and nearly died? If you followed them, why did you not call out to them, and run and embrace them? Did you dig out that poor buried doll to stare at it, did you dress yourself in that root-caught dress? Did you find that doll, and with your own ears hear the live birds singing? Did their plank pass you nodding empty in the channel? Where did you find the third doll broken among the stems? When the belly of the tree blazed red, and smoke poured upward where were you, lifting your nostrils to its flavour? Did you see those eaten husks among your hoard, when you were at gathering? Did you finger those abandoned slings and wonder at them, did you tear at them then, and start away at the round wordless shouts from under ground? Did you tread overhead to stare at the embers of their fire? Did you know then they were so near?

II.
The Ungreeting

Tared

Ah, we would all tell this part of our Tale! Ard and I singing as twins into each other's mouths and Ask making the loud clapping! For it was into Atwar's presence we emerged—that was the morning we first were sure of him!

How can we say what we felt in our hearts? Now such time has passed by, and so much is changed, how can we remember what it was like, that emerging? It was not a greeting as the scholars intended! It was an ungreeting, such as no fond scholar could have imagined. We came out, Ask first, crawling on our bellies over the hard surface, and saw Atwar sitting on our roof, at our fire.

He ran immediately away.

We all saw him, indeed we all insisted that we saw him, and for each of us there was no doubt but that it must be he. We were so surprised we uttered no sound.

We had not even stood up—Ask was still on his feet and hands, having squirmed out of the house and the passage, and I was directly behind him, pushing myself up to a crouch, and Ard coming with more difficulty after us. We could scarcely look over the top of the course.

Sometimes I suspect she did not then see him.

What Ask saw was that he looked directly across us, and sniffed, his lip lifted over light teeth; his head went back and his chin went up and his nose went up and his eyes were lower than his nose. Ask said he was big till he stood, with Betwar's big head and shoulders; this is what Ask saw, and that he was dressed in something but Ask could not tell what it was and his hair was divided, the same on each shoulder, and of two colours interbraided, light and dark. But it had seemed to me like a sleeve, not hair. I saw his big head turned aside as he got up and ran away. He stood, and turned from us falling forward in a slow spring, running like Ask on his feet and hands, but low on the ground, and very surely and gracefully. I thought his dress was light—there seemed, across his shoulders, some light cloth loosely spreading. None of us saw what his legs were like, or that he limped, but Ask and I said he was not tall when he stood. Ard said he was very tall, and naked.

We scrambled up where he had been, and saw that our fire in its pit was still burning—and beside it, pressed flat and folded over, lay one of the dolls. None of this we saw well, for the light was so strong after the days of near-darkness that everything was blanched on our eyes—that is why we could not tell what colour Atwar was, or the colour of his hair or garment. Even as he went off it was as into a pale, toneless scape—the shadows themselves seemed light to us. Also, he moved soundlessly.

There were long scratches radiating from the fire, as if he had scraped the ground clean around it with his fingers. The fire burned low and hot; it was banked with earth, and what burned in it seemed to be a kind of earth also. The ground itself felt warmed. We stood trembling.

Ask picked up the doll, unfolding it. Ard said that it was doubtlessly hers. I thought it was mine, the one I had buried for Saska near the sward. But I was not sure. Did Atwar follow us all that way, or find it by chance?

We touched the doll, handing it back and forth and looking at it carefully. There were two even rows of marks in it, as if Atwar had carried it folded tight in his teeth. Holding the doll made me think without argument that Atwar knew of us, and had willingly drawn near to us. Then it was not a desperate necessity to run after him.

Yet he had run from us.

We crouched at the fire and told each other how he had looked. Only Ask had seen his face, his expression.

"He sniffed, or he looked as if he sniffed." We could not remember hearing any sound. "He looked across us—not into our faces."

I said, "Our-father reminded me, that Atwar does not know of us at all. We were born and prepared for him without his knowledge, long after he went away."

Ard said, "He knows of us now. I think he has gone to prepare for us—then, he will return and greet us." Her voice

THE TAMING ○ 85

broke—even she dared to glance hastily far into the forest, where he had gone.

We waited tremblingly at his fire. Ask tended it, laying on wood, careful to bank it as Atwar had done. Where we had trodden on his marks, we smoothed them. After some time, Ask went back into the house and handed out the rest of the fruit, and the lamp, and the yeast wrapped in leaves.

The surface of the channel ran, the trees steamed and seeped. The colour that was drained out of our eyes returned, and the scape began to look clear and bright in the transparent air of the second morning.

○

But Atwar did not return, and we grew restless. He had run south, but we all thought he was turning west, the last we saw of him. Ask went back and looked out over the basin and saw no sign. He said when he returned, "Let us go west past the stone, to the place where I fell. There we can see a great way into the next barrens—perhaps we will see him."

None of us thought we need stay here at the fire, or watch for him in this one place. Atwar was everywhere, swift and knowledgeable, and would find us again, when he was ready for us.

The channel was awash now and slippery, and the soil soft and black as the air warmed. We walked among the stems, and past our old slings, and saw them black and rotted and hanging in shreds, though their knots still held. We came to the open glade under the stone.

Ah, it was sweet in that morning! When we stepped out on the pool, it swung and dipped under our feet. So we walked over, and near the other side it cracked, and became islands in the runny water, but we went so lightly we did not fall between. We crossed the top of the other culvert, to the place where Ask had fallen. A hardened waterfall stood out under our feet, its surface steaming. The shade of the forest stretched some distance across the barrens; then the sunlight lay on them, and their streams were already running through the reddish, uneven ground. The great stones hung as they did over the basin, almost invisible against the black sky, but the sunlight traced their edges red as the vales. The World was Twarwerd, waning.

Our lungs liked that air, and we breathed deep—it was fresh and tasteless, and of the most perfect coolness. Ask said, "Out there—it would be a good place to leap and run!" and I understood. It seemed, we could have floated off that jut of rooty bank, and the air would have taken us into its embrace; we would easily have been able to reach the low mountains. Only Ard crouched and squinted—"Say, if you see him. I do not like to look." The Moon's limb frightened her when she saw how close it was.

○

We did not however cross to those mountains then. So low they were, they seemed but an extension of the barren hills— and we thought the Cape was farther off. We imagined Hadley as a great peak, having seen from the World the shadows he cast, when the terminator neared him.

○

So we were held in a kind of attentiveness, there where we were. We lived in and over the water in slings, making a complex network of them in those hours of days, though we had to begin again each windfall, for they did not survive the night. They were most rudely black and torn! Ask rode the flood—it was he who first stood and followed it, fearlessly! He began to learn then, on that lesser current, what he would later play at and teach us, in the great flood-bore in the west. We ate and harvested and stored the fruit with us, hiding in our house at night when the Moon hardened. Some time we spent there also in the days of afternoon, to be out of the great heat. More slings we took in with us, and improved it greatly, making a good, wood floor above the mud, and pockets for the yeast and fruit.

I began to farm as I had planned—we dug shallow wells that first morning, out on the barrens. And the yeast throve. Here was almost no soil over the rock and that soil thin and lifeless, so we carried out black earth from the forest. It was on the rock itself that the reddish plants grew, spreading a loose, covering on the soil, seeming not to take nourishment from it. They were tough, not to be plucked, though Ask tore a great strip free at the side of a stream and it lifted easily.

We did not cut it, however, for it was living, and he smoothed it down again. When we looked closely, we could see innumerable tiny flowerets growing in it, shaped like spouts or short reeds, the same red as the foliage but paler and more intense: they look in the morning as if they were floating, but they are toughly stemmed. Later in the day they close. The air was most sweet, in the cool mornings, and Ask and I found it good to be among the farms while the forest shadow was still spread over them, and as the water gradually loosened itself in the grove, and came pouring out of that culvert where he had been dragged and harmed.

We looked ever out after Atwar, and he did not yet appear, and Ard said a little angrily, "We could as well be scholars, in our unluck in seeing him!"

○

We thought we could not have comfortably entered that open land in the heat of the afternoon, and we could not swim its courses, which were spread and shallow and dried quickly away. Out there the red foliage became browner, the flowers closed, and the good air lost its moisture after the mid-day; there was great dry heat and no shade.

It was then I had to venture out to harvest the yeast and close the wells. I threw my hair over my head, to go forth into that air! and I remember how I wished that my farms were against some east-facing grove, so I could harvest in shadow! Yet if we waited till the Moon's evening, the flood would have washed them away. We kept some yeast alive overnight, in the lamp's heat. And I cleaned myself most gladly, when I saw how it throve, and never again kept it with my body—ah, I lost my taste for it, but the others liked it as much as ever. And they came to think it was my task to farm, and be its keeper in the Moon. And I began to be used to tending the wells alone—to be alone is indeed something strange in us, which we cannot make you understand although we try—I think we had it from our father Betwar—he did go out alone, and it did not harm him.

○

Sometimes we spent the worst of the afternoons inside Ask's culvert, the one that spilled into the open lands. It kept its coolness somewhat and we could go deeper from the openings, to the very centre. The pool was by then utterly drained and dry, its bed a cracked field, and it had to fill to some depth—about to our breasts—before it entered the culvert. This we were able to hear clearly, the bore first entering the pool with that clamour of voices. So it came at us slow and dispersed, and we were not endangered.

Our bodies began then, I think, to slow themselves in those hottest days of hours, and to rest much—thus we endured that time, which was dark where we were; it would have been as if to invite worse heat in, had we lit a lamp. We found no Outdead seams, or doors, in that culvert or in the other one, though when they were dry Ask searched them from end to end.

○

Ask played with the shards in the morning, and saw how, by looking through them, he could more comfortably see the World. We would sit shaded by the fall, in under the water-scoured roots, with the very cool water spilling out of the culvert overhead—it was thickish and gray, not yet fully flowing. Up at the pool all sizes of white and greenish blocks still floated out of the course, and crowded against the outlet. Ask said that some of them were so even they seemed as if Outdead-shaped; but he was ever noticing the shapes of things. He would lie above us at the brink, and hold a clear shard directly in front of his eyes—he said he could see the World clearly that way, for it diminished the brightness.

One morning he was sure he saw at the limb Shelik's promontory and the Fu-en coasts, high at the terminator as the World turned his face, and darkness overtook them. For it was now Darkening in the northern World, with already more night there than day. He had told us how, as Darkening advanced there, it would be even harder to see our home land—but then, perhaps, we would see the lights of the city. As for the south, it was lifting itself towards us, but very bright—he said the sheath-edge lifted like a skirt and there was perhaps only sea there: yet, at the limb, something bluish and darker that might be a great land. He let me look but it was still too bright, and Ard would not. So he would watch

THE TAMING ○ 89

till his eyes ran with tears, and the shard ran into a slip of nothing between his fingers.

○

And the birds lived, and returned at every windfall! They swooped among the falling fruit, and talked with us in their unspeech cheerfully. They were more graceful now than when they had first attempted to fly in the Moon. They liked to eat of the fruit we had opened, though they could open it themselves. We were sure they knew us, but none came as close again as the one who had stood on Ask's shoulder. We had no idea how they lived. Surely, their consciousness is more intelligent than ours and they had already an understanding of the Moon's ways. We saw them become restless, as they were in the World at the last, and, when they had eaten and greeted us they flew sturdily away, ever north by west, out over the barrens as the terminator passed.

We watched out alertly for Atwar. And we made no permanent dwelling-places in that grove, neither over nor under ground. We were almost happy! for we trusted that he would bring us to his mansions—or, I played that I trusted, if the others were in earnest.

○

Those first two nights, we left the fire burning over ground when we went into the house, and made new careful scratches around it (for the flood had slurred them) and left for him plenty of wood. But when we hurried to look in the morning, the fire was long out and the wood untouched. There was no sign he had been near. After that we stayed there two more days, as they are counted in the Moon—all those days together would be, in the World, the half of Lightening or Darkening—that is, a fourth part of the whole year.

○

On that fourth morning, we came out and saw joyfully that Atwar had been there; he had himself scratched at the fire's bed, and turned out the slings. How we ran about, chattering, looking for other signs of him! Then Ask mourned that we had not left the fire burning for him, and Ard was angry that we had taken back the doll. We looked in the softened soil for his footprints, but he must have walked there when it was hard and left no trace.

We hurried to the pool under the stone, and saw there a another sign—two long, gray parallel marks crossing the surface of the water nearly where we were used to cross; they were already softening and obliterating. We came out of the trees and stared after him across the terrible brightness, our eyes still unused; but we did not see him.

Ask resolved then, that if Atwar did not greet us in that day, we should make him a fire, and go out of the house well before dawn to meet him, however cool it was.

"We can make garments of many layers, and cover ourselves."

"We must leave him the fire and the doll," I said.

"And other good things," said Ard eagerly, though what they should be we did not know. We agreed however that we would leave one of the lamps burning for him at the fire, and a bowl of yeast, of those small vessels Ask had been shaping. We argued also whether we should leave him the knife as a gift—it was Ask who suggested it—"for should we not give over to him every thing, even as Betwar did?" Yet the scholars had entrusted us with nothing useful to offer to Atwar.

You know that in the World, people do not readily give gifts, from that saying, *You are not allowed to give your life for your friend.* For if you cannot give your life, what other gift is worth giving?

"He has everything he needs, and will provide for us also," said Ard confidently. "But the doll he likes, that we took from him again. It is, anyway, a Sanev knife, and the Sanev meant if for us; they are our friends, not his."

But it was long till the next morning, and we were now very impatient.

○

I strove at the wells, and I thought Atwar near, or played that he was. We appeared then more acceptable than when he had first seen us, also! for during that night under ground we had cleaned and restitched our dresses. All the black in mine I had picked away and patched with leaf, so only that green

THE TAMING ○ 91

and the last clear blue of the cloth remained and I was dressed in the colours of water and forest and distance all intermingled. We had found that the leaf paled, and if we scratched it a waxy layer came off easily and left it almost white underneath, and supple. That night in the house Ard scraped the leaf that joined her garment, in a pattern of long broad bands, and Ask lay in his sling with a section of leaf and cut deftly in it with his knife. He made a row of little Worlds, as the World had appeared to us since we came—first the crescent, then Twelwerd and the Full, and then Twarwerd, and a thin circular mark for the World at New, as many times as we had seen him. So Ask played, and left space for more Worlds, but not enough. Later he was to use more leaf, and mark also the World's Darkening and Lightening as it occurred in the north, and the nudge and eclipse of the Sun, and many other things. But then we did not do more, or think of making other marks—or of writing; we did not dare.

As for me, when I had made my dress quite clean, I put it on again, and set about the slings also—so we were well occupied; and we gathered the waxy scrapings and burned them in the lamp for oil.

○

I was still thin and bony—very much thinner than Ard—indeed I could not see my image in my sister any more. Her face was puffed and rosy and her breasts very round, and she was tight in her skin—it looked bruised about the eyes, and bruised easily. Her voice was loud but rather dark, and unmodulated, and she still shuddered sometimes, starting with a great yawn. She looked down for the most, when we were outdoors, or sometimes directly into our faces; she said that to look up, or away, made her sick. Sometimes it seemed we treated her as if she were blind, for she would close her eyes and reach out after food, and we would feed her, or lead her about by the hand. She was ever glad to go under ground, and then she looked all around her. And her mind was ever clear, since we had learned to protect ourselves from the worst seasons.

○

What were my secret thoughts of Atwar then, as perhaps he warily circled us, warily watched? At first, such a burst of gladness had filled our hearts—it was more than ordinary joy—it was a confirmation. Our purpose was fulfilled. And the fact of him! He was, in that brief sighting, so large, heavy and real! Perhaps this should not have surprised me. The songs and images repeated him as he was when he went away, but his Doll in the city was big, higher than many houses. And he was big in the mouths of the scholars and all the people—so much had been made of him, so big he was grown in the World he had left behind! That Doll was made with white cloth teeth, and now—Ask said he had seen—this solid adult body with lifted lip had child-teeth as well. For Atwar had gone white-teethed into the Moon.

Like Ask—Ask would grow up so. No one would take the swartroot to his teeth and beautify them when he became adult; and he would look childish even as a man, like Atwar.

So I strove gently at the wells, in shadow, before the sun reached me over the glade; and I laid the yeast down, and cleaned myself of it in the stream. The good, cool unsmell of the furze rose around me, that air my lungs were gladdened by, and the good space spread away from me after the long constriction under ground. Indeed I thought then of Atwar's look, his eyes on me. For now we knew he was near, and was considering us. But I doubted my sister's complacent trust, when she said "He is preparing his mansions." Was it not unreasonable, if we thought of it, to trust in Atwar's care? He had been alone in the Moon for many years. Here, he had ever been alone, with only the speechless consciousness of the trees and furze for his living companions. If Betwar in the World so mourned the loss of his twin, how much more had Atwar lost! Betwar could take his children into his arms when he chose. And, as Betwar had told me so insistently, Atwar did not expect us, and did not even know who we were.

That time past noon we stayed at the edge of the grove, looking up at the World and singing. We sang I think all the songs we knew—except *Atwar's Grief*, for not to offend him—and there were many. We sang the *Tale of Tasman* from end to end, and Ard and I sang lovers' songs also, into each other's mouths, as real twins do though we were not so good at it, our voices breaking and rounding. Ask sang in his clear voice the *Song of the Four Children*.

"Perhaps he is listening."

The sun began to nudge the World. But we kept ourselves inside the shade of the great roots, crouching back within them, and so looked outward.

The World was at New with his round edge foamy and soft against the black sky. That sky was even blacker than the arms of the root-portal that embraced my vision, as if I sat inside a door and it was pulled down, the cloth walls drawn close together, and I was squinting out the narrow space between. And the World stood in the sun's way and would not be budged. He was reddening, red-black, with the light across all the Moon's barren lands dimming and reddening. That was the first total eclipse we saw from the Moon, and we slept and did not see it all, because it was very long, twice four-or-eight hours, being at the middle of that time as dark as a cloudy day and very red. There was no fiery sun's corona, as we have seen from the World around the eclipsed Moon, for the sun was quite hid, traversing the sky behind the World without flagrant display. Gradually, in that dimness, could we emerge from the roots and look into the World, gradually.

To look into him was to look into a milder darkness, into the hazed red of his covering air. Mild, yet it exhausted us, because we had not learned how to gaze at him. We forced our eyes, and so our desire, by striking so fiercely outwards, prevented any thing from reaching us. Ard knew better yet scarcely would look, though she kept the World framed by the crossing roots, and glanced only for very short moments. Often she went away into the trees, restlessly. She said she saw fires. Both in the north and south, some momentary and some enduring. But Ask and I could not see them.

So we stared, and sang, and slept as the heat increased.

Did Atwar hear us? I played that he did, that he came near and listened to us, and remembered the old Tales, and learned of us from the new, and was made our friend in his heart.

○

Beautiful we left that fire, when we went underground! Ask strove to make it as hot and deep as Atwar's had been, and covered it carefully so it would last. He chose the thickest wood, bringing broken planks and roots from the basin, where they were left against the culvert by the floods. And we retraced Atwar's scratches as we remembered them, radiating to a certain distance, with the soil cleared of its debris. Ard laid the doll where Atwar had left it, folded as it was found. And Ask carefully pressed a little burning lamp, his deepest, into the ground; it was filled up with oil, and I set the bowl of yeast between it and the fire, also deep in the soil where the warmth would keep it. Then Ard undid one of her pockets—"Let us fill it with fruit for him to eat!" As if he were hungry! but this we also put down into the soil, with leaf under it to keep it clean. Indeed we saw that pouch now, such a humble, useful thing, with clearer eyes. It was sewn double along the inner side and the bottom, the seams sturdy and even. Though it was scorched here and there, it was otherwise scrubbed and clean. So white it was, and finely worked! such smooth, even cloth! each hole for the bindings stitched close about with thread that had been strengthened with human hair! The ordinary cloth of the World is indeed beautiful and serviceable—and already we had so little left.

○

That night we took much leaf with us into the house, and worked it into garments. Perhaps it was the handling and turning of the leaves, as much as the scraping, that made them malleable. What we made pleased us at the time; we thought our clothes very fine! We made hand- and footgloves, of several thicknesses, for it was in our limbs the coolness most harmed us. And headsleeves of long bands of leaf, that we could pull up over our faces. We tied into them large pouches also, and filled them with fruit and yeast—for what if we must quickly follow Atwar? Yet perhaps this was all in vain: the coolness rotted the leaf.

"If we cannot bear it, we will go back into the house."

"We need not all of us watch for him, at first—it is best if I-go earliest", said Ask.

We had one fright in that time, for we were not cautious with those waxy scrapings that fell from the leaves, and some drifted against the lamp and ignited, and the fire fell into the floor—we saw it soon enough however and cried out, and Ask leaped down and tipped the yeast over it, before it was spread. After that we were more careful.

It was difficult to judge whether dawn was near. Could we have watched the World—but the foliage there was too thick to see more than a diffused, whitish light. He would wane in those days of hours. But as surely as his light dimmed it would seem to us more and more bright, for our eyes grew used to the darkness.

Each time we slept, we would insist when we wakened, that it must be the Moon's morning!

But finally we agreed, from the many times we had slept and eaten, and filled the lamp—and from our great impatience—that dawn must be near. We dressed Ask in all his garments and pulled apart the top of the wall, and pushed him out.

○

What terrible coolness met us, and rushed in upon us! It wanted to fill the house.

"Ard, Let us dress ourselves also." We began at once, standing and helping each other among the slings. To put on footgloves was frightening to me, and made me think of the bindings—you know that the scholars had crippled us in the World to keep us small, so we could enter the cars. Ah, my legs were most thin and bald yet, though my sisters' had thickened. And our feet were strong but not healed. When I bound them now with leaf, the act was easy; my hands remembered too well how it was done. If Ard thought of this also, she said nothing.

Ask did not call out to us. I was ever afraid for him, especially after that time he had left us, and was eager to climb out after him, when we heard him at the entrance.

"My sisters, I am not coming in. I am going to the pool under the stone. He has not taken the doll, but he was here. He has made those strange lines on the course—I will follow them."

"Is it close to sunrise?"

Ask made some noise that meant he did not know. "From the stone, I will look at the World."

I got into a sling and climbed out, the first breath of that air burning my lungs.

"Ard, do you not come yet! Block up the gap if you can, and keep the lamp!"

She would be made sick if she came.

○

I stood in the course, my footgloves slithering. It was smooth here where the calmer water had hardened, and on the sheathlike surface those two gray marks extended—they ended just at my feet. I could see also Ask's newer marks, sharp and narrow where he had set out, then a big smudge where he had almost immediately fallen.

I looked back at the fire, and saw it with joy—alit and glowing low in the soil. I did not look any closer but set off after my brother.

○

Oh World and your watchers, if it were easy to see you we would see you, and speak with you if we could! But our gaze has fallen into the cauldron of your air, your air is cooking it. How can these eyes see with their ordinary skin, and not be cooked away?

Often must Atwar have watched how the reddened World ate up the path of the sun, and the Moon was soaked in his dyes. What has Atwar seen, that he should answer you? Yet you intend him to answer you!

What have you intended? We are near him, what is our concern with you? How can we answer you out of this violent place, to which we have in violence bonded, in order that we can bear to live? Steady you lean over us, but your features are blurred out of recognition, as if you were already dead, and wrapped in cloths for the burning!

Ask

Now, this is how I found Atwar that second time, and how we followed him. I walked along the course—with the gloves on it was very slippery, but not difficult, helped by the lifting air. Ah—that air was at its most extreme and bitter coolness! My body had not forgotten our first night, and became quickly angry—it did not want to breathe and feel within it that chilled burning! I suppose the leaves gave me some protection as long as my body was warm in them, but soon the coolness entered at every fault in the stitches, at every seam! But I thought, I will follow these marks and see where he has gone.

It was far to the pool and I was glad when I saw the marks turned aside into the south bank. I could see by the cracked soil that he had, as I thought, climbed up and walked towards our slings.

Again they were overturned, all of them, ragged and black as they were, and there were many marks on and under them, yet I saw then how much more blurred these were than mine, and whitened over. I heard Tared whispering from the course.

We conferred whispering—for we dared not call him—as if it should be he who first called out. Even singing we had not called to him directly, even when our songs had named him by name.

"I made Ard stay. I said she must stay—this will sicken her. It is still very bright."

"No—only that you have been under ground, and it seems so—it has grown dim. The sun will soon rise—"

"He is about!"

She stared around her and back at me, her gloved hands two lumps on the bank where I stood. Indeed she looked most strange—so thick and squat in all that leaf, with its ties wrapping her into a clutch of fat bundles! Her narrow face with its harsh, black grin peered fiercely out of the sleeves.

"Have you heard him?"

"No—he is silent—"

"Will-we follow him to the glade?"

"He is nearer! Let us go back and hide in a root, where we can watch the fire." Afterwards, I understood she read his traces as though he had come towards the fire, not away from it.

We returned along the course, I doubtfully, for those marks were indeed not new—our blundering marks were darker. We stood with our arms on the bank and gazed at the glowing fire over ground. Tared shivered and whispered, "I will tell Ard."

"Go in and warm yourself. I will hide in that root, and watch if he comes. I will say it."

○

So I crouched among the roots of the tree nearest the fire, that stood south of it—a young tree as I thought, for there was hardly room for me inside. Almost, I was near enough to stretch out my hands and warm them—but I felt no warmth. My body trembled. My hands were in some pain, then I felt the pain drawn out of them, deadening.

The fire still glowed. Had I been clearer in my mind, I would have reasoned: so long it could not have burned without our tending. My mind was dulled by the air's chill.

Yet I was stubborn! I would withstand, and not give over this watch to my sister, if I could help it.

My eyes returned ever to the fire's redness in all that white, and I had a great desire to crawl closer—almost, I slept, and dreamed I went to it, and awoke again in the tree, and again slept and seemed to dream—but before I woke I had gone to it unawares. I was huddled with its heat on my face, seeking into my neck and breast, and good heat reached up into my feet out of the black, warmed soil. I slept again, I think, for the first I heard was a kind of sniff, and when I looked I saw Atwar crouched beside me, on the twarside. The sun rose then behind him, and all around his head its light caught in his hair, like rosy fire!

He was so close—I could have touched him. His look was as before—across my face, not into it. Something blue he

THE TAMING ○ 99

held in his teeth—it was the doll. His teeth were dull white—his broad lip lifted over them. All this I saw in an instant! He looked like a terrible dream of Betwar. His browhair crossed over his eyes in one even line, and he smelled of the barrens, the dusty Moon. I thought I said his name, but now I am not sure if I spoke aloud. His head lifted as before, and he was up and away, leaping rather heavily down into the course, and setting forth—

This was how he made those marks: his hands and feet slid forward twar then twel in unison, smoothly without lifting. Swiftly he went from me.

"Atwar! Atwar!" I shouted then, into the bright red morning—all red-and-white it was. I saw clearly his twocoloured hair swing its two thick strands, and his broad body, even his hands and feet, all covered with a thick, brownish garment, and over it, across his shoulders, a patch of cloth was flapping, a patch of brightest blue!

My sisters came out then, falling over each other, chattering and staring.

"Is he here?"—"Have you seen him?"

"He has run away down the course! Ard, he is wearing your dress."

We set off after him.

○

We crossed the barrens in four days as they are counted in the World, in a climate of great sweetness in the Moon's morning, following Atwar.

○

We had searched quickly about the fire, and found that he had indeed replenished it, but not with our wood, and that the pocket was gone as well as the doll. But the yeast he had not touched.

"Are these marks his or ours?"

"Ours, surely—as I remember—"

But we could not remember. We covered the fire up then, and Tared took that yeast, what had lived of it. She also sent me back for as much fruit as we could carry, and the bladder and lamp. I took also my true-book. So we started.

The air began to warm almost immediately, as we walked

along the course, and I pulled off my hand- and footgloves. That surface would not harm me. My sisters saw that I walked easier and pulled theirs off as well; so we went forward and discarded more and more of those garments. But Tared rolled the best pieces into a bundle and made me tie them across her shoulders, fearing we should want them. The ground darkened; whiteness steamed from the stems.

They asked me many questions as we went, about Atwar. They thought it most strange, that he had come so close to me, yet not stayed or spoken.

"How was it that you were not hiding, but sitting openly at the fire?"

"My body was so chilled—it crept there even while my mind was dull and asleep—I thought I had dreamed."

"But you did not dream him!" said Ard, "for he took the doll, after you had seen it." Without that evidence, she would perhaps not have believed me.

But also, there were two rows of gray tracks weaving through each other, the first pair dim, and the newer blurring too with the gathering surface water, continuing straight along the course after the first ones turned aside.

"Ah—our day-slings! Why has he turned them?"

"Our goodly little house! Will we come here again?"

Yet we believed that Atwar would show us a better dwelling place. For he knew the Moon and thrived here. So without more regret we followed him.

○

As soon as we emerged from the grove, at the waterfall, we saw him—far out in the sunlight and moving low along one of the white streams, with that sliding walk he had—

"Look, Ard—there is your dress!" I cried, and indeed it showed on him, a tiny patch of distance on the ruddy lands, like a hole cut through them.

"He is quicker than us," observed Tared.

"No—for he goes more heavy and ordinary, " I said. "He is not lifted as we are by the Moon's air—see that way he is moving. But he is quick at it—"

I thought we could perhaps diminish the distance between us.

There were many hardened streams twisted through the lowest places, between the hills and humps of furze. For us there was no advantage in walking on them, and we crossed at random, Tared holding Ard's hand—for Ard would not look—leaping and soaring. If we gradually fell back from Atwar, it was because of Ard, and our general clumsiness on that uneven ground.

He did not look back, or rest.

He was too far ahead to shout after.

When we reached a stream we sometimes saw his traces, and followed them for a time. But out under the sun those surfaces were quickly turned to running water.

The furze was itself springy, its foliage rough but not sharp enough to cut us. At first, in the shade, it was curled low into itself, a dull earth-colour. So it was also under the stones. But the sunlight brought it into radiant life, and in those first hours it swelled and reddened, and smoked—this we had never seen, not having been out so early. The great stones too, seemed clustered about at their edges with dusty light.

That smoke made me cough, and Tared urged me to walk upright, for we were not sure it was good for us. But it did us no harm, and the vivid motes danced in the sun—indeed, it almost harmed us with goodness, it was so rich and heady. So when we leaped we laughed aloud—and we called those barrens *Glaygras* (the fields of joy), because they made us silly and joyful. Yet it was a sorrowful joy too, because and my body ever turned to call out to Saska in play. He would have laughed here, as he seldom dared to laugh in the World, for he was ever timid and wondering. How gladly and tremblingly he had looked forward! And if I laughed now, it would be the same as if I had taken the joy that should have been his—ah, I wished to strike myself; I fell back from my sisters, and struck myself bitterly, for taking his joy.

We slept under the third stone. Even here the furze was awakening, but we found that if we lay face down the dust would not trouble us—and the stone's shade was welcome to us.

Tared sighed. "We cannot keep pace with him."

"Perhaps, when he looks back and does not see us leaping,

he will wait for us." Ard was the most tired, and it seemed to me Tared had been impatient with her, pulling her along more quickly than Ard would. And now letting me feed her, as we stood above the dusty furze, Ard with her eyes squeezed shut. Tared went over to a stream.

"Fetch Ard water another place; I am washing myself—I am bleeding," she said when I came with the cloth. And when we lay down, she turned away from her sister.

"I am bleeding," she said again, louder. It sounded ugly still to me, that Tared used such words; it would have been seemly to say "this-body is bleeding"—so we have ever spoken, for the language does not take us into account, who do not share our body with a twin. Yet Betwar would sometimes say I and not this-body, as I was now also determined to do. Even so, what Tared said was repugnant in my ears. Her body had first bled some days after Ard's: that was the sign we should go into the Moon. And I remember how angry she was then, that Ard should become adult before her, when she Tared, by scrambling first out of our mothers' womb, was reckoned the older.

Ard did not answer, though Tared had spoken to provoke; and I did not then understand them, except to think that we were tired, and therefore Tared was quarrelsome. The air, however, would not allow her to be serious, and she gave a sudden sneeze of laughter. Then Ard began to laugh too, in her new darker voice, very loud, and I rolled over on my back and laughed with them, yet not understanding, laughed and coughed with the happy furze smoking all around, and the stone hovering.

○

When we wakened again we could not see Atwar, but from the top of the next hill we saw him. Ah, how our hearts were gladdened then; even Ard looked, from under her fisted brows, her eyes catching at him across the distance. He was farther from us and had left the streams, and was walking along a flattish hill, past the next stone and a little north of it—he was so distant that, even in this clear air, only the bit of blue showed, flicking, and the flick of his shadow under him.

"See how low he walks."

Indeed, he walked against the ground, not leaping, but touching the earth often, as people walk in the World.

○

The furze had ceased to smoke, and the Moon's day advanced, the air still comfortable and clear. Only overhead, above the stones and behind the mountains, a haze was gathering, and the waning World's face was slurred and uncertain. The distant grove filling the vale ahead was now hid in a low bank of white. Yet the sun's light seemed even stronger, and we threw our hair over our faces, when we came out into it, and squinted, and Ard reached for Tared's hand.

At this time the furze flowered, a flush of dense, bright pink spreading rapidly across the darker red. Looking down I could see the tiny flowerets opened, in some places set so close they quite covered the foliage, in others separated, as if floating on it here and there. And when I looked up, the distances!

We walked underneath eleven stones before we reached the grove, that I, as children, counted carefully. On either side were many more, and those stiff cables also, set in rows in each direction. Because of the hills, some stones hung higher than others—it was no even scape overhead, but cluttered: their different shapes and heights, their flushed, sunbright sides, their bumpy gray bellies. Overturned, that sky could perhaps be likened to an archipelago rising out of a dark sea, with its coasts foaming red; and the sea, in the high haze, afloat with innumerable watery lights. As we neared the ranges and the land lifted, the stones hung also higher, as on a steep beach—a shoal of boulders.

I could not then have described it so; I am trying to make it visible to you, remembering as I write the familiar look of the World. But to us they were then so strange they compared to nothing.

If looking made Tared and me a little sick, we would not admit it. I think she chid her body, feeling discomfort but determined to endure. As for me, these sights filled my heart with dizzying joy, so that even when they made my ears sing, and my belly turn over, I was daring myself to stare, to take courage—not to miss such wonders!

Tared too, from time to time, would say almost to herself, "It is wonderful."

○

We glimpsed Atwar sometimes, as he crossed a rise, but we never saw him rest or look back. Once I thought he stood to piss and when I said it Tared rebuked me.

"Would you watch our father piss?"

"I was not watching for that purpose."

Ard said, grinning, "The scholars would be very sorrowful to hear that Atwar pisses in the Moon. There are no songs about it."

Tared said he was probably stopping to take food out of a pouch—"Our pouch, perhaps—" and we remembered that he had not taken the yeast. I said, "He does not smell like us, or of yeast; he smells of the barrens, that dust."

○

We would advance on him; then while we slept he would draw away, each time a little farther. When he was nearest we could still see clearly the blue winking of his dress.

"Watch the dress—he limps, as we do," said Tared. For the wink was even yet uneven. Ard, squinting ever down, went forward holding fast to Tared's hand.

"Ard, remember how amazed we were at that colour, when we first saw it?"

She answered: "In the Sanev hands! the bird, that died when they caught it."

"And the sapphire dust they found!" I said.

"Nevi stirred that, in my palm."

"Ah—Nevi stirred well—" echoed Tared scornfully; then, I did not know why.

I said, "Saska immediately smeared it down his white dress!"

For that blue was the first blue we had ever seen close by in the World, and that was the first time it was used on cloth. It was the colour with no name, except the word for distance. Saska's colour.

Tared said, "Atwar delights in that colour as we did, when

we first saw it close to our eyes. Therefore he carries the doll, and when he found your dress he could not help putting it on. Look, Ard, how it winks at us!"

But Ard would not look. "I will see it when he greets us," she said stubbornly.

After we had slept again and eaten, which was under the eighth stone, we could not see him any more.

So we continued westward, going over an uneven plane and then a level vale, the land around us ever a little rising. The streams had ceased. Here there was no water except in seeps and trickling hollows, and I filled the bladder, in case even these would soon be dried away. The mountains were close now, and cut off the Moon's limb, so it was easier to look ahead. Then from the top of a rise we could see the extent of the approaching grove—it seemed to be swimming in the last strands of mist, that rose like lampsmoke behind its hills. The trees spread northward along the foot of the mountains. That more northern range was very low, or farther away—it looked more blue, as if the grove was poured between the two ranges and separated them.

At that time I began to say it was the Cape, and this nearest mountain must be Hadley, though it was so small. Tared argued, but as we came closer I was sure of it. The grove filled the plain between the Cape and the range to the north, and Hadley was as he was, squat and smooth. The sky beyond him was clear of stones, and the distant plane to either side of us also: no shadows darkened it and it had a lifeless look, drained of vegetable red. Ah, the habitable Moon was here very narrow, ceasing behind Hadley and again over behind the northern mountains; this was the meeting place of the two great, seeded *maria*. The Outdead had covered much of each one with their great roof, held down by the cables and stones, and this was the pass between, forest-choked. From the World, it appeared in the eyes of children as a dark river, but from Fu-en Book we had seen that forest magnified—the desolate mountains closing it north and south. When the terminator passed it had appeared craggy and wild. Even now we were greeted, having named it with those familiar names! It had ever seemed to us the most beautiful place in the Moon.

○

The grove that sloped over the horizon was frothy and high; it looked greater and sweeter than those we had come from, its roof of leaf denser, grown farther down the stems. Bright it looked, its shadows cool and wet, pressed against that close, black sky!

"There is water, surely," I said, for it looked so drenched compared to the barrens. The furze was now brittle underfoot, the tiny flowerets bursting where we stepped. Each time our feet set down, flakes of pink drifted from them in slow, dusty splashes.

We hurried, but it was more than a day of hours before we reached the grove.

○

The ground grew more level, and the bristly furze crackled as we stepped. Ahead was all vertical shadow—among the stems such green, such welcoming darkness! The World was past New, black against black overhead behind the high haze, its crescent the faintest blur of light—its curve seemed to me like the after-image of a burning reed, cast in a perfect arc by World-children, at play on a night-beach in the World.

We passed under the tenth stone. Then we were so near that the last stone occluded the treetops.

We crossed a place where the furze was marked and flat—then a wider, stronger mark intersected it. It was surely Atwar's path! Here and there I saw little dry stream-beds half-hidden by the furze. Their world-tree pattern told me these would flow westward, into the grove.

It was good that we should come into the glade soon, while the air was still temperate; for the shadowless heat of the afternoon we could not have endured. And we had drunk up all our water.

Ard had endured from stone to stone, her eyes clenched shut; she stepped clumsily forward.

"Walk upright, Ask, and take her other hand."

I did so, and went on, staring forward ever at the tall shadows, the thought of water.

We walked in his path, and nearing the trees it followed the twarside of a larger stream bed, that came from the north. This was not Outdead shaped but followed the hollows of the ground, with smaller tributaries opened into it. Some of these crossed the path in rough dips or tunnels under the flattened furze.

"Atwar treads with wide feet," observed Tared. For we did not much touch the ground then, in our fashion of walking, or need such a broad, level road. It was as big as Semer's Way, along which the quarriers dragged their heavy rafts of stone and sapphire to Fu-en City.

At the grove the ground dropped off abruptly under an overhang of furze—I stepped into air and stood surprised on the hard soil below, having fallen about the height of grown men. I stood in a rounded, shady space, almost a little room, with the furze squeezing over it, and past it the great roots of Atwar's forest rising.

My sisters came down together through the gap, Ard sitting back against Tared, and pausing—when she grasped the tufts of the furze on either side, they looked for a moment like ordinary twins perched between their mothers' heads, grasping their mothers' hair.

"Here is where Atwar comes and goes—this is his door and this is his grove!" said Ard gladly, when they were down. Her eyes opened into the comforting shadow, that seemed almost as darkness. Ah, our burning eyes began to rest and widen, and tingle at the outermost corners; they gazed with their soft unfocussed cells into that pleasant gloom.

The flooding stream would fall here over its brink. Gray rock and scoured soil showed at the base, deep in under the furze—perhaps it was an Outdead bank—we were not sure. So we entered Atwar's grove on his well-trodden path.

○

Almost, we did not dare to speak aloud. Here were the same plank-sided trees, but they were older and broader, more widely spaced. Their white roots arched like rooms— some, I could not have put my arms around, they were so thick. Under them the soil was very black and smooth and clean. There was no debris on this open forest floor, but I saw tree-patterns of the receding flood, and the stream-bed itself was deep, worn into a ravine, the path going along its south side between the spaces of the trees. We could see far into the grove.

The air became more and more thick with moisture, the trees slick with it. At last I saw a little water gathered in the stream bed, and quickly filled our cloth. After that there was more water, trickling and filling small pools, and it was clean.

Ard was sweating now and very tired, but she smiled and we continued, helping her, till we smelled and heard the running water, and reached an Outdead watercourse flowing from the north.

Like the trees, it was on a bigger map than those in the other groves, broader from bank to bank. It was not yet mist-hidden, though some bands of greenish vapour hung on it; and it flowed very smooth and slow, the surface hardly moving. Atwar's path followed it, but we got into it and swam, looking ever about us and talking quietly.

We rested over ground and the heat increased. When we awoke the air was nearing that sickening, soaking heat Ard could not bear, and the muffled course was almost dry.

Then I stood up, and looked about.

The path was like the rest of the forest floor but harder, its surface less black and porous. It would surely take us to Atwar's mansions, so purposeful it looked!

"Come a little farther," I said to my sisters, "There will be a cool house for us surely, at the end of this great path, or a way under the cool ground—"

And we found a house, as we thought—made within a very great tree which leaned across the straighter ones, so its near roots were pulled farther out of the soil—stretched like rope in many strands. All the soil inside was dug away to make kind of well. I put my head over, to see how deep it was.

We were cautious to enter his dwelling; it was not seemly, before he had greeted us. But in our necessity we did so, and slept there, out of the long heat. It had a down-sloping room dug into the west side, under ground, and the soil in there was smooth and wet and black, and the air a little cooler.

Tared lay down at once with Ard and fed her, and I left them talking seriously together. I took the bladder and filled it at the course, which was already boiling away, and full of choking mist. Then I stood on a root inside the hole, for I would hold up my head as long as I could, and looked about.

○

My sisters slept. What if Atwar were angered, that we had entered his house? My hands smoothed the worn brim. I did not think, from its appearance, he had been in it since the last flood waters, for it was in places crumbled, and its floor, though we had now marked it, had kept no trace of his body.

Perhaps he had many such dwellings here and there and would enter them as he happened to be passing? Perhaps he was just now returning along his path with that heavy, silent tread! I listened for him with such energy that my ears began to whistle in my head, but I did not hear him.

○

The rude flood reached us there, spilling over the muddy sills to fill up the well. We rose with it to the surface, splashing and coughing. The bore had passed, and the water was already spreading out calmly between the great roots, and lying level all around us.

○

Ah Atwar, even then I did not really think you would be angry, when I remembered your look—I had only to turn my mind towards it, as I had twice seen you looking at me— looking across me! My sisters had not yet received this look, this gaze I had to admit was strangely indifferent! What if I were to gaze at a tree, would it perhaps think of my look like that, which does not choose to look at that which is tree-important (I mean, the cells striving, the vertical push, the seemly rootedness) but rather sees it as a source of shade or food, even as useful wood that perhaps could be burned against the night's chill, or in mourning? Would the tree not think my look as strange, as I thought now Atwar's?

What then did he see, to look across my face in this way? He had come close to me and crouched down. He took and kept the doll and the dress, as if he wanted to have something to do with us, some shy intimacy. Twice he overturned the slings—that was a strange act! they were not to his liking!

He did not speak.

If I had been Atwar, would I not have searched this childish face for the likeness of Betwar my twin? Would I not have stared longingly into these eyes?

But I was not Atwar.

III.
Two Voices

Ard

We lived in that grove and Atwar was there, but he seldom came near us—it was long indeed before Tared saw him close, and even longer before he greeted me in any fashion. We lived in the skirts of his domain, and he came and went as we supposed, though he may have ranged farther—we did not see him nearly a whole morning, or even at harvest any sign of him.

I was no longer fearful to look around me, after we came in from the bright lands. The trees closed us about, and the course-water flowing between its banks was calm and familiar. That first afternoon when we curled into Atwar's hollow, and I felt against my body his firm rounded wall, I thought, *He has lain here*, and was comforted.

○

I thought also then, *If you will say any thing, Tared, say it immediately and quickly, or in this coming heat I will be turned from you.* A mind's picture—the rearing belly of a stone—poured upward against my eyes. I had kept them closed as much as I could in all that journey—as much as I could, to prevent this. And even what I had not seen followed me still, I was rocked in its wake, or as in waves after the wind has long passed—the slow stepping forward and the fall, and the press of the furze into one foot, and again into the other. My mouth, as my mind turned in sickness, refused to heed me, and spoke what it would.

It said aloud, "Tared, I am not as children, whose delight is in counting!"

○

Yet I knew this body was at the four-or-eight now, as women call it courteously in the World. At the four, we had lived yet in that second grove, in the little culvert house and among the slings—it was then the babies first quickened in me. I began to wonder if this was more than the private sickness of my body, however it jerked and shuddered in the miserable hours! The Siri too, I remembered, had such hard, round breasts, when they were gravid in the World. And now as we came into Atwar's shade I was swollen not only in legs and breasts, but also in this belly—and Tared saw it and knew what it was.

She did not ask me. Perhaps she did not think that I myself knew, perhaps out of courtesy she would not speak before I spoke. Or out of anger! Ah, for some time, even before we crossed the open land, she had been pricking me with her look, and with short words! And I also—because my mouth desired to tell of it, spoke ever of the Sanev, if I had a chance. "I am bleeding," she had said under the stone—making much of it. Before that, perhaps she had watched me.

It would have been shame in the World!

It would not have occurred in the World. But that they gave us no root.

Now as I look back, I can admit that Tared and I knew each other very well. We need not have been afraid to speak or to be silent. So well we knew each other, even in these unnatural, separate bodies! We had despite our birthfault grown in the same womb, cried out together two-voiced at our birth, together lapped our mothers' breasts! And till recently we had been very like, so that each saw in the other's face that image of herself. Tared's hair was more unruly and I was a little heavier; yet these differences were slight—only our father and brothers knew us unerringly, and the Sanev and our closest friends. Even the Ng had to peer twice sometimes, if Tared had succeeded in slicking back her hair!

Here in the Moon we had become unlike indeed, yet our minds knew each other as well as ordinary twins do; and even though our bodies are apart they have ever listened acutely to one another, without our being aware.

Tared knew how this body was, nearly as soon as I did myself, and it did not matter whether we spoke or no.

○

And here is something wonderful, that we were not harmed! In the World, the Ng had prepared us for another, darker promise; in those red rooms they meant to submit us to a terrible thing! Even this, in our growing understanding, we had both known, and taken into our hearts in our own fashion, and could not speak of it. Yet Tared never doubted me, that I too had escaped their cruel scheming! With Betwar our good father we had deceived them; we had come out of those rooms as we had entered them, and so come into the Moon. Tared never had to ask me, whether it was the Sanev's babes I carried under these ribs—she knew.

○

Ah, she was ever jealous in the World! Even when we were small, it was she who spoke aloud for me in Book, and for our brothers, and was most rigid in following the scholars' rules, and arguing for anything we others questioned. I did not care to learn that rote, but she learned it all. Sometimes she protected me, and answered for me when they asked. She was ever determined and serious!

Much softer she became, after that last ceremony; she repented then of all her ardent trust. Since, she has spoken more than once of Saska's dream, of the City with no ceremonies and no Doll, and everything made clean and new! We were children then and when he stammered and told his dream, she had struck him.

Yet now we laughed in the fields! She was much changed.

○

As for that more-than-milk-play with our friends—she was ever as eager as me, but she pretended she did not care for it. And in those last days it was me the Sanev carried with them far into the marsh-forest, and Tared knew it but was too proud to chide me openly. The Sanev were become men, and would perhaps soon be short-bonded. Perhaps they were already now, I thought, for they were ever lusty even as boys. Then, I had looked in the streets—I can remember—into the faces of women who might soon take them in bond! Their mothers said it to me openly, such-and such women are ready to look at our comely sons! because they suspected what we did. Ah, I loved and continued to love them, good Nevar who had my heart and Nevi who had the wetness of my sex—his secret smile! Their body that insisted.

At first I did not like the very act of it, but in such a short time as we had, they taught me well. And I liked it despite myself, for every cell in this body was swelling towards it and trembling.

That was in the World. Rude, wild twins—they loved to range; what was dangerous delighted them. If they could have come with us—and Saska—!

○

So now Tared said in the hollow, giving me water carefully, "Look how this drinking cloth is tearing—it will soon be two small cloths—we ought to stitch them." And then, "Are you lying close against the wall?"—settling herself against me irritably, her knees and elbows sharp as sticks.

Yet all the time she was saying into my mind *I know that you are gravid, that you carry the Sanev's twin babes in your belly; I have known this almost as long as you.*

And when I answered, "If you will sew one cloth, I will sew the other," I was speaking other words into her heart. Her hand pushed the hair back from my ear.

"Ard, sleep if you can. Ask is watching, and now that Atwar has brought us here, everything begins to be made new."

○

The watercourse ran southward, and we waded to it and swam down the flood. Wind came out of the barrens, and the great trees rocked and groaned, but none fell; then it rained as it was used, cloths of fine-rain sideways in the wind, and the heavy rain after. Farther in we came to a glade and a stone, where another course joins this one and they flow together in one great channel towards the west.

Here we stopped, and harvested windfall after the rain. The birds we heard, but they did not tarry—Ask said they were in haste to follow the wind. But later they came near us, and ever fed with us.

○

It was hereabouts we lived, finding everything we needed. Between the courses, as the waters fell back, a low island appeared. It became a half-island when the courses ran within their beds, a sharp-ended peninsula where the waters joined.

Under it we found many passages. They were protected against the flood—I will describe them as well as I can.

THE TAMING ○ 117

This is what they were like then: they opened into the the half-island, under the two most western trees—the point at the very joining of the water is bare, being under the stone. When we found them, we thought they were as the first of Atwar's diggings, only a scooped-out room. They were then well banked: all the soil he had taken out must have served to raise their mounds, for the roots above ground were covered up. The two trees stood to their planks in hard soil, and the highest rooms were that space within the roots themselves. We could see it was no Outdead work, for theirs is seamless and even; yet it was made with hands.

The room to the south was very large, enough so we could all lie down in it together. The other was smaller. For each, the door was a gap between roots, just under the stem—it was Ask who first slid into the larger one, and told us, "Here is a great room!" There was a passage, with air coming through it, between the two trees (for Ask came grinning out behind us at the other door), and under ground four low openings to other passages, cut in its westward wall. In the afternoon we did not go so deep, and it was some time, that first night, before we understood the pattern of them, and their extent. Ask dared to go first, and we left lamps at the joins and turnings.

One passage went deep indeed. The lowest room opened there, its floor of stone, and the small passages past it had stone floors also. When we looked at its roof we could see here and there uncovered patches of Outdead gray. We had crawled far, and understood that we were out under the course.

Yet the walls were firm, and only in two places did any water seep down—in one, in that great room's west side, the floor sloped to form a little stony pool, and it was clear water—there was surely a way for it into the rock.

In the shallowest passages, the walls were a tangle of roots—above, thick like those over ground, then thin and ropy—these strands had been tied back or cut away, but some hung across the passages. In some places the walls were woven of those mazy strands, as if they had been trained back to give room, and their whiteness lightened them, throwing back the lamps' glow. Here and there gaps in the root had been stuffed with old furze.

The steep floors were of worn root and new root and soil, with a rill in the centre. Small, sharp stones were pressed into that soil, and lay loose in the rills; these were the first stones we saw in the Moon.

Farther in, there were no roots. The air when we entered there was thick and unused, and there were no husks or mats of furze till we came. The farthest range of the passages under the course we did not use; the air was very bad, and the roof had fallen in—Ask crawled back and said to us, "It smells sick, and I could hear the watercourse."

During the flood, the water closed over our half-island, and some entered the passages; but it ran through, and they were not filled. Deep underground, we were kept safe from the terrible lunar night, as well as from the heat of the day.

○

That first morning Ask climbed out and saw far off on the great course a strange pile—he called eagerly to us, for it was unlike the rest of the surface, that was rough and jagged: it was almost Outdead shaped, though made of the same hard water. Ah—it was not only Ask who recognized any shape that does not occur, but is made! We knew immediately Atwar had made it. The surface of the course had been scored into and oddly cut, and what was cut piled up over the depression to make a house. Atwar had surely lived there!—he had burned some kind of taper for a lamp, which was now but a twig of ash, and his mats or clothes lay on the floor, that was cut deep into the course—we saw then that he dressed in furze. The door into the house was one seeping stone of water, lifted out and laid aside. When Ask tried to fit it back it was already too small, and fell in. "But see—how he has pressed furze into the cracks in the roof!"

Atwar's marks however did not show well on the rough course—Ask scrambled a good way on, among the green-white jumble of hills and boulders, and saw what he thought were those twin gray traces of Atwar's passing, but could not tell from them where he had come from, or gone.

THE TAMING ○ 119

That dwelling broke up and floated away—but not before Ask had climbed into it, and touched it to remember it, trying to discover how it had been made.

He also tried with his knife to cut deep into the hard water, but without great success, and he did not know how Atwar had done so. He was determined to find out.

○

Tared and I were satisfied with the passages. That first night we had not gone deep, nor had we been very comfortable; the one sling we managed to make out of our clothing would not hold us all, and we had slept on the ground. Now she was eager to go back into the barrens and fetch furze, and use it as Atwar did—"See what he has done with it: he dresses in it! The underside is thick and soft, and even an arm can be pressed through, without stitching." Then she had quickly withdrawn her hand as if ashamed, and put the rough garment down—but in the end we folded it, and laid it carefully on the bank.

"He has taken your blue dress with him, however."

Atwar was near, and we must accustom ourselves, because we did not know what else to do. We were in his lands, and we had to wait, and learn from him what he wanted of us.

○

We brought furze from the barrens in that cool morning: indeed, Tared and Ask found it more pleasant to come out of the trees and the increasing mists—and the air over the furze enticed us; but being east-facing it took the early force of the sun, and I stayed nearby in the shade under the bank, and closed my eyes. Out there Ask was happy, though it was the air that made him so despite himself—and Tared, if she tried to be surly, would begin to laugh, especially if we were out early, when the foliage was smoking.

That first time Ask stood up on the bank, and looked about him, he reasoned that Atwar must cut the furze without harming it, because it was one consciousness—"See, how it lifts off, and the tendrils conjoin and have no ending. To cut it does not cause it pain—it is no different than when gravid women cut their hair—"

He said this lightly.

Then he and Tared went farther out, away from Atwar's path, and cut furze in the bright morning. This was to lay on the ground inside the passages, and to dress in when the night returned. They threw it over the bank, and we brought it back through thickening mists to the half-island.

Where he had cut, Tared made the day-farms just as she had done against the second grove, having brought out good soil for them.

Fruit we had also at our half-island, that we had kept against the lamp, and some leaf clothing—but now we liked the furze better. Ask however would try to burn it; he cut some away, crouched over there at the point, and lighted it. But it burned very slow, one tiny prick of light eating with no hunger or flame, and no oil came out of it. He lit the furze in four-or-eight places but it burned always like that, as we thought, diffidently. At the time we did not understand its properties.

But that stubbornness in the furze made it safe for us. Only later did we think how perilously we had lived in our culvert house, with an open flame, and the waxy leaf spread all around us!

We used the last of the leaf to make two slings there on the half-island, and filled them with furze, so the flood would not wash them away. Ask tied them round and round with fibres so they hung like round bags high among the roots.

"He may yet overturn them—"

"They do not look like slings."

We were doubtful. The rest of the furze we threw down into the root-rooms.

○

The water broke and flowed, and white-green boulders came bobbing out of the fog on both sides, scraping into the greater channel noisily. Ask was restless, and wanted to ride—he leaped out on them, and played among them, the water pushing them ever ponderously westward, and him with them; it was still thick with coolness. He clambered ever back.

"Tared, there is no danger here!" Even as he called out to us, he skidded, and lay on a tilting block with his feet in the

THE TAMING ○ 121

water, and then the block, and his black peering head, slid out of sight into the mist.

He was very curious. Indeed we did not feel that there was any more danger, now that we were in Atwar's grove.

○

At that time, as Ask played down the channel, I went under ground, not from the season, but because I liked the dark. It was already long into the Moon's morning, as long as what is counted three or four days in the World. But Tared was watching, and saw Atwar coming towards her along the north course, across the water.

What she saw of him, she told as well as she could. Ask had said Atwar's look was not attentive—or, attentive to something other than our own attentiveness—that Atwar saw him, yet did not look into his look. Tared afterwards called it an *unlook*: "Perhaps he is not intelligent!" Yet she meant something else. She could not describe what she meant.

"He stood up, and so I stood up also."

At that time I was asleep and heard nothing, till she came down into the passage and shook me to waken me.

○

Tared said that Atwar walked as he was used, as Ask does, but more heavily—yet he was silent and graceful. At the bank he stopped; seeing her, as she supposed, he stood up, with his unlook on her. The fog was then drawing off, and she saw him well enough.

"I stood up also—as seemed courteous—and so we stood, with the water between us. It was not such a long time, for I think I did not dare to breathe—yet it seemed very long! He was wearing some stuff—the furze I would guess—around his body but he had no headsleeve, or anything tied to his arms or thighs. His legs were bare—they are somewhat short as ours are, but black and well downed—what a big head he has! His face is like Betwar's indeed with that wideness, and heavy browline—

"But not like Betwar's!" She said this vehemently, and took a breath. "His hair grows back out of it, as ours and Betwar's; he is not bald-browed as the eastern folk. His hair is very long, and some of it is black and some light gray—it is more rough than mine.

"There was good time to look at him, speechless as we were! I will never forget him.

"Then he put his hand to the blue cloth, that I could see a little of, tied across his throat—"

"Tared, he saw you wore also a blue dress!"

"I did not think this was what he meant. He meant—"

But we did not know what Atwar meant!

"His hand was there, his twarhand, his fingers in the cloth, and so he turned around and away—with that same look Ask saw—that look I saw the last of near the culvert, in the other grove. His head lifted, I saw the white of his child-teeth, and he turned away. When his head lifted it was as if he looked carefully all the way up the plank of the tree behind me, and across its foliage, and over the great course and down towards the water! It was not quick, or changing—perhaps he is blind!" But we knew he was not blind, though at that time we thought he was in some way as if blind.

"Did he go off down the channel, towards Ask?"

"No, he went back where he had come. I saw the blue of your dress among the stems."

○

We stared at each other. Tared's eyes were very round, as if they would roll about in their bony sockets, and mine were surely round too, with the same wonder. Then, at the same moment, we each drew in a great breath. That made us laugh. How as it, that Atwar could fill our very lungs with delight?

"He knows me now, he will know me!"

But we were unsure. Such a look! yet we thought: if we have encountered that same gaze he bestows on his trees and watercourses, we are received in his grove well enough, greeted and welcomed.

○

We went out, and saw Ask returning; he was walking on the north bank of the channel, and went on some distance up the bank of the north course, passing even where Atwar had stood, and swam back to us with the flow. When he climbed out, Tared told him how she had seen Atwar there.

Ask must first listen, but later he told us, "I came to a

stone, and the course divides—there is a half-island—very high! It is bare topped—I saw rock and furze between the trees. The water branches—but the broad path continues on it. I walked there and looked for passages, but found none. The trees are smaller. It goes on as a great path. It does not diminish. I think it is the way to his mansions."

Ask marked our place on his leaf, close to Cape Fresnel, at the beginning of that narrow vale that led into the Sea of Rains—we knew, though we had not yet seen them, that the ranges closed in on us westward, north and south.

○

"Why did you not speak to Atwar, across the water?"

"Ask, you told him so many long and wonderful Tales yourself, as you sat beside him at the fire!"

Ask was silent. Then he said, "It is not so easy to speak. I called out, however."

"After he was gone."

We were under ground, because the heat was upon us.

We sat in the lowest room near the seeping water; there the air was coolest in the afternoon, though it tasted heavy. It was yet long till the flood, as much as three days as they are counted in the World.

We were very tired, for we had gone back with Ask swimming down the great course, and looked with him at that second half-island. We had walked in Atwar's path there, that winds south around its slope among twisted trees. Some smaller paths went upward, for it was high, and Ask wanted to follow them—"Perhaps he has doors overhead, into the ground—" and he went uphill, but found nothing except crooked ground, with a ridge sloping north into a smaller hill and one channel running under it, narrowly. Here the planks are not aligned; some are even turned around on themselves in their growing, and the foliage sparse overhead. Some dead wood we saw, but still not as much, or as newly broken, as in the eastern groves. The World's waxing crescent showed between the leaves, and Ask said he saw him clear from higher on the hill, with the shadow of night across his northern pole: now was the darkest of Darkening in Fu-en and Lofot and all those peopled lands.

We got into the water and it carried us. The course flowed rough and looked shallow but we were used, and knew it was deep. Farther on, the water was very broken, with standing waves and hanging foam. It made so much noise we had to shout to hear each other. There, the courses again ran together—it was an island after all. And from there we could see a second branching of the course around a second hill, and broken wood on the beach and Atwar's path—but whether that was island or half-island, we could not tell.

I would not go any farther. The foliage was so thin it did not cover the courses, and much heavy light fell on us, the heat also increasing. So we stopped and slept, and went back, coming into our dwelling when the heat was already great, and the channels full of choking mist and burned almost dry. Ask laughed when I came in: "You are indeed stout, Ard—if you eat more, you will have to sleep over ground!" I know Tared wished me to tell him then. But she said nothing, and after she had rested she sighed, and went to the farms.

We were in the deep room, where it was coolest. Ask had filled up the bladder, for that pool in the stones was then very small, though it never quite dried away. Now we laid our cloths in it, folded carefully (my sister and I had sewn that one rag into two, as we said).

O

Ask still wondered, that Tared had said nothing to Atwar.

"Atwar would have gone from you, had you offended him. He went from you at any rate. Tared, where was your mouth? In the World, you were ever complaining to him!"

Because we remembered well her insistence at stopping under the Doll, when we were carrying home from Book—and how often we must wait while she prayed to Atwar, or whatever it was she did.

Tared said sadly, "That is what I was taught, and do you not chide me for it!"

Then Ask was sorry. "I know that you are not so now, Tared. You are not strict, as you were then."

"If I were strict, you would not have stiff fingers."

Ask went close to Tared then, and embraced her. "It is nothing—they are healed. This-body is still as children's." He grinned. "When it becomes adult, do not think it will ever heed you!"

She stroked him. "Seldom do you come to us, Ask. Do not be, as I was in the World, striving to be ever strict and strong. Ah, I was as small as you, when I was in the World, and very serious, and mostly unwise—"

"I am not unwise."

"No, you are wise, for here you must increase your necessity. So much you have striven—too much, we have required of you."

Ask rested then and smiled, leaning at her breast, and I came close also. He let me embrace him, and said I was not so sharp to lean against as my sister! We talked for a long time about Saska, remembering everything we could of him, so the dark low room flickered as much with those dream-images as with the ruddy lamp behind us, that dragged and gutted in the stale draught of air.

Then I told him, stammering, that within the course of the Moon's next afternoon, or even morning, two more voices would be heard in the Moon.

O

We named them Selen, and after they were born, Atwar came nearer to us, and we began to have some communication with him.

They were separated twins like us, each with one body—very alike, so Tared tied a strip of her blue dress to the one's arm—and then afterwards could not anyway remember which she had chosen! That was however Itsel the first born; for I ever knew them, though I could not say how.

That birth was, as I had expected, in the afternoon, past the Moon's mid-day about two days, as they are counted in the World.

We had climbed out at nightfall against the running rills, and found the floodwater all around. Atwar had been at the sling—those bundles of furze were gone, which we had tied in it, and it hung overturned and empty. So we swam and harvested, and when the water fell, Ask and Tared fetched new furze from the barrens, but I stayed in the house. That night I was again somewhat sick. The furze was long in drying, and my body felt the coolness even so deep in the ground, with a stinking leaf-fire to warm us as well as the lamps. Tared was angry we had not secured the furze in slings in the passages, instead of leaving it over ground and on the floor. But towards morning it was dry enough, and we made clothing for ourselves and so occupied ourselves—Ask impatiently, for he wanted to be outside.

○

All the early morning Ask was down the channel, and over on the courses, looking for Atwar—he had gone out very early while it was still bitterly cool, all furze-dressed like a bundle. He saw marks near to our doors, but not against them, and gray traces crissing and crossing up on the north course, where it was smooth; but when they turned off into the forest he lost them. Far down the channel he saw traces also, earlier ones, but no clear direction and no dwelling. He went up into that crooked island, and walked in its many paths, returning only when the air became too thick with vapour to see.

So he and Tared again cut furze in the smoke of morning, and she looked to the farms, to replenish the shallow wells now black and dead with the chill they had endured. And again I hid nearby under the bank, to wait for them.

The babes leaped strongly in my belly. Tared had talked with me much in those days of hours, in the night house—and was ever asking me, whether I would make a pit, and where it should be; but my body had no idea of it.

I thought that perhaps, if I should give birth in the day time, before it was hot—I did not care to be over ground, yet here under the bank I was comfortable, with the gray water gushing into its stony pool and the air warming and good to breathe—if the babes were born here, and in such weather, they would like the outdoor Moon surely and thrive! But it was thought only. These hands did not desire to dig any pit there, or this belly to push; and the babes waited.

So in the end, it was in the small southern room the Selen were born, among the great roots, with the sun's light at the door.

Tared

*O*h my sister, what name could we have chosen for that bond, for it had no name among the names? Milk-play we ought to have abandoned at our weaning, but the Sanev were careless, their body lusty even as children, and ever our companions! I did abandon it—and was angry, yet I now know that Ard's way was the seemlier! For I was turned, not thinking of them, and by force I must be prevented—that doll in me prevented, from what it was determined in! Betwar gripping my arms, calming me, returning me to myself. Even then, my sister was already bonded! and in her body my separate body was as if bonded too, a clean bond as now I know.

What is called shame in the World—yet here it was clean as a well-bleached cloth. And remember how Tasman short-bonded did take those same twins the Sorud for her housebond. That was also clean. What would be shame for the ordinary people is clean for us—as now this life, this life, shame-made in the World, clean in the Moon, our first born, not strangers!

O

Ard cannot not tell it. Ah, it seemed to me she had died, and the babes, so sick she was, and they so very still at first, and small!

In the night I had said to her, "You are now older than Tasman was, when she gave birth to Atwar, and Betwar our father." I said this to comfort her, for it is not safe or seemly to give birth out of a body so immature, so recently itself the body of children.

"Tasman ate bad root the Say gave. That is why she became pregnant in short-bond," said Ard, repeating the Tale. All the Fu-en people believed this of the Say who were jealous, and who had been with Tasman at her initiation. But Betwar had doubted it.

"And you, because they gave us no root. But our father

said, it was so with Tasman because the root had no effect, because of her deformity."

"Then had we eaten root, perhaps even so—?"

Ask broke in: "There is no root in the Moon."

He was curious, but we could tell he felt it unseemly to question us outright. I would have said, *It is not our purpose here to eat root*—but I did not know our purpose any more. I think he had some idea that the babes would be normal twins like the Sanev who had fathered them; because he said—"It will be easy for them to learn to walk, with this thicker air. They will not take four years to find it out, as twins in the World!"

"They will be as we are," said Ard.

"Do you know it?" I asked her. For though I thought it would be so, I was not sure.

She put her hands on her belly. "So it seems, when they move. And they are male."

She was right about their being like us, but they were girls; and I think in that she was disappointed—our brother was at first, certainly.

○

I had asked her more than once in the Moon's night, about digging a pit, for my mind ranged, and I did not want to be afraid, but to think of everything needful. She was again sick, shuddering, and we could not keep her warm. I made Ask light a fire of leaves, as well as the lamps, but from it the air became very bad. Then he went into the upper passages, coughing, and cut away some of the living root. But it was hard and wet, and did not burn with much warmth. If Ard gave birth now, there would be no pit, because the floor was made of stone, and no pit-pool either, only that little stony seep against the wall. Yet I was sure she would choose to be under ground.

Ask worked true-book into the leaf with his knife. It was already past *Kaamos* in the northern World, when we went into the house, in the dark part of Lightening, and he marked that little-World on the leaf with the darkness covering the north as we had seen. "And for the southern folk, white nights!" he said, showing us. But for the people in the north, gradually, the days would lengthen and the cool darkness shrink away. "When their white-night is passed," he said, "We will have been here one whole year."

All this he could describe with his markings in the leaves—he kept them with him in the night, so they would not blacken; but in the day, if he did not want them, he put them into pockets in the high room, cut into the root.

Towards morning we made clothes, and I made two little garments that had, for their legs and arms, narrow inner gloves. The furze was indeed soft inwardly, and kept that softness. I made the headsleeves narrow too, though Ask argued, "Such a small headsleeve looks foolish!" Then, he set about making one garment with a big, ordinary sleeve; perhaps he still thought they would be normal twins. Ard did not make anything for them, but she made Ask's clothes, so he could go out before dawn and look for Atwar.

○

Ah, we talked also of Atwar in those hours! Ask and I telling over and over how he looked, till almost we might have forgot him in the words' image! But if the details were dyed, the way he looked at us was not—that unlook—it was too strong to colour with words; and also, we had no words to describe it.

My mind could see him easily, and Ask's as well. He said, "Atwar is in a space between my thoughts—if my thoughts hold their breath for a moment, he appears there clearly between them." This snow I could see—it was so with me also.

And Ask spoke often of Atwar's dwellings, that he called mansions; he was very eager to find them.

"I know, that he lives well, and can build many things! He has been into the Outdead house at the sward, and there he stopped the fall of the Moon, and he has seen every thing they made! He lives hereabouts now, but he came there and found us—and brought us to his domain."

Ask thought then that perhaps Atwar had seen our fire, or its smoke, when we had inadvertently burnt the tree. But perhaps he was already in that grove—would he not have seen us coming in the sky, if he had been looking?

"All this we will ask him, when we are his friends!"

Ask did not then wonder about Atwar, that he had as yet not spoken to us, and had looked strangely, and run away. For Ask, then, Atwar was as Atwar was, and would do what he would, and in his good time befriend us—he had already befriended us! bringing us into his grove, sitting beside Ask at the fire! Did he not wear Ard's dress? and had he and I not, with the water between us, seen each other and stood still?

But I wondered much about him.

O

Ard went into the passages, and slept, though it was the time of the Moon's morning and pleasant. I was in the farms as long as the shadow stayed, and then above ground on the half-island, in the fog—I was as restless above ground as she was, down in the passages! And I went down to her sometimes, and slept some hours beside her in the big root-room. I brought fresh water to her from the slick on the course.

When Ask came, he told us he had been as far as a second meeting of courses—and that a third island lay beyond the second. Atwar's path on the third island was even more wide, Ask said—"I went to the top, and Hadley stood over the water and the trees, back behind its barren hills—the leaves of those shorter trees spread even so, as high as they can. But the roof dips—and the stones and the cables under it. I saw Hadley through that dip in the roof, and that skin blurred it—for it is much scratched and pulled—indeed, I saw the upper surfaces of the stones—they are as red as the barrens!"

"How is it they hang?"

"They are held into the grid—it is all in a patterning of six and six, for I counted—the canopy dips like a navel to each cable, and like a great bowl with a black lip over each stone."

His eyes were wide and a little scared, and he glanced away, and rubbed them, before he went on.

"It was very bright on that hill, and on Hadley also, but the vales were filled up with mists. I saw many paths, and looked within the roots, if there was any door under ground, but I saw no mounds, as here, or doors—or his traces. Yet does his way firm itself, and broaden. His mansions are farther west."

I could not then understand how the scape had looked, over the trees and mist, with that dipping of the roof and Hadley rising. Later I saw for myself.

"Could you see westward?"

"One more large island—or half-island—its top north west of where I stood—then the Moon's limb. There was a stone in the way, but its peak did seem to be Outdead shaped. There was thick fog under me, even there, and I think it must be forest. I heard the first noise of the water breaking, and turned back." He paused. "How is it with Ard?"

"She is under ground. She is not making a pit, or doing other than drowsing and sleeping."

"Is she sick?"

"No."

○

The courses were clanging and changing—and again he rode those greenish rafts—when he came back, he said that his legs were tired. I think that was the first sign, that the air was becoming less buoyant under us. But he had gone far in those hours of days.

Ard's body did not find much suffering in labour— perhaps, because we had already seen her so sick in the Moon, we thought this slight. As for a pit, she was till the end uninterested; it was past the Moon's mid-day when I looked down, and she was vaguely spreading the furze about—

"Will-we dig here?" I asked. She was in the smaller room with its stout root walls.

"Dig with me if you like, as sisters dig in the World -" Ard pushed some furze aside, and looked around her, still dissatisfied, and at the hard dirt floor.

"Here is no pool," I said. "Over ground, we could make a pool in the bank." But I knew Ard would not want to be over ground.

She stared at the roots. "This is a pit, I have felt it, I think, ever since we came into it—this room now more than the bigger one. Atwar has dug it for us—"

"Such a great, broad pit—" I said. But I could see she was decided.

"We will fill it with furze! and from here, we can take the

newborn with safety deep under ground."

Then Ard climbed out with me, and Ask came also, and we went to the barrens. I took the yeast then though I could have waited, and Ard went out also, in the short shade, and strove, tearing at the furze herself as if she could not wait for what Ask was patiently cutting. And carried it, her back arched, in great trailing bundles held over her belly. We knew then that she was near giving birth, from her fearless striving.

Ask brought back much also, and I too after I had stored the yeast; we pushed that furze down through the door, till the room was stuffed almost full. This was the time when the flowerets dried up and crumpled on their stalks. Ah, that whole stretch of Atwar's Way, from the barrens back to the door, was laid with pink. I beat the furze also, before we took it inside, so the last of the ashy petals would be loosed; and a drift of them lay all around the door. Ard looked out—"You are dyers' colour!" grinning. And so she was as well—her hair dusted with pink, and pink flakes stuck in the sweat of her face.

O

Perhaps it was this colour that Atwar saw, that brought him close to us; perhaps he was curious what we were about, and why we had strewn his path like a celebration.

There was not room for me, and I lay over ground beside Ask and looked down through the door. Ard struggled with the furze to turn it and order it, till at last she had a pit to her liking, lined with the soft underside of the furze, and deep. It was messy and easy.

Yet, my sister had dared to go out into the barrens, and carried much furze home—for her this was effort indeed.

O

I said, "Will you cut your hair?"

She lifted her hands to her head, and opened her mouth wide and wailed. "Where are they, who should cut it?"

Then I was sorry I had spoken, for it was what the Sanev should have undertaken, the fathers of her children.

But Ard stopped her wail suddenly, as if in great surprise, and sat still. "This belly clenched," she said.

It seemed, during those clenches, that she was ever more

THE TAMING ○ 133

surprised and attentive than suffering.

I stayed with her, and Ask coming and going gave us water. I think, holding her, my separated body felt as much as she.

The babies were born before it became really hot. Only at the last did her mind turn from us, after the first was born and before she understood—her eyes rolling away and her mind as if sinking back inside her body, and she grew slack and still.

Ah, I had never seen quite such a new creature—the Siri twins were three days day old and ruddy, before we had seen their goodly body and their two round and satisfied heads! But this little one was wet and shrunk like old fruit, and one-headed and made no sound. I put it on Ard's belly.

○

They say that when Atwar was born, he waited for Betwar to be born before he cried, so that even though they were separated, their two voices were heard together in the World. And so did this babe wait—yet I would have desired it to cry, for it was surely lifeless! I put my finger into its tiny mouth, and I put Ard's hand over its downy back as it lay, but her hand slid off again.

Was there but one, as Tasman?

Then Ard's body released the other; not clenching or crying out, but with a long, sorrowing sigh. It sounded—it was as if she died! even Ask heard it so, chattering in the door, "Shake her, Tared!, shake her awake, shake-them," because he was afraid of the silence.

"Bring water."

Ask was back, naked, and pushing down to me his dress, which he had soaked in the course. He crouched there over ground at the door in the mess of pink petals, his teeth clicking in agitation.

I did not know what to do with that water! I had put the second baby with the first, on Ard's belly. The cake lay in blood in the brown furze under her, but I saw it not then. I pressed Ask's dress over them, squeezed water on them, rolled them to and fro anxiously. I shook Ard and whispered.

○

Perhaps such a long time did not pass. Perhaps it is ordinary, that women in giving birth are so tired they seem for a few moments dead, that children after such striving will rest before they utter! How silent it was! A little earth rolled down from the door. Ask said afterwards, that to him also the time of stillness seemed very long. And he was looking in so desperately, so attentively, he did not notice Atwar there beside him.

○

Were you then wondering what they had done, why they had strewn your path? Red on it where you walked, a fragile red, the inner colour of those infant mouths, their palms and footsoles, their sex that proclaimed them. Though the furze had been shaken the petals fell into the pit, then there were petals of blood. Spattered, stringed when she held them towards you, the ropes unsevered, whitepink looping. Your face, your oval, oval of love.

IIII.
Shadows

Ask

Atwar was crouched by me on the twelside, a little behind me, and very slowly I learned he was there—my body learned it, for my attention was all in the pit, with the new babies—my mind came back slowly into my body and quieted, knowing he was there. But I dared not acknowledge him in case he ran away. I need not have been so careful, for he had come in spite of my chattering, and agitated running to and fro. He was close enough to see into the house.

Almost, I could have burst into loud tears when my mind, from the edges of my eyes, received the shadow of his dress!

Then I looked covertly, and saw his downy twelfoot close to my arm. I looked at it, I think, for a long time, for still I remember every detail, the first I saw of him clearly, the fierce black hairs springing out of his long toe-knuckles, the hair growing (like mine, like Saska's, like our father Betwar's) across the high arch without no ordinary strand of foothair bound around it, because like us he had bald footsoles and palms. His nails were very thick and uneven, and there were pink petals stuck between his toes.

Atwar smelled good, of the furze, but it was an unsmell too; he did not smell human as we were used. Even as I was gazing at his foot, the babies began to cry weakly. Tared sat back on her heels and looked up, and saw Atwar.

The light spread on her thin face, and on that haggard grin she had that was not a grin but somehow became one; and she laughed out of it. She grasped the babies and held them up—she was still laughing—and they were all legs and arms and blood, squirming meekly between her fingers.

"Move aside, Ask, so they can look first into Atwar's face!"

And I did, and he stayed, the two babes held up towards him in the pit—though whether they saw him or not I do not know, for it seemed they were busy crying and their faces were squinted over their eyes. They were indeed female—I looked—under each belly only a scored pout. I was disappointed, then!

I tried to laugh too, for I knew the custom, and coughed, and Atwar did not run away at that, or at what Tared had said. She put the babies on Ard's belly again, and put Ard's two hands over them, and my dress.

"Ard, see your children! Atwar is here, and I have shown them his face."

I saw Atwar now; I had moved close again, but he stayed where he was. I think he was looking as we look, in focus, but I am not sure—his face in profile was very still, big as Betwar's; the mouth muscle was bigger and the expression entirely different, as if washed away. His hair had on this twarside a thick streak of white that was wound about the black hair in a long strand and tied at the end tightly, like a bandage. I could see Ard's dress across his shoulders, over a thin dress of furze—the inner stuff of the furze it was, scraped or beaten so fine it resembled coarse brown cloth. It must be soft, I thought, for it lay in folds and wrinkles where he crouched in it—it covered his knees. I could see his twarfoot now, that his good foot had crossed and hidden, it was the one the snake had lamed. It was smaller, malformed as if it had been crushed from the toes towards the heel. His arms were behind his knees and his hands folded together at his throat.

Ah, I desired then to speak to him, I who had chid Tared for her silence, when she and Atwar stood across the course—and now I dared not! How fearlessly Tared had held the babies up to him, and loudly ordered me out of the way! That was as good as speaking to him, almost. She had laughed aloud as she ought, which I could not manage.

Now I heard Ard laugh too, in her darker voice, and Tared's voice comforting her. I stirred. Atwar gave a great sniff, and released his large bare arms that had been pressed against his chest. He put his two hands on the ground. His head turned towards me—he looked across me, that unlook, very slow and deliberate, then out towards the steamy courses. I saw the doll, tied within the blue dress, fastened at his throat.

What did he look, was it sadness, or an absence of sadness, an equivalent absence of joy? His mouth lifted back across his dull, white teeth. I felt my own mouth answering his—I began then, I guess, to learn his look, as infant twins learn by copying the looks of their mothers—I would learn it little by little long before I knew what it meant.

Atwar! He went away slowly, and I followed him.

○

Another full day would pass, as they are counted in the World, before the greatest heat set in. But the channel was already dried up, its last mists dissipating. This was the time of the bad air, when it was too thick to breathe willingly, and the body gave away water and could not in all that wet find any end to its thirst. I licked my hands, and sucked my soaking hair, and followed him at a little distance. He had gone heavily down into the course bed, and was moving along it westward, but I leapt up on the north bank, for not to step in the simmering pools. He did not heed them. So we walked, both of us low as we liked, and my step was lighter—I floated then between each push of hand and foot—but his pace was more graceful.

We walked as long as a day's hours and the great sun was still high, smearing the treetops, and the heat increased terribly. Atwar entered the first island, and followed his way under the peak, and again heavily over the channel beyond and into the second, and still I followed him, but I was now very hot, and sickening. Sometimes I saw his blue shoulders, and at the ground his hands going forward and his swinging hair, and ever I saw his short, limping legs under the furze dress. I half-dreamed that I fell down, and that he turned, and picked me up and carried me. But he did not look back.

We passed to the third island and came to go down its western slope. This was farther than I had ever been. I had not seen the fourth except for its top over the fog. It was apart from the others, across a wide stone-shadowed glade, and now I thought I could not go so far. I sat down in the path, and saw Atwar crossing to it over the bed of the channel.

Then on the other side he stood upright on the shore and

turned around, and looked towards me. So I got up somehow and followed him.

○

That smallshadow, that tired one, a fire in my side casts my shadow upward on the dirt. The pools eat themselves, that soften my footsoles, I pull away the layers of skin in the night to chew them inside my cheek. That shadow leaps, then I was small and leaping, then when I laughed, and there was no answer. It is unwise to make a noise in this world.

He has a very round look, a secret Betwar look in his wrists, his wrists are my fingers' shadow. I push my fingers through my cloak, it is tramped thin, I roll a long nightwick out of the furze root and dip it in the tallow tree, my fire burns all night, not those fires. The tree flamed! Twice, the first time worst, the whole grove black afterwards under the leaves. I buried the bones of the stems, they buried nothing. For days I ate ashes.

Tared

We named them Selen for their birth and separately they were called Itsil and Itlin and they were, from the beginning, long-limbed and their skin pale, but it darkened. At first their colour was as our palms or clean footsoles—of that lightness—and their hair rather sparse, the down on their bodies sparse also so we could scarcely trace the crowns. They were like us, narrow-shouldered. Ard was surprised to see they were girls; she said wonderingly, "They were ever female in this belly, even as I was saying they were male."

It was already hot and I tried to persuade her to exert herself and come deeper under ground; she would, but she slept again, so I took an armful of fresher furze and went down, and then returned and carried the babies down, wrapped in Ask's dress. Then she followed. Now we were away from the heat in the lowest room, with a small lamp lit at a distance from us and the air heavy but bearable. Here lay the old night-furze and we lay in it, and Ard put the babies to her breasts. I watched.

Ah, my sister was unlike me in the Moon, both before and after she gave birth! And after, I think I was closer to Ask, in my thoughts and ways, than to my separated twin. I believed, when she gave birth, that I shared in her striving, and it was I who had gently directed her about the pit, and watched over her as she crouched down, and as a world-mother received the babes. But now it was as if she had gone through another door and I could not follow. There was a kind of darkish light around her, which I did not see but saw with my mind, that enclosed the babies as she lay holding them, and stretched to enclose them when I held them also. I was not within it.

We spent those hours of days quietly, Ard ever stronger, and well occupied, enough that she did not notice my impatience. Often I took the twins and held them, also when she was eating, or doing up her hair. I helped to wipe their skin when it was time to clean them of the slick birth-oil. And we looked at them together, to see if one of them had any peculiar mark, so we could tell them apart by it, but we could not find any thing. Only, as with us, the whorls of their central crowns turned in opposite directions, as they do on twel- and twarside limbs of ordinary twins—but with us, the crown between the shoulder blades (as the crown of the head) is as back-to-back, and I am from it a kind of Twel, and Ard Twar; of our brothers, Ask is as Betwar Twar-crowned, and Saska was as Atwar—a kind of Twel.

So we laid the babies on their bellies across our knees and could say, this one is Itsil (the Twar) and this one Itlin. I think Ard saw it unthinkingly, how their skin-down lay, for she ever knew them, without doubt. But I tied a slip of cloth around Itsil's arm, from the seam of Ask's dress, because otherwise I could not tell her from her sister. Even we stretched their puny limbs out, trying to see which twin was the longer, but they squirmed and were made unhappy and would not allow us. Then would Ard, when they cried, lick them and fondle them tenderly, and laugh over them! As is seemly, one or other of us held them ever, until they did swim, and when they slept we wrapped them against each other in the cloth of Ask's dress, so they resembled ordinary twins, and had the good of each other's touch. And Ard from the first was joyous in stroking them and in all that milk-play; her milk spouted and was plentiful, and she smelled ever of milk. The furze stank of it.

So it was that for Ard to see, or for me to tell of it, I was as near her as ever, almost as near the babes as I would have been, had she and I from one body given birth like ordinary women in the World. But this did not correspond.

○

We did not know where Ask had gone—he had surely followed Atwar. Ard had no energy to think about her brother, but for me his absence was another part of my unease. As soon as the rills ran in the passages, I went over ground to look for him.

Our half-island was submerged; our two doors on their mounds were two tiny islands and the spreading flood moved slowly around them, carrying the whitish petals in long strips on its surface, that had lain along the path. The mounds were ashy with them still. I slid into the cool of the water.

The sun set with the Moon's wind and I heard the birds before I saw them, high among the swaying trees. Ask said that they followed the terminator with the push of the wind, and thus they lived; but we had also seen them fly north, not west, and in his true-book he had begun to make some charting of their journeys—he said that, when they were farther north, they had not to fly so far, for the path of the terminator is shorter. That they came to us was because they liked us, then, if we were out of their best way. However, there is no air at the poles or any seeded area north of the mountains, except the Lake of Death. So he could not yet understand how they came to us ever from the east, with the wind.

I heard them with gladness, and breathed the cooler air, and watched the red fade into dim blue as night fell under the half World. The first cloth of sweet rain touched my face. Down the fruit would fall, and we would eat its ripeness!

We were grown large now, a city, a multitude! Now we could say in truth, *we are many, a family.* Not four-or-eight twins, as they call a large family in the World, but four-or-eight even so! I could see us in my mind as a city, a cluster of fires, to make a sign across the space between the two worlds.

Ard should bring the babies over ground, for it was already late to swim with them—I wondered whether they would have forgotten how.

We did not see our brother then, but he returned while I was still at harvest, as Ard swam with the babies between the two island-mounds.

◯

I had fastened up some slings of leaf-fall and was filling them. The first I knew of Ask was his voice close behind me—"Mind the fruit does not strike the babies on their heads!" and he laughed.

We gathered between the doors, standing about to our waists, and laughed and ate, Ard holding, it seemed carelessly, a foot of each squirming babe in one hand, and eating with the other. Good juice ran out of our mouths.

"See, how they swim!" said Ask.

"And yet they were born in a dry pit, and were not in water till this day. But they have not forgotten how they swam inside me!"

Ask caught them up, looked over at Ard, as if he dared her to allow him to drop them into the water. But she was as calm as ever. He ended by sliding them gently in, towards Ard, who received them as they came kicking upward, and lifted them spluttering. "Ah, you are diligent, our-daughters!"

I said, "Ask, where is Atwar?"

He did not answer, but went on chatting and playing with the babies. So I ate, and did not ask him more. Later I bundled the slings together and took them under ground, and hung the harvest in the passages. Ask lay down on the earth outside, and immediately fell asleep. There was a long scratch on his leg, in one place deep—it was clean from his swimming. I put a water-cloth over it, perhaps only to say *We see you have hurt yourself.* He did not stir.

After Ard had fed the babies she slept also, in the root room, but I swam, out over the course and west through the silent, flooded forest, looking for Atwar, telling myself I would surely greet him in words, as soon as I saw him. But I did not see him then.

O

Why did Ask not tell us of Atwar or of that afternoon? He chose to talk of nothing except the babes, and to busy himself over the lamps, and when at last I demanded an answer of him he said, "You know yourself that Atwar does not love to speak." As if, in the matter of Atwar, Ask had determined to be speechless also. I suspected that he had been disappointed in something, that Atwar had disappointed him and he was ashamed to tell us of it.

"Did Atwar house you from the heat?"

"You see that I have returned in health."

"Where were you then?"

But he fetched down his true-book, and turned his back.

He worked long over it; later I looked when he slept: he had marked a map of the islands in the pass west of us, and the courses, and in the centre of the fourth island drawn an Outdead shape with straight sides, and a finer, curved mark all the way around it, and two short marks joining them. Later he told us about it, when he had made the image of it several times and was satisfied with it.

I saw in his behaviour some change also, for he rubbed much at his legs, and said they were tired and he could no longer leap so far. He had swum home against the flood, after its strongest surge but still with difficulty. Also, he would from time to time imitate Atwar's face, in that he lifted his lip—and on Ask this looked very foolish, but I did not laugh at him. Whatever he knew of Atwar, it made him the wisest of us. But Ard said when she saw it, "Do you not teach that ugly face to the babies!" not recognizing it was Atwar's look—ah, one of them learned it after all.

The night had not set in before Atwar came, and after that he was seldom away from us long. So we began as we thought to tame him, which was not as the taming of children, but much otherwise—and yet we believed that we were diligent, and that we prospered in it.

○

That night, after the water had fallen back into its courses, and was beginning to form its skin, I saw Atwar swimming in the great course, his head moving black in the bright water out past the shadow of the stone. I called the others and they came up, Ask with a lamp and Ard with the babies inside her furze. We stood on the point of the half-island and stared after him. His head would appear, and be gone again, and appear somewhere else—

"There he is!"

"Now, Tared," said Ard, "Do you speak to him, very loud, as you have intended!"

So I pulled much chill air into my breast and shouted, "Atwar! Atwar!" but he was already gone again under the water.

"Wait till we say it—then tell him to come to-us."

"There he is!"

I shouted again, "Atwar, swim to-us!"

"Tell him about Betwar our-father."

But I could not put those words on my tongue. "You make me into a doll that opens and shuts its mouth by a string in your fingers. Now he is gone again."

Ask said, scornfully, standing beside us, "Do you think Atwar cares for your talk?" And Ard went back with her babies into the house.

Ask and I stood and looked, the water glinting; we thought then he was swimming away from us, but it must have been a bunch of leaf—for he appeared again at nearly the same place.

"He is harvesting," said Ask. The fruit would then be on the bed of the course.

I said carefully, "He has heard us talking, Ask, and was not afraid, when I told you to move aside so I could show him to the babies. And the crying of the babies he did not dislike."

"He does not love speech."

So we stood silently on the point, and I thought that my brother had some reason for this stubbornness, and that Atwar had been mute, or had made him some command of muteness that my brother thought he must follow. I had nothing more to say either, as we watched, as if Atwar's silence were starting to spread among us. I looked over at my brother; he was lifting his lip and his teeth glinted.

Then we saw Atwar go up on the southern bank, and into the forest. He was naked, but we saw him later dressed in the furze.

O

Twice I went out during that night, once at Full when it was again a little warmer, when I did not see him, and again later, very quickly and well wrapped. I went again to the point and saw him out on the course, a dark shape moving in the stone's shade on the white surface; when he moved, a red glow showed behind him on the south bank—he seemed then to sink into the course—then he emerged again pushing a block of hardwater before him. There under the surface was the smaller glow of a lamp, reddening the inner bowl of his pit. Crack! crack! went the forest, and away across the course a shower of shards came whispering down.

I ran shivering back under ground.

"He is there—he is making a house!"

But Ard would not come away from the babies, and Ask and I could not stand long over ground to watch Atwar, the air being too chill.

"Ah, he dares not yet come down into this house, yet it is his," said Ard when we told her.

"He had not used it," said Ask shortly. "Not before us, for a long time."

We warmed ourselves, beating our arms against our bodies. Then we lay down close against Ard and the babies, where the furze was most warmed.

○

Ah—we had seen him till then as wise, but now we were unsure—even Ask. This was the reason our brother would not speak of him, that Atwar had in some way proven himself unwise, precipitate!

But I had wondered for a long time, how Atwar was! Even in the World, I do not think I trusted what I would find, when they said he was a god, and we his god-bonded! and here in the Moon, seeing him and wondering whether he was in some way blind. We were unable to read what was in his face.

Careful, careful we had been of his planet ever, only inadvertently by the fire had we marked it—and in cutting the furze. Yet the furze lived, and this he did not begrudge us, or this house under ground, or the mild farms that did come and go—and he ate, also, gathering to himself and eating (as we had seen) fruits in the flowing water.

But that he would help us actively, or take us into his mansions, I now much doubted. And Ask had not yet told us of that marked Outdead shape on the fourth island, where I thought Atwar had taken him. Was it perhaps the only house Atwar had? did he live otherwise only in diggings like these or in the hardwater houses he made so cunningly? What extravagant thoughts we had allowed ourselves of his mansions in the *mare*, of Chmedes, Aristillus and Autolycus! Out there was the treeless barren land—why should Atwar venture there to live, and not remain within his goodly grove?

Now it seemed to me more and more that his consciousness was as that of a tree, as much as that of a man—his silence! what he did was seemly for this place: he clothed and sheltered himself, and fed himself, but even a tree does this much, and prospers!

○

Ard, caring for the Selen, had not so much thought for Atwar now. She had ever said confidently, *He is preparing for us, and will take us to his mansions*—almost, she spoke as I did long ago in the World—large words, so there would not be space for doubt. Now she talked to the Selen, though they had no understanding, and spoke to them more of their own fathers than of Atwar. If she was not swimming with them, she kept them mostly under ground.

"See, maids, I have made you ear muffs, so you can lie close and comfortable. Thus do twins lie in the World. Itsil, strike not your sister! this is your breast, there is plenty. Itlin, take not my hair into your mouth!

"Tared, do you bind back this strand of hair, that Itlin is eating! Ah—the Sanev would have cut my hair. Daughters, when you are grown, your-fathers will come and greet you. And by then I will have told you so much of them, that you can remember them yourselves! Tsil, I can see in your eye Nevi's cunning—why do you ever thrust yourself at the twar-breast? It is Tlin's, not yours. Were you twins in the World, I must then hold you upside down, so you lay across my mouth and I licked your small belly—should you insist on that breast!"

And this she would immediately try, for she was ever playful with them, giggling and rolling about with them, till sometimes I wondered she did not crush them.

"The Sanev will come with clean furze, they will joyfully order this room, and clean its air, and dig deeper under the course, and shore up that which is fallen! They love to range, they will go as far as the farthest boundaries of the vegetable Moon, and bravely climb to Hadley's peak."

I said somewhat angrily, "That order you speak of could you well help me with," for it was I who had cleared away her birth pit, and buried the placenta cake all stuck with furze, and down here I must ever drag the furze out and replace it, and yet the room stank.

Ask at book looked up then and said sourly, "Hadley's peak is nothing more than a round hill."

"Ask, let her chatter, it is her pleasure." But if it were not the heat of afternoon I would have gone over ground, for I was impatient with her foolish talk.

○

"Do you think," said Ask to me aside, "The Sanev will ever come here, or there will ever be that conversation?" For the scholars and the Tales had predicted, how the World and the Moon would be as twins, and there would be conversation between them, in those future days.

"Not within such space of time as could be comfortably counted by children. I do not believe it."

"The scholars are too stupid to devise it."

I laughed at him. "I am glad you dare to say this, what I have long known."

"Ah—you did not say any such thing in the World, Tared, if you knew it then! Yet, if the Outdead prepared that conversation—what they prepared, has in many ways come to pass."

"That knowledge is under-sheath now, if they did." I meant, that like Mosc's ruins most of their knowledge was buried forever under the vast, melted Sheath of the World.

"The Outdead were stupid also, in what they promised us of the cars," said Ask quietly, and closed his mouth, and bent over his book. I knew he thought of Saska in his heart.

○

Ard was not listening, busy with her twins. I remember how she was almost always then, her hair tied as well as she could out of their reach, her round face open and glad, the lamplight reddening it, her eyes ardent, the shred of blue sleeve-dress pushed down around her waist, her big, black breasts and her paler, squirming babes, the smelly mess of the furze-bed, her busy shadow on the gray roof over her, the wall seeping.

Now she said eagerly, "On Hadley we could make that fire you talk of, Tared, to tell them in the World—a letter, to tell of the generations."

"This we could, if Atwar is willing—but I would wait," I said, "till he willingly remains with-us—then we are indeed four-or-eight, a large family. And we could make that constant fire as he makes them."

For we knew then how his fire burned indefinitely -in the night, he need scarcely tend it, it burned till morning through all those hours of days.

Ard said, "Even the fire over the culvert, but what we had made went out."

At these times, we would pause for our brother to speak— we left such courteous, open spaces in the paths of our talk of Atwar, not thinking what we did. But till then Ask would not walk in them. And now he said only, "A fire was never seen from that mountain."

○

As Atwar began to stray near us, and we learned more of his ways, we could not see that he had any purpose or intent, no particular greeting. He was at the edge of our eyes, and then nearer, whatever we were about, but he did not look at us except with that unlook. He did not eat with us, or swim with us, and he never came into the house.

That dawn, Ask and I had gone out to that hardwater house, and peered inside it. Atwar was not there. His gray marks, broken by the rough course, were old and westward— his fire glowed low in the south bank, with the soil scraped in those radiating lines around, hot to our feet even though the crumpled, stoney furze was dulling and extinguishing.

The doorstone was set aside, and I climbed down into the house. There as before was his furze-bed, but no lamp, only the depression where it had stood, when I had seen its glow— he had taken it with him.

"Ask, I called, "come and see, how comfortable it is!" But he remained outside.

Later, I saw my brother on the course, when it was breaking, climbing about on the house, opening it up, pushing the loosened blocks into it. Soon they floated off down the course with the other unshaped blocks and shards.

○

THE TAMING ○ 151

But Atwar was near that morning, and he watched me as I made the farms. Ah, I had pretended he watched me, at the first wells—and now he was here in earnest, from this day.

I saw him first as I went out carrying the yeast. He was beside the path, near that first root-room we had lain in, standing upright between the stems, with his hand on one of them—he was wearing the night-furze and I could see his legs under it and his bare feet. At his neck was the doll, and Ard's dress.

My feet stammered. Yet I did not stop, but continued walking lightly forward, carefully towards him, and set my feet so I would pass him in a slow bound—I think I held my breath! He was as near, when I passed by, as when he had looked into the pit. I did not hear his breath. He gave me no greeting.

Then from the barrens I saw him again, north along the line of trees. There he stayed as I went about the farms; and as the mist thickened in the grove he came a little out on the furze, so I could see him still. His hands were at his throat. Was it as Ard had said? was he again showing me that he, too, had a blue dress? Then I desired that mine were also on my shoulders, but I was still wearing the furze.

After that I ever remembered my dress, and wore it also when I was clad warmly—just as he did, tied at my throat and hanging.

When I looked up, he was as often as not looking away, turned towards the barrens and the other grove, or northward. So I, too, did look more about me, and quieted, though I had not learned to look as he did, which is not looking but receiving. My hair was thrown across my face, for the sun struck very bright despite the coolness of the air; it blazed on the wells. Atwar did not protect his head; the light made sharp ridges on his cheek and along his nose so his face was part-coloured like his hair.

Most cautiously I planted out that yeast, for not to disturb the Moon more than I must! Then, I had a set of four wells in the cuttings, about the breadth of my two arms, and shallow. The flood carried off much of the earth that I had brought to them, and more I had to bring each morning from the grove.

All this I did with courtesy, smoothing the ground in the grove also, because of Atwar's presence.

The furze had long since ceased smoking but the air was very pleasant; this was the time of its rapid flowering—sometimes I tried to see how the more intense pink spread across the duller red, in a wave to cover the low uneven ground, towards me and widening. Ah, the unlook receives such changes, but I did not then know how. Bands of mist trailed over the small courses, that were already running freely again in their hidden rills, to where the main course broke through the forest cracking and grinding. Inside the grove the fog was at its thickest, and I threw back my hair and walked in Atwar's path from stem to stem.

○

He stayed near all that morning. I persuaded Ard to come out a little; she would still keep the babies far under ground, not bringing them outside till the fog was dissipated, and that would be more than another whole day, as they are counted in the World. But she agreed and we dressed them, and she stuffed them into her great furze—she was then so round she could scarcely get through the door. She herself was not swollen any more, except her breasts. We went out on the point under the stone, where we liked to stay to watch the breaking courses gush together—it was like a quarrel between them, as if World-children were quarrelling violently in the water—so the green blocks came slowly tumbling forth from both sides, and struck one another and rolled as the courses joined.

"Where is Ask? Where is Atwar?"

Ard pulled down her sleeve so the Selen heads could peer forth. The twins were both awake and blinked at the light, and coughed at the freshness of the air.

"Ask is on the courses. Atwar is near—look! There he is, over behind his fire."

"Where is that house that he made?"

"It was in its place, it is gone down water. Ask climbed on it and broke it in on itself."

"Why does he do that? Is it because Atwar breaks our slings?"

But Ard asked diffidently; she was already looking into her sleeve, seeing to the babies.

○

The fog was thick and we could hardly see the farther bank. We stared to see Atwar, but he had stepped back into the forest.

Then soon after we hear his sniff—he was here on the half-island, behind us where the stems began, nearly hid by fog. His furze he had before him in his hands and his body was bare except for the blue rag of dress. We could not see his look, or whether he watched us, or looked out across the course.

"He is ever coming nearer!" said Ard. "See, maids!"

"Nearer but not to-us. He is still perhaps afraid."

Ard stared. "Why should he fear us in any thing? Soon he will sit down with-us."

"Will you then greet him?" For Ard among us had never said any word to Atwar, but we had called to him, both I and my brother.

"He ought first to speak, as is seemly."

"Ask says he does not love words. Perhaps we have received his greeting already—I mean, as he has behaved to us."

"To us, he has scarcely behaved in any way!"

"Well, he comes ever nearer. And there is not much use in shouting towards him when he will not answer."

Yet we spoke low; it was not seemly that we should speak of him in his hearing.

I said to Ard, "You see how stubborn our brother is, and will not tell us how Atwar took care of him, over in the islands. I think he is angry at Atwar."

"Ah," said Ard, rocking her twins, "he is angry that Atwar is not Saska. Remember how angry our-father Betwar was, sometimes, but then he wept; it was for loss of his twin he fiercely grieved."

It surprised me that Ard would say this, and it seemed to me wise what she said.

I said, "Indeed, it was Betwar's way! And Ask has anticipated so much, of Atwar—to find a kind of a brother in him—a child-Atwar as in the Tales—I have thought this before."

It seemed to me now that Ask had gone through a door, that I saw him from a distance and could not be sure I understood him.

○

Itsil coughed and Ard drew her sleeve up over the Selen heads. "They are too cool, I must take them under ground. But Atwar is in the way!"

"I have walked past him in his path. Come, let us see what he will do."

We walked then from the point towards the trees, and when we came close to Atwar, he stood back, but only a little, and we passed him, so Ard's clothed shoulder touched his arm— for I was beside her and did not swerve. He sniffed, very loud; then we were past and among the stems, and hurried down into the house.

Ard was giggling. "I did touch him, with my arm, against his furze-clothes that he was holding."

"Did you look at him?" She had plunged away ahead of me into the passages.

"Yes, quickly I looked up, as my arm touched him."

○

One lamp was burning. Ard brought it near the seep, and settled with the babes into her usual place in the thickest furze, and began to unwrap the babies.

"Maids, what a big head Atwar has! It is broad as Betwar's! He was looking past my face, not at you, my maids."

"Ah—you had wrapped them out of sight."

"He has an unsmell. I saw the doll close. It is flat and torn - it looks somewhat like Saska's, when Saska played so much with it in the World. We mended Saska's doll."

"Perhaps he will allow us to mend this one."

"Perhaps it is his plaything." Ard giggled. "You and Ask chide me that I have never greeted Atwar. But none of you has touched him, none but me."

Then I took an armful of the stinking furze with me, and threw it up into the birth-pit room (for here we had begun to

THE TAMING ◯ 155

leave what we did not want, and it was filling and settling and we did not use it as a door any more). Ask had said he would burn that fill, or bury it where it was, yet we did not dare to close a door to Atwar's house, that he had dug out with so much labour. I went back after the drinking-cloth and squeezed it out, and said to Ard, "I will not give you of this sour seep, I will bring fresh water." I disliked her talk, though she meant nothing by it.

So I went outside, looking all around me.

◯

This wick burns the water, the water submits and falls back weeping, thus piece by piece I make my night house.

They have turned the trees upside down, to grow with leaf and fruit close to the earth, this is not the intent of trees. I search in the water before it closes, there is the fruit best and the belly satisfied.

First I found the cloth ball, small-world with its feet and its eye, with it and another I called down the living. And the dress. Two others.

Of them I found a plank that smelled of their bodies, and their fire-ash smells of their bodies also. It is not sufficient. When I returned over Tolcus he was gone. I have smelled the place where I put him. It is not wise to make a noise in this world.

For them are there not any balls of cloth. Here, there, they leave their imprint, it is old, it remembers. In the dirt beside their extinguished fire it lay darkening with leaves over it, noiseless and potent. I did not touch it.

Then I saw the small-ones, offered towards me out of the old night-house. With this I will tame them, wearing this at my throat. Gradually, so they are not afraid, gradually.

Ask

Now it was no remarkable thing to see Atwar, for he was ever about, even in those seasons we avoided. Not in their extremes—then he was in his night-house often in the course, and in the heat of the afternoon he must have sheltered also—perhaps in that fourth island, where I had been with him.

Difficult it was, to make any order out of that place in my mind, and before I could speak of it I marked it into my book as well as I could. I knew that Tared, who was curious, looked at those markings. But it was easier to say nothing than to say a little. If I had said a little—what would I then have said?

The island was not high, even Hadley is not high, and this was but a small hill in the valley of the pass. But it had a sort of peak, and set into it an Outdead house, and there I stayed out the heat of that lunar afternoon, though I remember little of it.

When Atwar turned to wait for me, as I thought, I got up and went forward down the slope, though I had no strength left—I think I fell forward rather than walked. Then I had no remembrance of it; but he must have taken me as I had half-dreamed he would, into his shelter, into that place.

There was light when I woke, but no water. Atwar was there, and in handling me he had wakened me. But he did not give me water. I found it later by myself, when I again awoke for thirst; I drank it by myself with my face in it, for there was none to squeeze it into my mouth. I was alone.

O

I was not where I had first awakened, for I had crawled away, and again slept and then started up, as if at some sound. There was no sound. The place was dark, the air hot and bad. I smelled the water. How can I describe what I did not see? What I had seen had been enclosed with darkness—

only a small circle of light, and now the light was gone. Every surface I touched wih the whisper of my fingers was seamless: if it turned, it turned more sharp and even than an arm bent at the elbow. The floor was covered with thick dust, and the water lay in a kind of trough—as I put my face and arms into it I could reach the bottom with my hands. Its surface was a skin of dust and its floor a layer of mud which I unsettled with touching—but in between the water was drinkable. I had no cloth, I was naked, I let water enter my mouth.

Then my body recovered, and returned me to where I had first slept, and the space seemed perceptibly lighter there, though I cannot remember having at first seen any thing. I was very afraid.

That place was higher up, over a passage, a rising row of Outdead surfaces, too small to step upon comfortably—also, its roof was low, and slanted upward evenly. So I ascended into an almost indiscernable lessening of darkness.

I felt with my hands forward, and stopped; my body told me the air was larger here. I remained at that opening for a time, on my knees, listening for Atwar. But it was utterly silent, I could even hear my hair scrape loud at my shoulders, if I turned my head.

He was not there, or he would have found me! so I began cautiously to explore that space, my body recognizing its breadth I think by its air. It was low—standing I could mark the roof without stretching out my arms—Atwar would have to crouch here. The breaks in its walls were also Outdead-smooth, so my hands went up them at each side and sharply across. Those openings led into passages I dared not enter; the dust there was also very thick. So I went all about that room and across it and it was not empty—in the centre was a high furze bed, and that furze fresh: it smelled of Atwar, and a little of me also for here I had lain.

Along the east wall I fell against a jumble of sharp objects, and cut my leg—they seemed in my hands broken, the made shapes of the cables or the old branches of the cars, and their smell was sharp—then I tasted my hands: it was that Outdead flavour in my mouth, the redness of the Old City and the broken machines in Book. Then I would have wished for a lamp! It was not till much later I saw what they were.

I did not want to hurt myself more among them, and went back into the space of the room, and so at first missed that door. Then I found it, and went again upwards, there were more rooms piled one on top of the other, with those slanted passages between them, and lastly a room full of the faintest true light, and terribly hot—it smelled of the forest.

When I went down again, seven rooms I counted exactly, until the trough of water—indeed, when I went down I could not understand that I had seen any light there. Now, all the rooms appeared to me utterly dark.

I stayed many hours there, drinking and sleeping. Once did I go up, too soon, but the second time I ascended it seemed to me that the dim light was a little rosy, the air perhaps less heavy. Ah, this highest room was very broad, with no corners, and I walked its edge with my hands and lost my directions; so when I came to where I had emerged it seemed farther around, at the south, even when I had struck my body to make it correspond. In the centre I could discern a shape, it was as big as a Fu-en house, and I touched its curving surface. If I looked at its detail overhead directly, I could not see it at all. Then, at the east wall (though my body said south) I saw over the door a swollen pallor, like the most blurred World—and with my hands I found a high opening partly stuffed with earth, and ordinary. Its passage had roots for walls and led upwards, towards that bloom, that redness.

I leapt easily up and came over ground.

My head settled; I was indeed at the east side of the house. The World was at Half through the sparse trees, and the terminator approaching. I heard the first glad noise of the flood waters.

○

So despite the heat that took away my breath, I did go out, and let myself fall towards the valley through the stems, and reached the course as the divided bore rounded the third island and foamed together at my feet. I rolled into the coolness of the water as it rose spreading around me, and though the current pushed against me I returned in health to

THE TAMING ○ 159

my sisters, swimming among the diminished islands into the cool grateful wind and rain, and under the happy fruit falling.

Of Atwar I had no wish to speak, and after that if I saw him, those first days, I did not tell of it or acknowledge him.

○

I would try to describe him, as he was then, yet a stranger to us. Even then in the Outdead house he had a lamp, and by it I watched him, but me he had not cared to see by lamplight: it stood away from me on the floor.

So looking at him I saw much of how he was, and though I could in no way understand him, my face received his face to remember it.

Ah—we learn early from our mothers and fathers those human looks in all their intricate changes, for every muscle of the face has a name, and its own power of meaning when with others it contracts and eases, pulling minutely or grossly at the skin. This is a proverb about the human face: *We can see your anger in your hand and in your shoulder, but only in your face can we see its reasons.* The heart feels, and the face changes, for only the muscles of the face insert into the skin—in darkness they hold the visible skin in their fingers, and they play with it as the heart dictates, and they obey the heart.

So we know Twel from Twar be they ever so like. So also do we foolishly mask our feelings sometimes—foolishly, for we cannot—the eye sees through that dissimilitude and will not be utterly deceived, though skilful tellers pretend it. And they say there is a place in the north, Novaya Zemlya, where one family through all its generations has so perfected this, that people could be deceived! but this family they put into a particular house, if they will practice it, and the people can go and look at them, and if they are deceived they can say afterwards, *It was only in that house, so we are not ashamed!* As for the tellers of Tales, none are so clever, none I have seen, that I could not nod and say to myself, this is the wailing of a Tale, evidently!

And so it is, also, if any mind would hide what is felt; first, the shared heart reveals it through the body and the twin, and second, the muscles of the face being so delicate and so finely interwoven, and our eyes so trained to read them, some small truth even so breaks through! Thus, when Tared was most thin from the yeast's eating her, and her mouth was pulled into a kind of smile, we quickly learned that it was no smile, and to see her real smile even so, if she was glad of any thing. And when she cared for the babies I saw that she did not always like them, as did Ard, but sometimes smiled even so, and this they would learn to read—that smile that is wearied of smiling!

Children are ever beautiful, because they have not learned to dissemble, but weaned children learn it, and use it, and become ugly. Ah, I was then at such an age myself! So when I had been with Atwar did I endeavour to make my face into his stillness, and this was partly the reason, that I would not speak of him with my face as I would not with words. Tared read this as stubbornness and disappointment and Ard as anger—for I had not succeeded in erasing my look: I was indeed stubborn, not to speak of Atwar, and angry in my heart, and in some measure wished to speak—it is these quarrels in the mind and heart, that make the look ugly! And I was disappointed indeed.

O

Atwar had in those years laid aside his expressive and changeable face—I suppose having no twin or any others to answer him, he had discarded this language as unnecessary, and out of long disuse had forgotten it. So his face had fallen into that unlook which now we received and which disturbed us. He seemed unwilling or unable to answer our looks, then. We had looked at him with great surprise, and joy, and longing! Perhaps he could not read such looks any more.

What was it in his face? I thought it was the absence of what he felt, so that we were tempted to believe he felt not any thing. This was surely an ordinary conclusion for us, who lived to look into each other's faces, to read them closer even than the words we spoke, for they tended ever to correspond.

O

So I had watched him as he sat by his lamp, and its light fell mildly upward on his face, a little from the twel side. No more did I see any thing of Betwar, in this man-face, this

THE TAMING ○ 161

tree-face with its leaves of white-black hair!

He looked at nothing and at every thing, with no judgement it seemed, or desire to make any thing he saw into importance over any other, as under the sun's indifferent light *the leaf does not increase itself above the grass*. Yet he moved without stumbling, he chose the fruits, he had dug the house we comfortably lived in. He devised the shape of his hardwater blocks, to match them cleanly together, he cut furze, and made clothing, he took the doll. His look was most deliberate, even so! At that time I saw that he had two dolls tucked at his throat, the one less torn than the other.

He made lamps also, that I knew were more enduring than mine, and lasting fires. Yet his touch was as if he were blind, or saw in some way that was to us as different as blindness.

It was not his eyes in themselves I meant when I said "his look", for the eye by itself has no look; it is ever remote and cold. Only the surroundings of the eyes tell us their look, and these surroundings were in Atwar's face motionless and therefore unreadable.

○

He was as Betwar single-browed, yet his face was wide, with an opening lightness in the space between his eyes I remembered not in Betwar, and at the outer edges of his eyes some bareness and opening of the muscles—this I could not read, except that my eyes liked to rest on it. When he sniffed his nostrils flared, the wings lifting strongly. In the World, this would be have been disdain, but yet it would require as well a narrowing of the eyes. I am telling all this though you know it, because I want to explain his look, that it was different; his eyes were quiet and his brow and upper face did not change. Isolated it was, and without meaning, like the sniff of children when they have wept, when their body desires to pull back into itself the wet of their weeping. So they scrub at their eyes and sniff inward and swallow.

Also, that he ever lifted his upper lip—it was not as we would screw up our faces at a bad taste or unpleasant thought. It was a slow lifting and it lingered. He turned back the inside of his mouth, the row of his teeth showed big and rough, adult yet unblackened, and for us to see that was particularly strange. We had to see it as a sudden childishness in his face. It was then our hearts were most open to him. A tenderness wakened in us and we wanted to protect him.

Yet this was not his look either. We could not read it. I know that even then my facial muscles began to practice him, answering this widening at the edges of his eyes, this snarl-sniff that was without threat, this rolling back of the surface of the mouth. I was after all some hours in his presence.

○

I had cried out, when I wakened with his hands upon me, but he immediately put his large twar hand over my mouth, and held it there. Then he did pull his hand suddenly from my mouth, so my outcry burst like the sound of his brother's name. And this is the sound of my brother's name, spoken in haste so it slipped past his hand before he could prevent me.

"Betwar! Saska!" over and over till I gave it up weeping, and he went away.

○

Did Atwar leave me then in Four-Island, to go into Tolcus intending to return? But I escaped! Earlier than even he would have been out on the surface of the moon, I emerged, and leaped in that burning towards the flood that would come.

I was not his brother Betwar. I could not be that brother he had lost. It did not occur to me then, that I was perhaps as disappointed as he.

○

I showed my sisters the house as I had marked it, and described it to them as well as I could, but I did not let them question me. Of Atwar I said only, "When I awakened he was gone."

And Tared watched, to read through the silence of my face whatever I had not said.

V
Tamings

Ard

This is most ordinary. And past the babies, past their heat and smell and breathing, is nothing important—not Tared and all her concerns, not Ask and his roving, not Atwar over ground. Tared takes and brings the yeast and sorts the fruits and slings, and sighs, and renews the furze more often than is necessary, that she might sigh over her task. And Ask roves, tying on his bundles and returns and writes it in book and it is not important. Only when Tared comes close, and takes the babies into her arms talking softly with them. Only when Ask, as we swim, lifts them and tosses them, and they soar, their eyes big with wonder, and fall gently into the water, him thrashing after them to lift them again—ah, he makes them laugh, and they are not afraid—only then is Tared important, is Ask important.

○

So we began a kind of new life, in which we were many, a large family, with the twins, and with Atwar also, as much as he would allow.

That was a happy, careless time for me, too careless! Our house was comfortable, and the twins throve. They swam a little heavy, which I thought was from our not bringing them immediately into water when they were born. We carried them still so we did not know whether they would move as light as we moved—but we leaped not so far now, and after those hours of days in the house, and before the water returned into itself, our legs angered us much to swim again.

We saw Atwar often now and were used to him, and no more surprised. He was away early from the course, but not longer than what would be counted as a day in the World; when the air began to mist he was with us again on the half-island, and he watched Tared at the wells, and watched us at harvest—but he did not himself eat or harvest then. Once he swam among the slings, when we were not ourselves close by, and dumped out all the fruit we had gathered. Then he was gone! and we scrambled to untie them, and bind the fruit into them as well as we could, and took them immediately under ground. After that, we made bags for the fruit, that we tied under water, and as soon as we filled them we pulled them after us to the house. This fruit that was left wet tasted more intense, and lasted best, so we learned not to hasten so much in the harvesting, but to eat well and later to bring the submerged fruit up from where it lay.

We had good time, and did not repent the slings; under ground we still used them, tied across the passage that led from the smaller door. Atwar had not yet entered the house.

He would build his night house on the course, but not every night. Ask said that he built ever in that place because the bank was his fire-pit, and indeed a stretch of the south bank was sunken now and full of burnt furze, that looked like twisted rock all melted together. We still did not understand how he kept that fire—for Ask, the furze would not burn. In the morning the ground there was ever smoothed and finger-traced, and black and warm where the fire had burned; Atwar had pushed earth in over the pit and then flattened it. Later, the floods dispersed that earth and that pattern. His traces showed here and there on the rough course, in the early morning, where he had walked west.

○

In the evening we would see Atwar swimming and as we supposed eating in the course, when the water had fallen.

Because he did not eat with us, or come into our house, we did not swim out to him then. And we did not go near his night-house except after he had abandoned it.

One morning I took the twins inside to see it, and they stared at the glassy light.

○

Once, Atwar did not return the whole day—which is many days as they are counted in the World. It was at that day's harvest (as Ask marked it, so we would look for it again and know what it was) that the birds came to us much agitated, so we could not understand them. Ask said, "This is how they were in the World, and then they withdrew themselves into the bluffs." After that, we did not see them any more, until we saw them in the west.

Atwar was back to make his house in that night. And the next morning he came nearer to us, so that Tared began to think we were close to having tamed him!

Mostly, I kept under ground—if I took the twins up briefly when it was hot they were not harmed, but when it was very cool, and their breaths tasted that first air, they startled against me. So I did not like to go early over ground with them, even when Ask and Tared had been long out, and tried to persuade me.

"Ard, they are as used as Atwar is, and more, for they were born here. Let them *learn the turns* as we have done."

"They were born under ground," I said then. I was proud, and believed I was very careful of them, so that no harm of any kind could come to them.

Later into the good morning, I took them always out after Tared towards the farms, as far as that dip at the barrens, where we had first come into Atwar's grove. I was happiest there of all places over ground, sitting with the babies against the bank, with the living furze hanging over us like the shadowy hair of mothers, keeping out the harsh sun. I could hear Tared's steady digging, and sometimes she came down and rested with us, and we gave each other the sweet water. Then, refreshed, she would go out again.

The stream spouted from the thicket, over the brim in a steady rounding gush, still gray with coolness, and the mist gradually thickened in the dark grove. The babies were well wrapped and I nursed them within my furze, and talked with them, and looked into their faces. Overhead was the boundary of the forest, with its bright pale stems and leaves against the black sky. But I did not heed it. I said to the twins, "Daughters, you think all this is very ordinary! for you know of no other world."

And it saddened me a little, that they would grow up in that harmony with the planet I could never have—surely I wished it for them! Yet it separated me from them—it would separate me from them. Those dangerous scapes, that I would have protected them against, they would thoughtlessly accept, and when I stood back sick and afraid, they would go forward carelessly. Ah, when they were big they would crawl after

Tared right out into the sunlight! But I could not then imagine them as big, as moving about on their own—so far my mind could not picture them, that could hardly think of them past the pricking forth of the next little tooth my thumb felt after, when it rubbed their gums.

○

Sometimes I saw Atwar among the stems, and once he came close—I lifted the babies against me, for them to see him. He was walking low as Ask did, but with his head lifted towards us. He stayed still a moment, then crossed the stream to its north side, and came up to the pool—very close he was, across the pool from us—there he drank after his fashion, with his hands holding back his hair, putting his face against the water.

When his head was lowered I saw my dress across his shoulders, and when he raised it two dolls at his throat, the water running from them. Ah, when I was so close—it was as Tared when she stood across the course from him, yet so much closer we were now, that if I had stretched out my hand, and he had stretched out his hand, they would have touched across the water! Then he turned his lip out so I saw his white teeth, and I thought he would speak. He stood upright. He wanted I think to go on his path over the bank, but I was sitting under it. So I scrambled up with the babies, and went a little back under the stems, and gave him room. And it was so—for he stepped across, and went up into the barrens. It was that day he went to Tared.

○

Ask was not always sullen, or bending over book. He loved to ride the flood-bore west, with loud cries! then, he was not silent—and he would teach Tared to ride with him, though she would fall back, and swim. Once he insisted I go over ground and see him come past—and I left the twins with Tared for that, and covered myself with my drenched dress, and when I heard the water followed him up. Tared never emerged into that heat till she heard the water, and so ran to it as it passed the half-island, but Ask dared despite the great heat—he leaped away towards it, far along the dry bed of the southern course; he said he did not breath that air, but held his breath against it till he reached the flood.

And now he came as if floating towards me, standing on its very brink. The other course was still empty when he passed the point, but that bore came soon after, overtaking the first, as Ask was carried laughing down water—I saw him tumble back into the slow brown waves. The flood now rose around my legs with its wonderful coolness, and I sank into it, and under it, and swam back to the house—rising, it lifted me almost to the door.

○

Ask at this time began to rove, taking with him fruit wrapped on his thighs as travellers do, and we grew used to his absences though we did not like him to go, and Tared was I think always a little afraid.

He went down that south course. He thought there were caves near Hadley—"A mountain ought to have caves," he said—but he returned having found nothing, before it got too hot. He saw also small stones there—not as small as those in our passages. He brought two back—they were like the dolls of the great stones, uneven and gray, about the size of his hand.

"With this," said Ask, "we can place things on the ground, and they will stay despite the floods." For much leaf he had lost, that he had prepared for book and left over ground. He gave stones to the twins to examine, and they tasted them, but Itsil cried at how her stone knocked against her mouth.

He went north also, a good way, but west only with the flood. Atwar did not follow him.

○

The Selen were now well grown, being—as it is counted in the Moon—from their birth eight days old, or an eightmonth as it is counted in the World, that is, half a year. I would be glad when we could leave over to them all this counting! though it still occupied Ask—he was, when he was in the house, often at book, and counted all the Moon's days and the World's phases—now, he said, we had been as long as two eight-months in the Moon, more than a whole year.

We had come after white-night and that Darkening had now passed in Fu-en, and one Lightening, and it was again

Darkening there, moving towards Kaamos, that season when it is coolest of all.

"In Fu-en they look forward to being comfortable, in Kaamos they think it is very cool," he would say, looking up at us from his markings. Then he would show us his marks that he said was the World, how it looked, with Fu-en in the light—and he spread out all those little-Worlds from the beginning, to show how our fastland would again darken. But it was not much like what was in the sky.

○

He would not talk of Atwar, but I thought it was a sign of his age, for it is usual for weaned children, as they near adulthood, to be sour and secretive. He was growing long in his arms, and he complained of his legs and rubbed them often—he said, "They are growing, now they are unbound, but they are brittle—I think, if I struck this leg with a stone, it would crack."

"Then do not strike it," said Tared. I knew her legs, too, were angry, and her feet, but she did not say it, only rubbed them. Our poor legs were still bald, but perhaps they were growing, and our broken feet were straightening somewhat, in the moving of them, the freedom from the bands. The salts from the husks strengthened us, we thought, and we gave husks to the babies to gnaw on. The twins took otherwise only my milk. They did not like water, or need it—the milk was enough.

○

Itsil was the more forward even then, and she was stronger. She weighed no more than her sister—and almost, they had no weight in the Moon—they loved that Ask tossed them, slow, high, over the water! Itlin had a softer weight, and she was more willing to settle against me—Itsil was the more active and curious. They both put everything into their mouths, our sleeves, our hair, even the furze—they had a long reach, especially Itsil, and grasping fingers. Ah, they were different already, but still Tared could not tell them apart, so we kept that blue band around Itsil's arm. She grew stouter and twice we loosened it; it was loose when she was taken.

We wrapped them, when the air warmed, in Ask's blue dress, which he said they might use—he went naked in the heat, and otherwise dressed in the furze. We had not yet learned how to make our clothes as thin and pliable as Atwar's, though we thought them well made even so, with their tunnelled arms and footgloves all of a piece, and no seams where the air could enter. I wore my great-furze at night, with the babies inside it naked, so they could lie close against me and each other as they were used.

They were not so pale now and their skin-down had thickened, and their sparse infant-hair was overtaken by heavier hair, still too soft and short to tell if it would be as mine, or more straight, as the Sanev's, or as Tared's tight and unruly. Slick it would not be like Fu-en hair. They had no Fu-en blood.

So I played with them and looked at them with my great care and knew every cell of their skin, and they stayed not as they were but changed and grew, and these changes I could encompass also, for I gave them all the attention I had. And I am sure when they first raised their heads, when they first laughed and babbled, when their first small teeth pushed at my fingers, that I knew them most perfectly—and yet through each change, without thinking it, new knowing overtook the old. Almost as real twins, they were together. Nor did I bleed then, with them at my breasts.

○

They saw Atwar, his face they were put to gaze into after they were born, to bond it into their minds. Only then was he important to me, that his face was turned towards them, when Tared held them towards him. I did not see how close she held them, or whether they saw him, or whether he looked with his unlook across their faces. And when I lifted them to see him by the pool, and did not care except that they saw him—"That is Atwar!" I said into the napes of their necks, as if I had said to them, "That is your mother-sister Tared," or, "That is a husk, and good to lick," or, "That is too hard for your mouths, it is a stone."

Tared

That evening when the water had fallen, we strove for some hours at the point to make a fire pit like Atwar's, and Atwar watched us. I had gone under ground to rest when the pit was finished, yet Ask would dig a little more before he was satisfied. Now I came up to find the glade much whitened, and the ground hard. The course flowed, warmer than the air, with strange small trees of mist standing out of each trough between the standing waves. Westward they seemed a little growing grove, dim under the stone, bright in the World's light at the farther edge of shadow. The courses gushed together—I saw Ask crouched, and Atwar crouched also, just south of him—with their furze clothes and large heads they looked more like than unlike, against the mist-stems and bright water.

More like—yet our brother would not have made that fire, unless I persuaded him. And when he refused to hear of Atwar, or to speak of him, I must find other words, and talk of the fire itself. How useful it would be to us, to have such a fire as "the one on the south bank", which would burn when the air chilled, all night through. He would not answer me, when I talked thus to him in the afternoon under ground, but towards evening he took a lamp over to the wall near the passage, and chose some of the freshest furze, and began to cut and thread its interminable tangled root into a rope—it looked a little like the wick we had seen Atwar burning. Ah—our brother had watched carefully what Atwar did in spite of himself, and his hands desired to be making!

He did not show it to me, or attempt to light it, but set it aside in the passage.

Ard spoke up with less caution: "Atwar will show us how to keep the fire alight, when he sees what we have prepared. As soon as the water has fallen back, we can begin—we have not had a good fire over ground since we came to this grove, only Atwar's—and that is across the water, too far for the babies when the air is chill. The babies would like it."

THE TAMING ○ 173

For it was my idea, that we should make it here on the point, where at night the World's light lies in a curve between the last leaves and the stone.

And I thought, too, of what we had spoken of, of Hadley, and what Ard desired—if we learned from Atwar, we could perhaps make a great, continous fire, in the open, to tell them up in the World that we were with him, one family, and as a sign of the generations.

○

When the flood came Ask went outside gladly, to ride it; and he ate his fill, and played with the babies swimming—so I watched, whether he would stay, and help me make a pit. I did not look forward to Ard's help. We played, and rested, and slowly harvested, gathering the fruit as Atwar did, under water after it had sunk down. Atwar swam and ate out in the course, after the floods had fallen. And Ask stayed, and we began to dig, but Ard did not remain long with the babies over ground.

When Atwar came to us there he was dressed dry, so I thought, he had rested where he had laid his clothes. Where did he rest?

We had never yet seen him rest. When he crouched and watched with that unlook, it was perhaps his rest—I had a thought of him in his winter house, not lying down to sleep, but crouching, with his eyes open in the close greenish light, resting after his fashion.

○

Our digging had raised a low mound like a polder between the pit and the bank. It turned like the inside of an elbow, for it was against the joining of the courses. Now Ask sat back, his arms resting between his knees. As Atwar sat across from him, motionless.

I began to carry out the furze from the root-room, and he took it from me. It was stiff and crackly but its roots still held it in thick wads. Ask packed the pit. Atwar watched.

Like Atwar's fire, this one would burn against an Outdead bank, and Ask pressed the furze into that bend—here was the pit deepest.

Then we waited, and grew cold, but Atwar did not move.

"Call Ard. Tell her to bring a lamp."

Ard came up with the babies hid in her great furze, and carrying the lamp before her.

Ask had watched Atwar as closely as he could. The ropewick he now unwound from his waist was similar to Atwar's. But it was not similar! Atwar's burned harshly even when it was wet, having burned into the flowing water—Atwar swung it deftly, as women will swing thread about at the end of a seam, to plunge it again into the cloth—so he would plunge that fiery wick into the course till it steamed and whispered. And we had seen him put it deep into his fire.

But Ask's would not burst into flame like Atwar's. Its rough endings glowed tiny and useless as stars.

"Put the lamp itself into the pit," said Ard impatiently.

"Atwar does not."

"Then he must show us what he does." The Selen were whimpering and Ard stood up. "We are going under ground."

I stood too. I said very low to Ask, "Perhaps if we go down, he will show you." Ask's face was very closed and sullen.

We left them squatting there—from the root-door they looked very close, very alike, with the lamp behind them reddening Atwar's twarside, Ard's twelside—hair, hunched shoulder, arm, gloved foot and knee.

Could I say Atwar watched us? He did not watch! His body he brought near us, his head he positioned at times in our direction—he attended us, I suppose. He attended our striving.

○

Ask came in a little later, after we had lain down to sleep. I moved back from Ard and the babies to make a place for him in the warmest furze. I could tell from the way he shivered and settled himself, as much as from his silence, that Atwar had not helped him.

But later he went up, and came in again whispering. "Our fire is lit and burning, and the night-house building!"

Ard turned and grumbled. "So it should burn, for all our trouble—and as for Atwar building a house, this he does every night he is here."

THE TAMING ○ 175

"But his house is here, at the point, right against our fire!"

I put on the thickest of my garments, and went up after Ask.

○

The World was just past Full and the scape brilliant white, our fire at the point deep red, its polder rising black behind it. There was Atwar in the course, his dark head and shoulders showing over the polder as he moved about—there were his shapely green stones rising!

Ask came out behind me. "See—there is only one fire—ours."

Across the course the bank was even and shadowy, the pale stems rising. Crack! went the far grove south and a distant crack! answered from the north west.

"Will you stay and watch him?"

"I will go down first, and eat." Ask was shivering in the terrible air. We went down, but as soon as he had eaten he left the house again and I think strove with Atwar, Atwar allowing him. Later he came in and flung himself into the furze. He said, "The night-house is finished and the door laid on Ard's spread dress. That was, to pull it into place, but I did push at it, and fixed it—I have closed the door."

○

So Atwar was with us, and we believed we had tamed him well. The next morning he was still in his house when I came out, and I stood on the hot bank, where the good fire still burned, and looked down at his house—I could see within it his shadow. Then I saw how he broke open the door, by throwing himself against it twice with a strong lunging, and came out naked with his hair loose over his head—he stepped immediately up to the fire, and crouched there, looping his hair with the white strands deftly, sniffing at the air—ah, I could tell, that it was good in his nostrils, as in ours, that warming of the air after the sun has risen! Eastward deep in the grove the first long threads of sunlight were seeking, and all the stems steamed and ran.

Atwar did not heed me, though I stood in his sight. He leaned into the course and picked up a handful of shards from his broken door, and put one directly into his mouth—snap! it went in between his teeth, and I saw him swallowing its pieces. Then he took more, and ate them also, and as I watched him it seemed to me good—for we were weary, long before morning, of that sour water under ground, and drank of the courses as soon as their skin ran. We had never tried to eat water. So I reached out the drinking-cloth, for I had it with me. But he gave me none; he went on eating, looking quietly past me into the grove. His feet were deep in the hot earth. There were long, single hairs on his legs, as well as down—so he was not bald-legged, as we yet were from the years of binding. I smelled his unsmell, and the close piss-furze smell of his body. In the hair of his skin was caught little brittle twigs of furze, from where he had lain—it was long since swimming had cleansed him.

And if I did look at him closely—they had told us, we would be his bond in the Moon! Yet, as he was, I would have been ashamed to think directly, "This is my housebond, to whom I am promised," or even to think as much as, "This is not my housebond." This was the body of men. But he was so very different from that promise—heavy, dirty, dense, silent, unknowable! That mind's-Atwar we had been taught so carefully did not smell, for smell cannot be taught, only remembered.

As it is said, *the mind has an orderly house for every little snow, one for the snow of seeing, and one for hearing, even one for the touching skin, and there we can go and find them, but the snow of the fragrance of childhood goes weeping forever out between the houses, and comes burdened with beauty when we do not intend, and cannot be persuaded!*

I heard the snap! of his white teeth against the shards. I drew back my hand that he had ignored, but in my thirst I had opened my mouth—unthinkingly. For it is ordinary to give water—you know that before we quench our own thirst, we do courteously squeeze the water-cloth into the other's mouths, and then open our own mouths to receive. He put a shard on my tongue.

Ah, then it was I thought, "*We have tamed him!*" The shard ran in my mouth, smoother and smaller, so I did not need to break it with my teeth, and its taste was sweet.

THE TAMING ○ 177

"*Tamed him!*" in the eating of that shard, in its sharp hardness diminishing into a little smooth stone of sweetness, and then into nothing, gently and adequately.

Tamed him.

○

Atwar was away the length of a whole day, as they are counted in the World. But again we began to say to each other, "He is preparing his mansions." After he had given me water to eat, he had gone back into his house, and put on his soft furze, and fastened at his throat Ard's dress and the dolls. Then he went ahead of me to the root-room door—for I had waited for him. I thought, trembling, "Perhaps he will go under ground before me, also." But he crouched down outside, his face turned towards the threads of sunlight that crossed through the weeping stems: one thread touched him on the mouth. So I hurried down and told the others, but when we came up he was gone.

○

At the flood he returned, out on the north course, riding its bore wave towards the point, and had the waves met (but the north bore was ever slower to arrive) he would have collided with Ask—as it was, Ask went through first, standing so high that it looked, from where we watched, as if he stood in air, and came forward in air, with his arms stretched out and his hair lifting off his shoulders and his white grin. The brown sheer edge poured under his feet and its skirts foamed along each bank. So went our brother past, and did not see how Atwar rode in on his twar side and followed him.

Thus did Atwar ride, as we ride rafts in the breaking water, but it was a plank, and he lay on it.

That second bore fell apart at the main course as an ordinary wave breaks into pieces in shallow water. I was used to sliding in then, between the bores in the cool brown swell—this time I stayed to watch Atwar, and leaped after him. So I swam, and let the current carry me some distance down the great course after Atwar and my brother, as far as the first island.

By then the flood had lost its forward momentum and was spreading among the roots. I reached Ask at the island's rise.

I shook my hair.

"Did you see Atwar?"

"He has gone up into the island with his plank. I think it is that plank we lost! The third, that did not burn -"

Ask was ever brightly looking at the shapes of things, but for me one plank was as another. Would such a plank be important to Atwar?—it had been indeed a good one, long and broad and new. This was the time when, in the other groves, there would be roots broken off and pushed by the flood, planks to be salvaged and even new leaves. Here the forest was clean, we saw little debris from the floods; it was perhaps that we were at its eastern edge, also that the trees were tougher and larger.

Then Atwar came down the island and entered the water, and we swam back together—that is, I swam steadily with Atwar some distance before me, and Ask all around us, binding us with his paths. Atwar swam over the north bank, where the water had already risen high on the roots, and I followed him there.

So we came back to the house-mounds, two little brown islands now in the dark flood-water, with their two great pale trees rising silent, waiting for the wind. Ard was there, swimming with the babies.

◯

Atwar did not yet eat with us, when the fruit fell and we ate quickly in hunger, but he stayed near. Then we saw, as in the course when he harvested, how long he could stay under water—Ask watched for him, counting.

"When I am adult, I will also learn this!" he said half to himself. For in the World, we did not think it any special skill to swim under water, and come to the surface to breathe when we would—so do babies and no one needs to teach them. But Atwar stayed under longer than any twins we had ever seen. If Ask deliberately filled his lungs with air, and submerged himself when Atwar did—ah, he came gasping up long before Atwar, and stared about, and began to count— and when Atwar finally appeared, it was without any loud breathing—he seemed as unwearied as ever.

"I did count, underwater, one hundred and nine, and for

Atwar, past that, one hundred and twenty—for I began to count again."

So Ask delighted in numbers, as children do in the World, and I was glad to hear him say Atwar's name.

We put the fruit-bags into those slings in the south passages, and rested under ground, and when the water had subsided we looked at the fire-pit on the point. The burnt furze was as in Atwar's, hard and black, and much soil had been washed through it.

"Now, where is Atwar, to help us prepare the fire?"

Immediately he came towards us, and I thought, he has heard me, as if because I called to him he came. This is how I reasoned then, that whatever he did, as he drew close to us less and less warily, was a step on a path towards the city. That city was in my mind, and was he not now between the cloth-walls of the first houses, with their bright doors opening to welcome him?

He was dressed in his soft garment, with the dress and the dolls at his throat. Ah, he had that wick-rope also around his neck. He came directly to the pit. We ran to fetch more of the old, stinking furze, and threw it down. It was nothing for him to bring it into great heat and red light. And then for the first time we saw him press new earth forward over it, almost to cover it, and smooth it, drawing it backward in long marks that were like the sun's hair in its eclipsing. Ard put out her hand and made a mark also, like his, which he later, after he had gone all the way round, erased and made over. Then he took off his clothes and left them a little south of us on the bank, and swam out past the stone to eat. Ask undressed also and entered the course and swam with him, so their heads came and went out in the glittering light; we supposed Ask was again counting, and filling his lungs, and striving.

Meanwhile Ard and I looked at Atwar's clothes. Ard said, "If we leave them as they were, can we not turn them and touch them?" so we carefully examined them, how thin and supple they were made—the furze flattened till it was as coarse cloth—yet it seemed, so dense it was, it must be warm.

"If we had such garments," said Ard, stroking it, "Then I could move easily with the twins—instead of rolling about in this cumbersome, ugly furze."

"He will teach us, as with the fire." I added, after a pause, grinning, "*This is the way it is for-us in the Moon.*"

"He will, surely! he sees how we are dressed. He has the best of the dresses, both mine and his own. Would you not be glad, Tared, to walk about in such clothing? Quickly it dries, and it does not flake—see, even its edges are firm, though there is no seam."

Indeed, next to the bulky furze we wore, Atwar's dress seemed very fine.

Ard had been smoothing and turning it, and now she put it aside, and reached for the blue dress.

"Look at my dress—it is very large—it is much torn!"

"That came from pulling you free of the roots. Atwar has kept it well."

It had indeed much stuff to it—the whole head-sleeve intact, and a great fall of cloth with only the one bad tear—ah, it seemed now between my fingers an abundant softness and richness, this cloth we would have held as nothing special in the World. Its dye had kept its brightness, and it was not patched with the wan leaf as ours were now.

"Ask's dress that he has given to the Selen is not larger than this one sleeve!"

"See the bird-dolls!"

"Tared, this one is mine."

"It is surely the one I buried, that he had folded in the other grove, over the culvert."

"No—this is mine, it is that one, the first he had, that he wore then, for he had it together with my dress."

So we quarrelled about it. Neither of us had much looked at those dolls, in the World; only Saska had his doll for many days, because he insisted, and played with it till it was nearly destroyed. Remember that we others were given ours in the ceremony at the last; and we did not care much about them, knowing we would bring living birds into the Moon. Why we now quarrelled was not evident to us.

We folded the furze-dress back carefully as it had lain, and put Ard's dress again beside it, with the tied dolls.

"Where is Ask's doll, then?"

"Atwar has not yet found it."

For we were quite sure these two were ours, though we had after all no reasons.

○

Was it not as a family that we ate yeast at the fire? I dipped my finger and gave it to the babies and they sucked lustily; then I dipped my finger again and held it out to Atwar. His nostrils flared, and he pulled back his head from it; so I gave it to Itlin in Ard's arms—but we ate again at that fire, when we were hungry, and even Ard came up to us again with the wrapped babes.

And Atwar stayed among us. He saw us drink from the cloth, that we dipped in the course, breaking the surface. Ard offered the cloth to his mouth and he let her touch his mouth with it, but the water ran on his chin; he did not drink. As for Ask, he was going about, busy to find the slivers of the skin of the water, to eat water also, as I had described—he had eaten much in the morning, after Atwar was gone away. Now he would show Atwar he had the trick of it, though as yet it was but fragile splinters he could find. Also, he offered them to Atwar in his hand, but they ran out.

Then Ard took an opened fruit, and smeared her finger and put it towards his mouth.

This he ate, so she squealed, pulling back her finger, and laughed. "Indeed, he is tamed," we said to each other.

And I would teach him to like the yeast; he had himself eaten it long ago in the World.

○

Our feet were deep in the hot, wet soil against Ask's fire, and it burned well. Atwar's taper was glassy with oil that he had dried into it; Ask had touched it and smelled it—it was leaf-oil, he said. We had not yet seen how Atwar made it, however—such a smooth, stiff rope, that burned fiercely and tightly without burning up, so hot it could cut easily into hard water and not be extinguished—this seemed to us wonderful.

"Tared, do you give him water again, and I will give him of the fruit!"

"Ask will give him a shard when he finds one."

"He does not like your yeast."

"Perhaps he has forgotten it. No, I do not think he has forgotten it -"

Ask had thrown off his furze and was swimming—up the south course to a small spit where the water would be quiet, and its skin thicker.

So my sister and I talked then, across Atwar, being I suppose used to his silence.

So we had talked of him under ground, and wondered whether, just as his face had forgotten its expression, his mouth had forgotten speech as well. I did not think he had forgotten.

"It is not of interest to him. He had no conversation for many years, and has no more need."

Ard had often said that Atwar would receive speech with the babies. "Now, they babble, but they understand many things." She had ever pretended they understood her, whatever she said to them.

Ask had said scornfully, "Will you speak to Atwar as if he were infants, with small words, to make him repeat them?"

Ard argued with him. "The babies understand our adult speech and do not need to hear small words," she said. "Yet when their mouths do begin to speak words, they begin with such small words, and call me *Mar* already, and call each other "*Mø* (maid)" because that is what they can form with their mouths."

I said, "Ask, it is the mothers who babble after the babies, more than the babies after them."

"Yes—Ard says *Mar* and *Mø*, very cleverly—whenever Tsil and Tlin no more than babble *ma-ma-ma*."

Ard said loudly, "And when Atwar speaks—if he should utter one sound—you will make a whole Tale of it, Ask, as proud as any mothers, I believe! Already you do sniff like him!"

"Atwar does not love speech."

Ard had laughed, and turned her back on her brother. And now she turned from me, and dipped her finger again, holding it out to Atwar.

O

Did it then flit across my mind, that I could love him? Was it Ard's dark laugh that warned me when my body did not? How small and insignificant, her laugh without meaning! She laughed in his presence, she braided her hair. Within her great furze the babies sucked and bawled, and she talked to them, absorbed and heedless, her head bent over them in laughter.

Ard

That night we were unwilling to leave the fire, or Atwar, and we stayed long, and slept in the soil, but when the air became too chill I went with the babies under ground. The others stayed by the fire, and I was restless to go up again, and busied myself, knowing I could not for the twins. I set about my furze, to see whether I could beat it smooth, as Atwar's. I laid it on the floor of the room and struck at it with the two stones in my two hands, singing. It was as the reed-blowers in the World, who sing and strike at the reeds—the one blows through the reed, the other strikes it with his wrist and sings. The furze became flatter in one place, but unevenly, and dust came out of it so the babies sneezed. At Full when the World's light tempered the air I again put it over myself and the babies, and went outside. I heard some diminishment of voices.

They were at the fire. And I think Atwar was even closer to the others than before. Their legs were deep in the warm soil, Ask's arms also, so he looked almost as if he were swimming in it. The heat was rosy on their faces.

"We have been singing for Atwar," said Tared, "as we did at the other grove." I crouched down beside her, with Atwar on my twelside. Ask was across from us, near the polder, where that patch of the World's light fell clear of the trees and the stone.

"He hears us willingly enough," Tared added. "Sometimes he does sniff, and when we sang the *Tale of Tasman*, when we came to the snake, he did put his hand across his forehead."

"That was however when the fire sparked," said Ask.

"He hears his name, and Betwar's," said Tared.

Atwar sniffed, and she looked at me proudly, as if whatever he did was significant, as if she were saying, he sniffs! therefore he understands.

I told them how I had slept, and beaten at my furze, and I showed them it—then I reached over and touched Atwar's yet smoother garment, where his arm lay across his knees.

Crack! went the forest, quite close.

○

Tared told me how Atwar had prepared his night-house blocks, cutting them from the bank when the water was yet unready, and cutting them again from time to time. She and Ask had watched, but also slept at the fire. For there had passed more than a World's day since I went under ground. Atwar had not slept.

"And if we disturb the soil over the fire, he rights it with his fingers," said Ask. "Do you disturb it—you will see what he does."

Ask had climbed a little out of the mud, and was looking through a shard at the World. He had found a great one, greenish, smooth as glass and with hardly any turn or distortion, and through it could see part of the southern lands—there was a great land curved around the pole there, he said, in sight however the World turned—one side was now much clearer, nearly to the Sheath—it was in the centre tawny, but otherwise forest.

"Do you see their cities?"

"It is too bright."

I scrambled around and took it and looked once, at the terminator, which seemed to me rough, as mountains, but so much I could have seen without shard, if I looked briefly. I did not like to look.

I gave it across to Atwar, to see whether he would look, but he did not; he put it on the ground. Later he ate some of it.

"He does not love to look along the path of strangers' hands," said Ask.

"He is not a stranger now," Tared said doubtfully. You know that it is not thought courteous in the World, when you make such a mind's path from the eyes along the arm and outward, if even your twin's eyes walk in it unasked.

Our brother rose. "I will go down with you, before the worst chill sets in. But almost, it is warmer here, underneath us and in front of us, as under ground."

"You are under ground already, so dirty you are," said Tared.

○

So we left the fire to go down into the house, and looking back I saw Atwar smoothing the soil, his arm moving in long sweeps outward, where we had displaced it.

Tared tarried.

"Come, Tared. Perhaps Atwar will follow-us."

Just as we were to go in, our mound-tree shivered suddenly overhead and shed a mass of glassy bits. They fell all about us in a white drift, chafing one another—the sound was like a fire of dry wood crackling.

Ask said, "See their shapes!" and picked up a handful. They were flat and even-sided, straight as an Outdead wall.

Tared said, going in, "A tree can also grow straight if it likes."

"And water make itself into such forms! They are more various and beautiful that Outdead shapes, even so."

○

He and Tared went up again later when Atwar was building, and once again—then, they went right into Atwar's house, because he had come out when he heard them, and stood out of their way.

"One wall is the bank, and temperate from the fire, and he has much furze, though we do not know where he cuts it. The floor is deep in the course. The World's light makes a pattern between the blocks, yet they are set close—in some places there is furze between them. He put in his head, so we climbed out again."

○

Towards dawn, Ask went up into the old passage for fruit. And Atwar had been there. He had turned out the slings and the fruit lay in the rills. When Ask told us Tared sighed, but then grinned. "There is indeed something about the leaf he does not like," she said. "He never has it near him. And often enough he has told us this, after his fashion. But now he has indeed come into the house! I think it is, because we entered his—that he bid us enter, by coming out—and so he is welcomed here."

Ask said, "Not much welcomed, the way he comes in! I was falling over the fruit at the turning."

But Tared conjectured happily, with much "perhaps" and little certitude.

○

And I played with the twins, who could now sit up, and roll about, and were sturdy—not stout, but rather slender, and long in their limbs, and their movements graceful. Ah, we had stumbled much when we entered the Moon, and even struck ourselves, our bodies not understanding! but they were ever in harmony with his thick lifting air, and his seasons— and though Ask said they babbled only, they did already call each other Maid, clearly, and me *Mar*.

"*Mø, Mø, Mø,*" said Itsil to her sister, rolling against her to oust her from my arms, and snatching at her hair. Ah, there was that slip of blue cloth around her wrist, and I saw it as I strove to undo the little clutching fingers, and scolded her gently! but that cloth I did not undo!

○

We talked towards morning of Hadley. In that day, if we could persuade Atwar, we would attempt it and make a fire there, a great one, to tell our presence to the World.

"Ard, it is little we can tell them more than that we are here, and alive."

"It will however be a sign." *Tasman sent word to Lofot*; it is courteous to send a letter of the generations, when babies are born in the World in another city—so do the travellers go from place to place telling letters, and some tell much slander as well, and Tales, but the great part of their telling is this: that So-and-so have given birth to twins and this is their name, or that So-and-so are dead.

"Those great distances in the World, they are very short," I said sadly.

Yet it seemed, with such news we had, the people would surely understand in Fu-en, if the fire were great enough!

○

So we saw in our minds that mountain and what we would do. Ask determined he would go up first, in the morning and see it, and Tared said we should persuade Atwar to go with him. But Ask said, "You can use that persuasion while I am gone, so he comes when he is needed."

Then Tared made bundles of food for his arms and thighs, gave him also the bladder and one water-cloth, and we slept, and Ask went away early in the morning, wearing an old furze which he would discard. He took also his dress, protesting that it stank much—in the end he let me tie it on his shoulders, so he could wear it later and protect himself, out on the mountain.

Ah, it was but mind's fire, that great fire on Hadley, and the news it would have told was not told—had any thing been told, it would have been other than we then intended! I slept even as he went away, and as Tared went about the room, for the babies had sucked much milk and slept heavily against me. Before she went out she half-woke me, and gave me to drink of the sour water. Then she went out to the farms, and again I slept.

○

Ah, why did I not take from Itsil's arm that slip of blue cloth, why when I let Tared loosen it did I not say, "Tared, leave her arm free!"? Why did I let her tie it back again loosened, instead of throwing it away? Or Tared could herself have worn it if she so liked it, tied to her ear! Why was she so ignorant in telling Itsil from Tlin—she could easily have done so now, and they so unlike in their ways! She was not ignorant, only careless; to look to the slip of blue cloth—that was simpler, than to look into their faces! All that was Itsil! Her look, great-eyed! And the sharpness of her corner tooth, Itlin had not that! Itsil bit at my breast if she was satisfied—she did look at me first, daring me—I plucked her off if I was quick enough -

In Atwar's presence did Tared retie that slip of blue cloth, and I watched her. I was more careful of the babies than was Tared, or Ask who tossed them over the water. They reached out to him and laughed. Itsil laughed in a little whoop, with the intake of her breath. Waking, she would lie and laugh so, before she remembered she was hungry. I believed I protected them. I did protect them. I would never willingly have given them from me except into Tared's or Ask's hands. Ah, Tared, you did not well, when you tied back that slip of blue cloth!

Ask

I went gladly up into the mountain, walking first south along the course, jumping among the hardened waves of its surface. I started very early, and passed the spit and went on farther than I had ever gone before, and saw many stones on the ground. The low sunlight came sideways across the barrens and through the stems, and the smoke of the furze reached my nostrils, for the course lay close to the edge of the grove. Streams loosened and ran in over the lip of the wood, and the trees steamed; the course grew wet and slippery under my hands and feet. I ate the shards, and sniffed the furze-smoke, and went gladly forward. It was good to be moving again after the night, and still the Moon's air did lift me, though not so high.

The mist closed in, and the course began to swing under me and sigh. The ground rose now to the west, so I left the water and went up among the stems.

There were now many large stones embedded in the soil and smaller ones on the surface. I rested and looked at them, picking up the small ones one after the other in my hands. Those pebbles on Fu-en we had played with were round and many-toned—Betwar told us the water had scoured them in streams and on shores for many thousands of years. These Moon-stones were sharp and colourless and I suppose ugly. Would the floods smooth them also in distant time, and roll them in the course beds till they were shiny and smooth? Who would then play with them?

I could not see farther around me than the nearest roots, so thick was the fog. I licked the backs of my hands where the water-drops clung all over the down like stars. The fog was yellowish eastward where the sun pressed. Before New World I must be turned back, and have come this far homeward at least. So I got up and went into the mountains, keeping the sunsmear behind my twel shoulder.

I reached the end of the grove and came out over it, and out of the fog as well. Here were the cables and patches of stone-shadow, the barren land under the black sky, but uneven and tipped upward, so I could see only a short portion of it—rolling hills rising towards Hadley, in the red of morning flowering.

A rill formed a kind of path—it was already nearly dried up, and I drank and filled the bladder from my arm-pouch. When I came to the top of the first hill I could look out over the fog of the grove. And when I reached Hadley's hilltop and looked south, I saw the canopy pulled down tight in a wall by its muscular cables—through it did I for the first time see the terrible mineral Moon.

Bright gray he was and lifeless, cut by the sharp black shadows of rocks and hills. Those rocks would never be smoothed by water. The low range curved off the limb—ah, Ard would not like to see that scape! I thought, meaning, I was myself sickened by it. Northward was our grove thick with fog, and out of the fog rose the tops of the four islands, and beyond them the other side of the Cape. So high I was, that I looked down on the sloping canopy, as I had from the island when I looked into the vale, but now I stood even higher, at the highest point in the vegetable Moon.

Red were those great stones under me lying in the light, and flushed with flowering. One was so close I could see that its covering was not even, as the furze, but sparse and blotched, like dye poured into the vat before it is stirred. Its colour in the sunlight was pink-red, more bluish on the distant stones—so they hung north of me and eastward out over the barrens and our second grove in its mists. I would count them, but they were too bright, and lay so uneven under and behind one another, that I failed in it.

I looked to the west.

There the grove ended and its fog, and I saw for the first time the great *mare* Imbrium, the Sea of Rains, turning away over the limb. The great course I could see also, steaming and shining, and other mergent streams—and, near the misted limb, rough rising ground that might be another grove, or the flattened rims of Autolycus, Aristillus. But the details of that scape were blurred and I grew dizzy in looking.

The light was very harsh though I had undone my hair and

flung it over my face, and squinted out through the cloth of it.

So I looked down at Hadley under my feet, and saw there was thin furze over him but no soil. I looked about, whether we could use any natural pit to build a fire, and found only a small place between two stones—yet, if a fire should be seen from up in the World, it would need to be as large as a city. The whole top of Hadley must be set alight. But how would a rope-wick do this, or how would we burn the living furze, or bring to it furze or soil?

Atwar had never made a fire here; if he had made any fires, as some scholars said, they were in the Sea of Vapours and the Lake of Death. Perhaps inadvertently. It would take a long rope indeed, soaked in much leaf-oil—I did not then know how he soaked his tapers or even how they were made. Even his lamps were only a twist of rope, not closed and runny as mine. Would Atwar understand what we wanted? would he not think it discourteous, to burn the mountain? All this we had already talked of in the house, and laid sticks across each other's paths. How could such a fire be quenched? The chill air, the rains—but it would not rain out here in barren land.

The floods would hinder its spreading, Tared had said. When it ran to the level ground it would be stopped.

No, Atwar had never made any fire here. How could we persuade him now?

○

So I argued with myself, sitting out of the sun between the two stones, squinting down into my own shadow. I squeezed the rest of my water into my mouth. Almost I slept. Hadley's hump was about the size of Fu-en city. Was this perhaps the city of Saska's dream? One day his dream would come to correspond, perhaps, here—our fire the first sign of that city, a family, a beginning—

But whatever I ordered to and fro in my mind's dreamy house remained there. We did not come to make that fire then, and what happened overtook us, as a flood-bore overtakes the husks and dust in its path.

○

HEATHER SPEARS

Ard's reed-striking song:

In the World, wrist against wood,
Stone against furze in the Moon,
Knock with me, daughters,
I will make you a soft garment
Soft as World-cloth, softer than our water-cloth.
Knock with me, do not be weary.
How diligently you knock!
When you are grown, you will wear large sleeves.

VI.
Gashed Light

Tared

First I looked for Atwar, and saw that he had come out of his house, for the door was pushed aside, and black furze was spilled on the course. So I set off for the barrens, eager for him with the edges of my eyes, but not seeing him.

With Atwar near and tamed would it not be my delight to go early into the farms? the furze smoking and the air with a chill-burn in it still, painful to breathe, but very sweet. This Moon's day, I thought, will bring with it great changes! Ah, I did not know what changes it would bring.

So I walked between the high white roots and the soaring stems. Ahead of me the sun stood over the limb, and its threads were drawn tight between the vertical trees. Indeed it was not the Outdead who kept for themselves all such straightness, such even crissing and crossing, and Ask said this to us often, in wonder, that the unmade are the most beautiful, the forms of water and light. Water lies down as low and quiet as it can, and light reaches forth ever straightly and will not be turned, and all this is without interference.

So do we as makers strive not to interfere; the weavers among our people drew ever the threads straight out of the fibres of the World. Women comb their hair, but it grows at its own pace, and no great uncouth or devious thing has our race ever made. But the Outdead would shape any new thing; it was their delight, and whatever was made they must have thought it first and spoken of it, I suppose, and made it in their own estimation pleasing. What pleased them was to interfere, perhaps.

Our race called them crazed and cruel, but we used what they made, and wondered at it—ah, we became as them in spite of all our reticence. And even we children of Atwar, even we when we looked about us in the Moon, however careful we were we marked it more than we knew—surely our sickness marked and diminished it. Such marks will not last forever.

And what is unmarked here? The vegetable Moon, grown frothy and obedient in the thought of the Outdead, made after

THE TAMING

its image in the mind of that race dead these three thousand years. *"So it will look in the Moon: fruitful trees will spring from rich soil, and flowers will enrich the air, and water will flow forth after its seasons, and stones hold down the pushing canopy. And there our race will live well."*

The last did not correspond. They died; their minds died every one. Did the ancient mist of those minds still mark this scape that was all their making? *They did not live in the Moon, but with great effort they put things on it.*

○

And Atwar came of necessity, when the Moon threatened the World. And now we had come to be with him, and of necessity we marked the Moon.

○

Going up into the farms, I thought again of Atwar, and understood suddenly how he was not like the Outdead, or like us—he did not mark the Moon! In some way he was clean, and did not interfere. In perceiving this, my mind received some knowledge of him, and of what Ask meant when he said "Atwar does not love speech."

Ah—these tales of ours, it is as if we have written all over the Moon, as carefully and completely as possible—we are doing this for you, so you will know what happened to us. Yet with language we were already writing then, as if we were great scholars and careless of what is forbidden. The pages of leaves, the Book of the Moon, the names, our voices—already we did stain the Moon with words, seeking to make a word correspond with what is. It cannot correspond. But it is all we have.

○

Atwar did not come, though I expected him from moment to moment. And I lingered when I was finished, and was half-angered, that he perhaps would not come before Ard, who would as I supposed soon come to play at the pool with the babies. I had completed the wells while it was still so cool she would not venture out with them, and in those hours he could have come to watch me, and be with me.

I lay in a stone's shadow, as the flowers opened, their colour stealing across the land, and the fog grew thick in the grove. I heard Ard's voice.

○

It was loud, and something was wrong in it, and I jumped up, and leaped headlong down into the path, almost falling, and met her as I thought coming towards me, but when I came nearer I saw she had turned around, and was running back.

Her hair was half-loose and she was naked. I could see a baby's head at her shoulder. She ran aside then, among the south roots, still calling aloud in a broken voice, but I could not make out what she was saying. When I came up to her she ran at me, turning and falling—her mouth was very black and wide—she had but one baby in her arms.

Then I held her so she must stop, and could not break away; and she became suddenly quiet, her eyes towards the mounds and very black under her brows; she said what I knew already—"Atwar was in the house. He has taken a twin." She said then what I did not know, that the one he took was Itsil.

○

Ask returned much later as the courses were boiling dry. I had gone some way to meet him and missed him, for he came directly down the ridges, and walked in from the western valley. So he heard it, and it was he who ran looking for me, up along the south course, when I faltered and was turning back. The air was then stifling hot, almost unbearable. We met at the spit.

He looked like an adult. As he gazed close into my face he told me, "There is left one doll in the house."

○

Ask should then have slept but he did not—he ranged in the room, and I followed him to give him water. He said softly as he walked, "Much, I should have told you. I think he would have kept me then, if he could. He is crazed."

"Say not this to our sister!"

As for Ard, it would have been even worse for her except that she had to give her attention to Itlin. This baby slept with exhaustion, and when she waked, looked aside immediately after her twin, and startled, as if she had been suddenly brought up into chill air, and turned her head away quickly and silently—it was terrible to see her. She had cried at first but now she was silent. And Ard's breasts spilled, for Itlin would not take milk, unless in sleep, and then only a little, from the one breast as she was used. As soon as she wakened and looked and felt after her sister she startled. Ard, from her breasts, burned in a fever, and wept with grief, and sometimes cried loudly, and we wept also. Ah, that dark light was bled away, that had surrounded her and the babies—it was gashed asunder.

The blue doll lay near the passage, folded over on itself. At that time Ard did not accuse me about the strip of blue cloth.

O

This was the worst for us, that we could not go out until evening for the heat, and had to remain under ground as much as four-or-eight World's days, unable to do any thing. Ask said Atwar would surely have gone west, and would be in the Outdead house in the fourth island. Over and over did our strangely adult brother plan how he would ride the bore all the way, and how we were to swim after him, bringing food, and Ard bringing Itlin tied on her back.

"Ard must come also, to bring Tlin as soon as she can to her sister."

Little Tlin was sick and growing weaker. And I reasoned, waking, that for Itsil it must be worse. What could Atwar feed her, that she would take? Even Tlin, who was here in a familiar place, and at her mother's breasts, was perhaps dying.

I would have erased in that time my mind's clear terrible dreams, and I could not speak of them, not to Ard, not even to Ask, for I would not frighten him when he was so old in his look, so determined! Before this I have not told them at all—what I dreamed in that time—

I dreamed that I saw Itsil tied at his throat. Such an image did not come out of my reason, but from the look of wan Itlin and perhaps from my memory of the dolls, and of Atwar's hands that, when he was near us, ever hovered at his throat.

I thought they must be Itlin's dreams—should any mind apprehend what happened to Itsil, it would be the mind of her twin. I dared not sleep for the dreams, and yet I slept, and in each dream Atwar stood in some dark place and could not be reached, and looked away, and in each dream was the body of Itsil at his throat more limp—she was become gray, fleshless cloth—she was as bones clicking in the wind.

These dreams made me, in my waking, more hard. With myself would I be hardest, yet did I shake Ard into silence if she wept, and Itlin's mouth I opened forcibly with my finger, and from the cloth impatiently squeezed into it that milk Ard's breasts had leaked. So pitifully did Itlin cough! So long was that Moon's day!

○

We did not find them at Four-island, or anywhere we looked in that grove, and we stayed in that Outdead house till morning. We had to shelter there, yet to enter it was horrible—its black, stinking air, the taste of its stagnant water! In that night we lay where Ask had first lain, and Ask made near the door a leaf-fire. I think it drew away the air more than it warmed us. We were listless, and slept much, and I had enough to do tending Ard in her restless sleep, and feeding her, and feeding little Itlin as well as I could. I could feel under my hand how her narrow baby chest heaved and fluttered after air. Ard had much pain from her milk, and pressed it out between her fingers. Her breasts were hard and knotted.

I said gently, "Betwar though he was long weaned, did suck Tasman's milk when their little sisters died. In the Tale—he was about the age Ask is now,"

"He and Atwar were her children. It is not seemly."

So we did not speak to Ask of this. But eventually because her body was so angered, and she wept from it, I did suck at that twel-breast Itsil had sucked, to relieve my sister, when Ask was not there.

He went deeper for water, and ranged about among the rooms helplessly, and came back and flung himself against us. Long before dawn he was repeatedly out to look, and would run in shivering. As soon as it was light we started west.

○

We came to the end of the fog and of the grove, with its morning shadow extended into the bright scape of the *mare*. The course lay wide now, spread white and straight across the level barren land. There were no gray traces on its surface. It was beginning to creak and tilt under us.

We quarrelled, because Ask would go on but little Itlin was very weak.

"Ard must bring her under ground before it gets hot."

"What difference does it make, where she is?" Did he mean, *She is as we are, and will endure what we endure*, or did he mean, *She will die anyway, if we do not reach Itsil*? Ard would have gone on, for she was past reasoning about it.

Indeed, what was reasonable?

In the end we all turned back, and because we hated the Outdead house and its filthy water and darkness, Ard and I continued, swimming as soon as we could, then walking again when the water began to steam away, and brought Itlin living into our own house.

Little Tlin, you lived, you were stronger than we thought.

But her hair fell away, and grew in white, as those strands in Atwar's hair but very straight and fine—this against her skin made her look very strange; her face was as if traced with clay, as ours had been, and her body clay-brushed, and her head's hair dipped in it—she became from that time truly a Moon's creature, like the Moon in its night aspect, bright and dark and colourless.

○

"An eight-month and more in Ard's belly/ to complete the pattern of the World, an eight-month and more from birth/ to receive the pattern of the Moon."

Ask

Then began my days of roving, and in them I became adult, and more as my opponent Atwar, growing tall and strong, beginning to take into me his looks and ways. My voice did darken into a man's, and my penis grew stout so I made it a comfortable pocket of furze, that it would not slap me when I ran.

I was much prevented in pursuing Atwar by the climate, because I had at first only Four-island house to shelter in. Yet did I rove—and when I first came to Autolycus it was well into afternoon, for I had trusted to find myself a shelter there, that would keep me alive.

We believed, when we were in the World, that these wide circular pits we could see in the *maria* were cliff-edged, and very deep—but there was no abrupt edge, and it seemed not deep—it was choked with mist, and I walked into it down a long shallow slope, in the spreading bed of the course, which was there very great. I walked not into trees, as I had expected, nor was there any black soil, only the furze edging the course-bed and the dry rills opening into it at either side, and on its surface large, uneven stones.

Atwar's path after Four-island had continued broad and clear to the grove's edge but after that was less clear, for the open land was flat and flood-ravaged; even the tough furze grew bent over westward and inward towards the course and the deepest rills. Now as I came deeper into the mist I began to smell water, and reached the shore of a lake. It stretched out of sight in its vapours and I knew it must be deep, perhaps so deep that it would never cook entirely away.

I stood frightened at that brink, for I knew I could not endure more than another World's day into that season, without shelter under ground. Already did the Moon press itself burning upward into my hand- and footsoles; I shivered, and the roof of my hair burned on my shoulders.

I could see a kind of path up along the north bank, and some structure farther along, extending and submerging—yet when I reached it, it was a ruin, and seamless. I knew that I must go back if I were to live. I took water.

At the grove I got in under some roots, digging as deep as I could; it was as good a shelter as that we had endured the first Moon's day, in the ravine. And now I tested my strength, and learned that I could outstay the heat over ground without real harm. My body had toughened—and it had learned the turns of the seasons, and would no longer be surprised by them.

Never would we learn to wander the Moon's surface in all seasons. Atwar's body could not—he still required shelter and a hoard of water and the cover of the furze; he too must go into house part of every lunar day.

So I was very sick but I lived, and the flood when it came was most welcome to me—it took me in its arms and lifted me free of the soil and I let it carry me out into the *mare*, having no strength to resist. I did not then swim as far as submerged Autolycus. But I saw across the wide, flooded scape a low range of land at the northern limb—that was the brim of Aristillus—worldlit, white against the stars.

O

I stayed that night in Four-island, and with a lamp looked at those broken machines, where I had hurt myself, and at the large shape in the centre of the world-shaped room. It was like a half-world on its face, but with no foothold, and set high up, and filthy, so I could not read it.

In the morning I returned to the *mare*, ever searching for Atwar's traces. White and glaring it was then, so my eyes burned to stare across it, the wide course and its many rills and streams, far out in the sunlight, that were beginning to mist and run. Almost there was more water than land, though the flood had fallen much before it hardened. These surfaces were smooth—had Atwar walked here I would have seen it.

So bright it was that I stayed skirting the edge, in the long thrown shadow of the grove. I went northward along a hardened stream, sliding forward hand and foot as Atwar. If I glanced west and northwest I could make out the rough, slight rise of Autolycus's rim, the sharper rim of Aristillus. Both lay at the limb—two low, uneven groupings of hills they seemed, with their white burning off to dull red. Out in

THE TAMING ○ 203

the sunlight the whole *mare* had begun to smoke.

I went as far as I dared. I reached the other side of the Cape, the ground rising there within the grove. So I climbed up among the stems, till I came over the fog—from this high ground I could see a little of the surface of the larger pit, past its rim. It was also a lake; a very great stone hung over it. It was even then white in its centre, under that stone—I could not see its farther rim for the turning away of the horizon. Ah, so deep that water must be, that the day's heat must work at it most patiently! Perhaps, I thought, it is in its depths ever hard—but then I did not know about these lakes—these three, for Chmedes was the third, and the greatest of them.

That scape I gazed on—here should be Atwar's mansions, as we had dreamed. Yet everything was blank and bare. Where had he taken Itsil, if not into the west?

○

One more afternoon and one night did I spend in Four-island, and in those hours of days that I could be over ground I roved the forest, but I did not return home to the half-island, because I had no sign of Itsil and I was ashamed. In that time, and in those following days, I came to know his grove very well, as well almost as I knew the marsh-forest beyond Fu-en. But the grove's extent was greater, and now I was not at play.

I learned those paths most earnestly, that Atwar had made, the marks of his coming and going; and I found other root-pits, four-or-eight, at a certain distance from each other, so after that I had no need to return into Four-island or our house in the hottest season. But none were deep as our house was, and in only one, on the north side of the first island, did I find any recent sign.

It was over the flood height and well hid, and within the ordinary pit was a deep, low hollow into the hill, almost flat and very smooth—here was a cloak of beaten furze and his smell. I slid myself into that hollow feet first, and I could lie in it, but scarcely turn about, so low and narrow it was around me. I searched for the fragrance of Itsil and thought perhaps it was there—but I could not be sure.

I found a sign of him also, up in the north course, there

where it had cut its own channel. The Outdead bank broken long ago, and the old straight bed filled up with silt and soil. The water flowed in a long curve westward (for the land thereabouts was very flat) and then back on itself to turn again close to the barrens, and reenter, at a low fall, its original bed. Some leaning stems I saw at those turnings— well-growing but, from the water, forced aside. There was one great tree that had been pressed so far down it was leaned almost horizontal; yet did it turn to grow upwards at last, and its leaves reached and mingled with those high overhead. I could see how its plank was shallowly grooved and worn— surely Atwar climbed here! so I went up warily, and easily, to where it was pressed between two others trees, and found there a kind of resting-place. Much furze was stuffed there, some of it flattened into Atwar's cloth, and folded over the plank. From that vantage I could see out over the eastern barrens, and Tared's farms.

There was also wound about one stem some length of the furze-rope; it was prepared, slick and thick with—as I thought—a wax of leaf-oil, and was about as much as twice my body's length. I was not glad to take it, for it was his even so, yet I took it, and cut small lamps, and from then I began to learn how to cut into the courses.

But as yet I had made no night-house I could live in, and spent the nights in Four-island, or with my sisters.

I was not much with them, and when I was I quarrelled with them.

Tared said, "You are wild."

This was because I drank putting my face in the water, as Atwar. Who was with me, when I was roving, to give water into my mouth? She did not yet say, remain with-us, it is useless to search for them. But I saw it in her look.

She kept Ard and Itlin. I did not like to stay and hear my sisters talking together, in their voices was so much sadness. Little Tlin received the language in sadness, and her own voice as she began to speak had a mournful, plaintive fall. I thought they had said angry words to each other also, that were not yet forgiven, for it was no easy sadness, there was a tightness in it. I was glad I had not witnessed their anger.

Later Tared told me, weeping, how Ard shamed her over the strip of blue cloth— "She said, it was for my stupidity he took Itsil, in not knowing the twins apart and in keeping it tied on her wrist, and that he did take that baby because of it, in exchange for the doll. And I grew angry also, when she had said this many times, and answered her, and said, Perhaps you would have preferred him to have taken Tlin? and after that for some time she would not let me touch Tlin, or help her!"

They were almost always under ground.

They went however into the farms, early when the furze was smoking. There they laughed harshly.

Tared asked me also, because I had said, He is crazed, "Did he ever harm you?"

"No—it was not harm—"

"Then he would not willingly harm Itsil."

But by then we thought she must be dead, because of his ignorance and the harshness of the Moon.

○

I was stronger to endure, but not yet as strong as Atwar. When I could not rove I wrote much book, not only those marks that signify the World and its phases, but words also, for the scholars had taught us to read in the World—and how could they now forbid me?

Those ignorant writings I have not kept. I think they were a kind of striking: thus I learned that it is possible to strike in anger in this other way, in the writing down of words. But such anger lies still on the leaf and is not dispersed—this is perhaps why we are forbidden to write! For to strike is as speech; that blow does fly away into the air, even what is repeated must be repeated to exist. But what is written is continuous and dangerous, long after the heart has forgotten.

○

"You do turn your face into his face, Ask—do not do so!" they said. "Do not show that face to Tlin!"

I did not stay much with my sisters.

○

Tlin grew, and walked as I did and Atwar, but her legs being long she would bend her knees to do so—Tared desired her to walk upright. So she would walk on her feet if she approached Tared for any thing, or to be stroked, or if she walked by Tared's side, but toward me and her mother she came on all fours. She did not leap—the air had no power to lift her, light as she was; yet she was graceful.

She had a kind of sweetness—she did not quarrel with me. If I had been away some time she was at first shy—but she was glad when I came in, and I held her much and was comforted by her. It was no longer a disappointment to me that Ard had given birth to girls, and in touching Itlin's narrow limbs my hands remembered Saska's—he died still a child, and I was now adult—he was more like Itlin than like me, as I grew farther and farther from his likeness.

My sisters I touched very little now, and I did not sleep between them as I had, but a little apart. Then Tlin would climb over them sometimes, and sleep in my arms.

○

So passed those days, those seasons—in Fu-en, the half-year of Darkening moved into darkest Kaamos, and Itsil had been gone from us nine Moon's days—more than an eight-month, more than half a World's year.

○

Now is the one tamed, now is the one with feet and hands quieted in touch with the ground, with voice quieted. She rides in the depression of my shoulders, swiftly we crossed the land between Tolcus and Chmedes, swiftly we swam that flood. Nothing have I forgotten. She lay against me in the cave, she knocked the bone of her face against me. She sucked at the nipple of my breast, knocked and sucked, knocked and sucked. Bone she became. Her hair fell though my fingers, in her fingers small weary handfuls of black hair. I tied it with the little-cloth, I kept it. Milk came out of that nipple because of her importunity. My one breast a tender hill. Her hair grew in white, her eyebrows as white leaf. We began to swim in the cave.

Swim forward towards me from the far ledges, the light is stem after stem rising, swim among the stems of light! Now you are tamed, there is no haste, we will return to the old place and fetch the others.

Ard

Atwar stood across the water, with Itsil in his arms.
My eyes did not immediately know her, and though Tlin was before me here on the bank, my eyes insisted that one was also Tlin, for she had changed and grown, and my stubborn body still looked for the small baby it had lost.

○

Itsil was also white-haired, her brow like a streak of clay on her bald, grayish face; she stared out of her hair as out of a night-whitened sleeve.

I heard Ask behind me whisper: "Ard, Ard, do not cry out! be patient."

Then Tared said low, "Let us continue as we were, and thus make him unwary—"

She took my arm and pushed me to squat down, for I had stood, and so we remained quite still, and my breast did ache, trembling, watching them.

○

It was morning but the light was darkening, for the sun had gone in behind the World. In the course one last small block of hardwater, floating deep, passed us where the north course flowed into the other, and swayed in the slow green meeting of the waters.

Then Tlin saw them. She had been playing at the bank and went directly into the course, at a place where the old polder had washed out and made a kind of shallow beach; there she stood up and faltered, with the water pushing at her little knees—it was as if she could not decide whether she dared to swim over. She was not strong enough—the current would have taken her farther down, past them.

She said "*Mar*," or "*Mø*"—for the noise of the water I could not be sure—and without looking around at me reached back with her one skinny arm, her hand opening and closing imperiously. I went forward and took it—she began pulling at me, to go with her into the water.

"Swim-over, Mar, want to swim-over," she said.

THE TAMING ○ **207**

Tared whispered again sharply, "Do not speak, Ard, or frighten him. Ask, will you go up the course?" and I heard Ask go swiftly back into the trees.

He came swimming under the far bank, slow as the current, letting it carry him silently. Red was the light now, and at its darkest. Atwar could not have seen him, yet he straightened, and looked as if he sniffed, and his lip lifted over his white teeth. We saw Itsil struggle a little in his hands, as if she would climb down, and he knelt forward, so close to the edge that Ask, in the water, pressed himself against the bank, grasping the furze to stay himself. As Atwar bent down, in the same motion, he slung Itsil easily around to his shoulders. They were both naked, yet he had the dress on his back. She clung to it, and to his hair, and he began to walk in his fashion away from us, down along the bank of the great course, along his westward path. Itsil's white hair was reddish in the darkened noon, more red and bright as they came out of the stone-shadow, going away from us.

All this time Tlin chattered and jerked at my hand, and now I could not help crying aloud. Tared called also, "Ask, keep them in your sight!"

He was already scrambling up the bank, and ran after them as cautiously as he could.

○

This was indeed Itsil, and we called her by name, and my mind became used to her if my body did not. Never could I give back to my body that time, I was sure, or convince my body, in its obstinate grief, that what was lost is returned! My mind said to me, this is Itsil my daughter, be glad! and my body crouched and mourned and would not know her.

I think, looking back, I had made Itsil dead the day she was taken. There is a kind of mind-wall, stronger than any ordinary housewall of cloth—an Outdead wall, it could be likened to, having no seam or door, standing across that day, and behind it was Itsil as I remembered her. This new little creature with her name must I love, so I told myself despairingly: *I must love her*, or, *I do indeed love her as much as Tlin*. Despairingly because I still grieved, having made a finishing I ought not to have made.

There are indeed Tales of beloved twins who were lost and who returned, after such ceremonial finishing, after the burial of love! In the Tales it is nothing to love them, for they are as they were. Had that round-limbed babe been returned to me, I would have known her and mourned no longer!

I was ashamed of what I felt, of what I did not feel!

It had seemed to me, in order to live, such a wall was the greatest harm I could do myself, for having allowed her to be taken; my shame made it necessary.

I was ashamed before Tared. I said more than I felt, and felt my face become ugly in deceit, and wondered at myself. I was ever uncomfortable with Itsil, and would say this-and-this easily to Tlin, and chide her, and this-and-this to Itsil with the same voice—but I must by an effort of will make my voice the same, for it would not speak of itself, it was but words.

○

But I am precipitate in the telling. It was not all at once we tamed Atwar again, or determined we had tamed him, and it was many hours of days before that daughter was returned to me.

○

He began again to come near, and to bring Itsil with him. At that sunset they came towards us in the blowing rain; he swam pushing Itsil before him on his goodly plank. She was naked, white-brushed, lying on her belly, with her arms plashing in the water. She was as Tlin but thinner, her hair more matted, her face concentrated—at first, it seemed she was angry—but that was her constant look; it had no change or feeling in it. I never saw that she did more than Atwar then—sniff, and lift her lip—ah, it was a small, pinched face, narrower than Tlin's, a little lighter, grayer. They were beautiful even then, my daughters, my white-haired Moon-children!

Tlin was near me in the water when they came, and squirmed immediately towards the plank, and I followed; I grasped her by the one foot underwater. She stared at Itsil fixedly.

I cannot think that they recognized each other. They

behaved as unweaned children when they are first brought together with other twins their own age—there is a recognition of kind, and great curiosity! I am sure too that the Selen's cells did yearn towards each other's fragrance, that their bereaved bodies had not forgotten—for the body remembers what the mind has put aside; all this is written in the blood, and its Tales told in every twinge and turning—if there are listeners! I know Tared wondered that I did not snatch Itsil, for I was near enough, and Ask had gone behind Atwar among the stems—we were indeed all around him. She said also, that she was afraid I would do so— "Yet, I think I would have done it, unthinkingly!"

Tlin stretched out and grasped the plank with her hand, and Itsil struck it away, and her lip lifted—ah, she was indeed wild!

"She is as wild as Atwar, now."

"Tlin can speak, but she cannot. Her face is empty as his."

"She does not remember us."

All this we said afterwards—it was so and so with Itsil, and we dared not take her.

O

"She would be made very frightened and unhappy if we took her now—we cannot—unless we can persuade Atwar to come as well—"

We could see that Itsil clung to him in trust. If she came near us, if he allowed her, if he intended her return—

Tlin would be the one to entice her back to us, out of curiosity. But how could we allow Tlin near her when Tlin could be taken also?

Atwar had drawn a little back, yet he still held the plank and his unlook was towards it, and towards Itsil. Tlin kicked at my hand in the water. Again she put her hand on the plank, and again Itsil struck it away—this is how they began to play. Then the fruit fell. We saw Atwar break one apart with his teeth and Itsil crept to him on the plank and he put from his mouth fruit into her mouth. We did not then see that strange breast.

O

We harvested and dragged the fruit to the mound door.

"Perhaps he will come in."

"Or make a fire, when the water has fallen." We had furze enough in the south room.

"He will make a night-house, as he has done."

We rested in the house but he did not come, and Tlin tried ever to go up into the passage. Tared took her back—"Will you go up to Mø?"

"Mø must-come into the house."

Ah, it was difficult that she walked so early, before she had understanding, before we could say, "Remain here," or reason with her. Twins in the World cannot walk until they have learned how their body can move in harmony, and until their reason can be persuaded to obey, and understand what is dangerous to them. But Tlin walked, and now she would absolutely go up the passage, and continued to run towards it, and to be very angry when she was prevented.

Tared said, grasping her, "Perhaps we should give Atwar that doll."

"He had no doll at his throat," I said, and Tared said very quickly, "No—there is nothing at his throat! he will not try to take Tlin from us."

We did not think this was his intent. Yet he had taken Itsil—ah, then I was alone with my daughters, here in this room, sleeping—

My twelbreast tightened and leaked. My milk had settled, and this breast was dried up, except sometimes, when a little would run out suddenly—Tlin sucked the twarbreast still. She ate as we did, and accepted water.

○

We watched diligently over Tlin, who was ever determined to go to her sister. When she was not sleeping, she was in a condition of concentrated activity. She would go, and was angry when we thwarted her. Nothing else interested her; her whole body was ever on its way to Itsil, she demanded Mø with her voice, and her feet and hands went on foolishly hurrying when she was held.

Even as she sucked at my breast, one arm waved back behind her in jerky circles, and she would stop and splutter "Mø there—" restlessly.

So, because of her, we were often close to Itsil and Atwar—and the twins would play in this fashion, that Tlin would make some approach, and Itsil would reject it, and wait expectantly, and this would be repeated.

Itsil was less wilful than Tlin. She kept close to Atwar, and if he set her on his shoulders she did not protest or climb down. Across the fire we saw her on his arm, pulling at his face.

"She does love him!" said Tared.

"Well," said Ask, "she has no one else."

Ask was dark now in voice and body. He said little. He had been away from us in the grove, living as Atwar lived, coming very seldom home, for half a World's year—he was not wild, but most silent. Often he scowled and would not answer us. Only Tlin made him smile. And now Itsil—now, he stayed with us.

We watched how Itsil pulled Atwar's impassive face about and then turned her head to squint at us across the pit. She was as yet naked though Atwar wore his furze. She seemed not to feel the air's bite.

Tlin was inside my furze—now she stopped sucking and clambered against me, and I pulled down my sleeve so her rough white head emerged—she climbed out shivering; she was naked as well.

Come inside my furze, little Tlin," said Ask, but she twisted free of us and got down into the warm soil. The pit glowed. "Take care!" Ask's arms shielded her.

Itsil was turned about to watch Tlin's progress.

Tared said, "Do you go with her, Ask, around the fire?" Before he was adult she would have commanded him, now she spoke courteously.

Big Ask between us! He looked at a glance like Atwar; he was almost as tall. His face in repose had roughly Atwar's look, but not Atwar's serenity—Ask's eyes minutely narrowed and opened, sharpening with intelligence and sudden watchfulness.

"I could walk about the fire, and take Itsil from him, as he did take her from Ard."

"No—not yet—" I heard Tared's voice break. I looked at

her—she was nearly weeping. As if she would say: how then is Atwar to live?

○

The twins played in the warm soil inside the polder, as the Moon whitened, Itsil crouching and crawling about between Atwar's furze-clothed legs, and against the furze on his body, and leaning back against his arm. Tlin, more active, crept around before her, with my arms ever shielding her. Ask was there also—he had stretched out his body in the earth so Tlin could not fall into the fire. And Tared sat near Atwar's shoulder—in protecting Tlin we were very near him, and he stayed.

Tlin's attention was all on her newfound sister. She would offer Itsil a handful of mud, and Itsil would strike it out of her open hand—this they did over and over. Tlin chattered and whooped, as a stream that tumbles forward, for she had received speech and would use it without needing a reply. Then, she had a habit of calling everything and everyone, except Itsil, "old"—I think in that word she reassured herself, that much was unchanged. Ask was Oldask and I was Oldmar and the house Oldhouse and the doll Old-doll and so on, but Itsil was Maid (Mø) only.

Now she held out the mud closed inside her fist, and Itsil took hold of it in both hands and tried to pry the fingers apart; when she could not, she pushed Tlin over backwards. Ah, soon they were rolling about, and in our care for Tlin we came to touch Itsil, and Atwar came surely to touch Tlin.

But Itsil would not approach us, and when we spoke she startled. She was not afraid of Tlin's prattle, and would pull her face about and put her finger into Tlin's mouth when Tlin talked—I think already I saw her own mouth rounding, as if she would try such sounds as well. Tlin never struck her, though she was much struck, and her hair pulled also. Neither would she retreat; she liked this rough play. But sometimes she cried out, if her hair was yanked hard.

After such bouts they would sit back, as if they were replete with food, in silence—at such times Itsil would turn to Atwar and open his cloak, and push aside the hair on his one swollen breast, and suck at it, all the while watching us out of the one eye with such a look—! for she had a look indeed, and from Tlin would receive more.

Ah, it was strange to see these twins together! Often when they had sat thus a while, it was as if Itsil were saying, "What will you think of now, Maid, to provoke me?" And Tlin would do something—if only it was to make a mark in the earth, for Itsil to erase with her foot.

○

Atwar began to come into the house. At first I expected to be afraid, but no fear came. He stayed at the passage; Ask took him a great bundle of furze, and himself lay across the passage near him to sleep. Then Tlin would go there; she got out of my great-furze, and climbed to Itsil—directly over Atwar, as if he had been an inert root. It did not help to fetch her back to us, so in the end we took our bed close to the others.

"Do not sleep," said Tared to Ask urgently. "Tell us first, if you will sleep, so we can watch her."

○

We saw in those hours of days how Atwar did not sleep and wake as we did, but from after Full Earth till dawn drowsed quietly—if Itsil did wake he put his one arm over her—she was sometimes restless but she permitted him, as if her body too had learned the turns, the Moon's slow diurnal changes, and closed into itself as the furze closes—she did "smoke and flower"—she was most bright and active—in the dawn. We others slept longer when we lay under ground, yet our bodies were still obedient to the World's day—we were children of the World.

As for Tlin, she began to follow Itsil's pattern. She could not provoke her sister into play in those hours, and became herself listless; sometimes she made the unface—I would make to strike her if I saw it, so she did not; I hoped she did not any more. Sometimes she sang to herself, small, repeating, breathless songs. Was Itsil listening? Would she begin to sing as well?

I was early up and about, and pounding the furze, and at dawn Atwar went out with Itsil. All was busy and hurrying, and Tlin wailing to go outside. Ask said he would take her. Tared packed yeast for the farms. Ask came down with an angry Tlin and a number of clean shards, and we sat and ate them.

"Mø—Mø—"

"Tell us what you want, Tlin, do not complain."

"To go outside again with Oldtared, to go to the oldpool and find Mø." She slipped free and set off for the passage.

Ask said, "Come, let us all go out, there is no rest here!" So I left the furze-stones, and caught and dressed struggling Tlin, and followed her scrambling up the rill into the chilly light.

O

Over from you at the badwater, in the light of the dangerous small lamps leaning, in untrod furze, in shard noise and moving, in the smell of remembering. The smell spreads. the other rooms it cannot enter—they are fallen in, with noise they fell in dangerously and a separation began to grow; I see it over the badwater—it is at present dormant. What is safe is a night-house over ground they cannot make. Still only one is tamed. What is safe is over Tolcus. I keep close to the outway. Here the heat reaches by day, the chill by night, this way is open to me, I go up, when I cannot bear it any longer.

His smell I can most distinguish, he lies closest, the least tamed, dangerous. Lying across the door and I step over him easily, as yet over him easily.

Tared

"Are you content, Ard, that Itsil does not know you?"

"Gradually she is coming to know us. Already she is making small sounds after Tlin."

"She grunts as do mutes. Perhaps that time to receive first speech is lost in her, and she will remain as Atwar, and never receive it."

"Sorud Twel learned the speech of Fu-en as an adult, and so did others."

"With effort, yes, but if we are to teach her we must catch her."

I could not understand my sister—had I been Ard, would I not passionately have drawn that daughter back inside the dark light of my love, so it was healed? But Ard was fearful for Tlin, I supposed, and afraid of Atwar—she was uncertain yet what he intended. And she watched Itsil as if she were a little frightened of her as well.

○

Itsil did not become any tamer. Only Tlin did she allow to touch her, besides Atwar.

He would himself have let us touch her.

I remember the plank, in the flood: Ask hoisted Tlin up beside Itsil and they lay across it, close together, kicking their skinny legs and grasping out after the fruit as it fell. And Atwar allowed Ask to steer the plank away from him among the stems.

Itsil did not look about for him—Atwar remained where he was. I suppose looking after her in his own way—but he let Ask swim with them some distance before he came—even then, he went out in the course, as they were over the point.

So did Itsil extend her infant-bond past Atwar to include her sister, but the rest of us she shied from: when Ask put his hand near her on the plank she drew back. She did not strike at it—that would have been to acknowledge him.

THE TAMING ○ 217
○

It was a great joy for me to see Itsil alive, and I gazed at her much and desired to hold and stroke her—until I could feel her tough-fragile body against me, I could not quite forget my dreams. Itsil dead at Atwar's throat! Now he did not wear the other doll, and the old dress he sometimes put around Itsil. His throat was broad and bare between the white-black strands of his hair, and his chest-hair black, and thick as furze. There Itsil nuzzled. She was, for all her fierceness in play, most obedient and passive with this strange mother-father, as he had become! His twelbreast—it was, over the muscle, swollen to a point, while the other was male and flat. Itsil did not fight with him, if his hand lay across her body, though she would go. She looked towards Tlin and would play, but she did not quarrel with him if, even in this passive way, she was prevented.

Whatever he wished of her she obeyed him in—yet not a look or word passed between them. Perhaps some look that we could not yet read passed between them.

○

One morning as the course broke he came toward us with Itsil on his shoulder, and set her down among us. And jumped out on the blocks and rode away.

At sunset he came back swimming, and silently she swam into his arms—he rolled over on his back and she floated against his belly and sucked at that breast.

Ard close to me said, "Ah, he is in pain from it—he is glad to come back to her!" She sounded almost satisfied.

○

In all those hours of days she was with us, Itsil had not allowed us to touch her. If we approached, she got up and went farther off. It was Tlin who persuaded her under ground, and there in her baby way did stroke her, and push her down to make her sleep. We gave Tlin the water-cloth, for she had often played at squeezing water into our mouths, and now we wondered at her deftness in giving Itsil water. But later Itsil crept around the walls till she reached the seep, and drank there after Atwar's fashion.

Some of the food we gave Tlin, she fed to Itsil, pushing it

into her mouth with her fingers. Itsil coughed and spat at the yeast.

"When she sleeps, Ard, do you go to them, and lie close to her and see if she will suck."

But though Tlin sucked lustily, Itsil would not, and when Ard made to embrace her she rolled away.

She had large eyes; because she was unnaturally thin they lay deep under her straight white brow, but very still and clear—like Tlin's they had the blue sclera of Lofot, their irises hardly more dark. She looked somberly about her in the deep room. She did not cry. Tlin brought her the doll, and laid it across her knees, and for a time this occupied her; she turned it listlessly, and we could see that Tlin was confused, that she had not flung it away to be fetched—at last Tlin herself snatched and flung it, and herself went after it and brought it back. Later, Itsil also did fling the doll, but without fierceness—perhaps with that kind of courteous obedience she gave Atwar—ah, I had a glimpse of her sadness, then! For we do act, to be as comfortable as we can.

In the World were we the small-ones who must obey, and we found ourselves persuaded in it, and were happy after a fashion, except Saska. I thought I saw in her throwing of the doll, and thus in how she was with Atwar, Saska's sadness.

Yet, Saska had hoped for great happiness in the Moon!

I would have said, "Ard, Ask, see how diligently Tlin strives, and loves her sister! we must make this a goodly family, we must gather in these threads as quickly as we can!"

For Saska's sake.

○

Often after that did Atwar absent himself, and left Itsil with us, and she slowly began to understand that he would return, and was less in despair, and began to let us approach her.

Ask tamed her first, in that he lay on the furze bed, where Tlin was used to play with him and be tossed, and laugh and tumble. As he lay still, Tlin brought Itsil to him, and began herself to climb about on him. Then Itsil climbed up too. But if he moved, she ran off into the shadows. Later she allowed him to stroke her, and he began to feed her also.

THE TAMING ◯ 219

Her face was with them more animated, and her mouth moved in trying to say words after Tlin. I thought she said *Mø* clearly, and she seemed to understand much of Ard's prattle.

◯

When Atwar came back he brought, the first time, supple furze that he had prepared, and after that rope-wick and tallow, and the other doll. When he went, he went swiftly, as if to prevent Ask from following him. Ask said, "I have an idea where he goes, and I am thinking to wait for him there."

But he did not go yet.

◯

Ah, Atwar was a strange house, and I could see no door, even a closed one, into his mind's rooms, however my thought ranged all about him! I had looked to Ask to interpret him, for Ask had imitated him and become like him, especially since he put on the same soft furze, and tied his hair as Atwar did, in two strands. The time he would not speak of Atwar was past—and for us all, that time when we did not know Atwar and expected much. We knew him no better than before, but our expectations were now more temperate.

Can I remember how we regarded him then? We had thought him tamed when he first allowed us to feed him, when he began to remain close to us. We learned that he was not.

Ard believed still that he took Itsil because of the blue cloth on her arm—because of the blue dolls and Ard's dress, left as if for him in the other grove. Yet were our drinking cloths also blue. And she and I still wore, in the heat, remnants of blue dress. I thought, perhaps he took Itsil because I held them out to him, when they were born. Had he forgotten so much of the World?

Why should he take one twin?

If he were crazed, as Ask said, he would do any thing. But he was not crazed; he had cared for her impeccably. She had lived, and that was much! when Tlin safe at Ard's breast had nearly died.

And now, was it his purpose to return her? would he stay

with us? He was well-tamed, surely. But I was not sure.

○

Once in the early morning Atwar got up and went out silently, and I ran after him up the passage, and saw him step out on the white course. I stood at the point. The sun was just rising, the air bitter. Tiny threads of yellow light pierced between the stems, and touched in dapples the near side of the stone. Away down the course Atwar stopped, and stood upright, his face turned back towards me, or the sun.

Who among us would follow Atwar?

○

Ard said, "Tared, will you be his bond?"

We were sitting close together in the house, sisters at sister-talk. It was yet too chill over ground to go up with the twins. Ask lay across the passage; they were with him, Itsil a little apart, motionless as she ever was when Atwar went from her. I had given them shards, and thrown down many at the seep pool. Ard chewed at one, and waited for me to speak.

"I have thought of it—no. For I do not know what he is. If we could know him—"

"Ask knows him better than we do, and does not like him."

"Yet Ask can make a night-house when he will, and wears Atwar's cloth."

"And loves him not a bit."

I burst out—"How ought we to love him, who took Itsil so cruelly? And how can we like or hate or love him, when he has no face and is ever silent? He strokes not Itsil."

"He holds her, and we may not."

"Tlin, she allows to stroke her—and Ask, but only as though she suffers it. She has forgotten her pleasure in it." Then I said, "Ard—when Atwar took her—was it his intent to take her only?"

"She wore the strip of blue cloth"—sullenly.

I asked her again. "There was blue dye among us nearly equally, Ard. And when I showed them him, when they were born, had he not two dolls? It is strange, that he would take but one twin, if he would take children from us. To separate them, that was most terrible."

"You speak as if he reasoned."

"I am trying to understand his mind. He was separated from his brother. Ard, if he meant you to follow—"

"Then he would not have hid her, or himself. We looked for them till we could not look any more. And Ask was a half year looking."

"Atwar did not, then—when he took Itsil from you—touch you, or make any sign?"

"Tared, you are stammering. No, he did not." She grinned. "The only sign he could make—if he made it, I saw it not. And how can he look lustily, when he has only an unlook to look with?"

But I thought of Atwar's body.

○

I was restless to think of that bonding I did not want, and of how we lived at present unfriends, not as a family or a city, though we were many and had each of us in some measure good will. Indeed, for all of us it could be said, "*To increase happiness was their desire.*" Why then did we fail in it, what was the fault?

We lived disparate, isolated, afraid. Who thrived of us here? Tlin, because she had her sister and her constant busy play? But how could she thrive, if all around her was uncertainty and despair? And her twin was no perfect companion, being still nearly mute, and scared and stiff in her ways. They had not the simple friendship of twins, which is never questioned, rising as it does out of perfect knowing. They had been separated too long; half a year is long in an infant life. They did not know each other.

We were a kind of shattered pattern, a pattern I seemed to see yet could not see, that would not fall into place. Across it did the light fall and join in different ways, and yet nowhere into a greater harmony. That light was gashed. Ard and Tlin, in the gashed light of their loss. Itsil returned yet not returned, unable or unwilling to enter it—uninvited! I and Ard, sisters, but we could not find our coherence, it was hidden under angry words, the unfinishment of our quarrel.

Atwar and Itsil—a tight bond it seemed, that would admit no other—beyond it they gave no love, or accepted any. I could not see that Itsil loved her twin. Itsil and Tlin, breaking their wills against each other—ah, they would find it out—did not many twins in the World, sharing one body, fight desperately before they found their own pace? The Sorud in the Tale, big, unweaned, unable to walk, staggering—that Twar did break his brother's arm in anger! yet later they found it out very well.

Atwar and Ask—this was also a braided thread for all its knots—both adult, both strong, perhaps enemies, perhaps brothers! They did range at the borders of our broken city—what was Ask's purpose if not to grow as great as Atwar, or greater? Did Ask acknowledge this, did Atwar?

And Ask alone, Ask Ur as he now demanded to be called—his thread ran between us—to divide us, or to bind us? Ask roving between the voices of the World and the stubborn silence of the Moon. What could he do except what he did, rove between us?

And we, without Ask? Now he appeared to me heavy, steady, a dense centre and his sisters the ones who doubtfully wandered. Whatever was happening to us, without Ask Ur we would never understand or be healed.

So hard did these thoughts, these snows of thoughts, press on me! and I was unable to order them. Was this as it would ever be with us? Atwar among us, but refusing to look or speak! The twins with Ard, yet without joy in milk-play and laughter, innocent, selfish joy!

And what of Saska's dream? Against its wide breathless light could I see how dark and small were the lamps of our minds, how confused and quarrelsome we were in all our doings, how confined! No more did the birds visit us, they had found wider fields. Would that we might build in the open, under the open sky! Where were those mansions, out where the great whiteness burned off in the morning, the laughing air, the good furze smoking? Where was Saska's city?

○

"Ask, what is it Atwar wants of us?"
"Perhaps nothing. Perhaps he is content."
"Yet he makes these journeys, he does not settle with us."
"He is used to moving about—I think he has ever roved in

THE TAMING ○ 223

the Moon."

We were at the farms. Despite the grove's shade the air was thick and wet, the furze already brown and the rill-water cooked away. I scooped out the yeast wearily.

"I am not content, I think of Saska's dream and feel in my body such sadness, such a yearning—we cannot remain as we are!"

"Much we have accomplished."

"Ah, in those things that let us live. Ask, you yourself are unhappy. What was his dream, if it was not to show us that we could live well?"

"We live as we must."

He dragged a bag of yeast aside, and tied it.

"Atwar determines how we live!" I said, "for we have ever been courteous to him, and allowed him any thing, in order to tame him—never have we stood against him and said, this or this we will not accept. Ah—we did desire—when he first appeared among us, at the fire over the culvert—Ask, do you not remember how glad we were? when he stayed by you then—remember your heart's joy!"

"I did not speak, I was frightened—" Ask said in a low voice. "No, I was not frightened. It was enough for me, then! That is how it was! Enough for me that he came near."

"Every small thing was a joy to us."

"Even that he turned out our slings. Ah, Atwar has with-great-condescension turned out our slings and spilt our harvest! What pleasure this gives us!" He laughed harshly.

"You are the most bitter among us, Ask Ur," I said. Yet you do wear his furze, and imitate him."

"I would become as he is, in my strength, because he thrives here."

He knelt forward, gathering the bags over his back. "Atwar lives in harmony with the Moon. If I can become as strong, and as knowledgeable—"

"What then? What are we to do?"

Ask did not answer. He set off ahead of me with the harvest into the choked grove.

○

To have talked thus with him, even this beginning of

talking with him, to hear that my discontent was perhaps nothing against his own! Ask Ur, adult brother. There was no ceremony for him when he became adult, no twin, no mirror held against his face, no blackening and beautifying of teeth. No short-bond awaiting him, for there were no women to take him into their body and love him lustily, here in the Moon. In the World, the Sanev surely became short-bonded, after we were gone—though Ard I knew would refuse to admit it. How their dull mothers had happily looked about, when their sons became adult, and emerged black-teethed from their room! But till we went away the Sanev were Ard's bond, secretly.

○

Dark light! light I could not see with these outward eyes! Patterns between us formed and dissolving! A tangle of threads to be tied, untied, unravelled, intricately woven! A heap of shards that, as they begin to run, cleave against each other, and change, and in the end become one shape, water against the ground!

○

That night, trembling, did I go straight to Atwar, and take Itsil away from his breast.

Why was I afraid? Often had he put her from him, gone swiftly away. She was among us going and coming as she would. Yet it seemed as I did this act that I was moving with the changes, that something between us would be changed!

So close to him I had never been, that my hands must touch his body in lifting her away.

He half-leaned, half-lay in the furze bed at the passage, and she lay along his belly with her mouth at his enlarged breast. He drowsed as he was used, and surely saw me come to him, his eyes open under his heavy brow. When I put my hands between Itsil's body and his belly he did not move, but Itsil startled, and her mouth clamped on his nipple, and her hands clutched in the hair of his chest. To lift her away was to pull him also towards me—yet I was quick and she released her hold, and his nipple slid out of her mouth with a slight sound.

Would he snatch her back? No, he did not, and I took her in against my furze, and carried her across to the seep.

She held herself rigid against me but did not struggle. I sat down with her there, and busied myself giving her water. Since she was taken, I had never held her. She spat at the cloth.

No, she would not have that water. She sat on my thighs because my arm strongly held her. Thinner than Tlin she was, sharp-boned. My heart beat against her nape. I put my mouth against the musty turf of her hair.

"Do not be afraid of us. Do not be afraid of us!"

I sat her between my knees, tightly so she could not run away, and began gently to wet and order her hair. It had never been combed.

"Stout little Itsil, do not be afraid."

As we sat at the seep I did not look back at Atwar, but I knew when he came; I suppose I smelled him. His arms reached down and he took Itsil. Ah, her fierce, tiny body immediately changed, went loose and passive at his touch.

So this game was begun as well as Ask's, among the small changes.

O

"Why do you take her, when she likes it not?"

"Ard, you might take her as well, if you would. Come, help me to order her hair."

Tlin would creep close to us also and try with her baby fingers to comb the mat of Itsil's hair. It was as a mound of winter grass, fine but very tough. Best it would have been to cut it away, I suppose, but to cut the hair of a child's head? Only children kept at Medical Book looked so, in the World, if the scholars must invade them to save them.

"There, a whole strand, and I have not hurt her."

"In perhaps two years it will be ordered," said Ard.

So did we sit together at the seep, and dress them and speak with them and comb their hair. But if Ard reached towards Itsil for any thing, or touched her, I felt the slightest tightening of her already tightened body against me—ah, she was wary of me, but of Ard even more wary! This pleased me and I was ashamed.

Yet it was I who brought Itsil into my arms to tame her,

and was this not some sign, that she was, towards me, a little more friends? Now also, though I held her, she answered and repeated Tlin's chatter, but to Tlin only, blurredly.

We made them fine clothes of Atwar's furze-cloth.

○

A little change came in the house, the fragrance of a change, because Ask and I had talked together, and from it other changes. Ask ate with the twins as he was used, and then took a lamp and left them, went over to Atwar who was crouched at the passage, and crouched also, directly before him.

"What is it Ask is doing?" Ard looked across anxiously.

"I think he will speak to Atwar, and make him speak if he can. He is sick of waiting."

We heard in that stillness Tlin's prattle near us where the sisters played, and Itsil's sometime answering. Tlin had a clear, plaintive voice. Itsil's was as if she spoke under water. None could understand her except Tlin. Or, Tlin invented a meaning. Yet did Itsil understand our speech. And she strove truly to speak with Tlin. Otherwise she was silent.

○

Some hours did Ask Ur remain before Atwar, the children coming and going around them. Then did I see Tlin take in their silence, just as she would walk towards each of us as we liked—near Atwar was she silent, and observed Ask carefully. And something in her face frightened me, a look passing off from Itsil, an unlook—and I thought, if Itsil was to learn speech from Tlin, might Tlin not as easily learn unspeech? She climbed on Ask and tried to turn his face, holding him by his ears with her two little hands. But Ask set her gently aside, and remained before Atwar.

Until then would I have said, "Atwar has permitted Ask Ur to sit close to him and look into his face." But in the pattern of changes it corresponded better to say: "Ask Ur has permitted Atwar to see him, and to speak to him if he desires."

○

If I took Itsil from him, I knew that soon he would come, and take her from me. His arms reached her over my head.

His hair knocked at my cheek. His unsmell fell over me—his dark light. Then Itsil slid from me up into his arms.

Once when I came for her (this was over ground, at the fire) she was wide awake, and clutched at him so fiercely—mouth, fingers, little fisted toes—that I could not lift her away.

"Itsil, come to me, do not be afraid. Come over to us, we will dress you in your furze."

Her face pressed and worried at his breast—I could hear her sucking angrily.

"Atwar," I said, "let her go."

Then his hands, that had been resting at his knees, moved to her body. But not to release her—it was my hands they touched, and took, and pushed away. He got up on his knees, put her over his shoulder, and went off towards the house.

○

He did not take her from us, only into the house. But I wept for his choice. I sat back on my heels and wept angrily.

Ask Ur called out, "Tared, do you go in after them!" His voice was sharp with authority.

"No, I will not."

His lip lifted. "Go, or I will go."

○

And later in the house, Ask Ur's adult voice at my ear, urgently: "Tared, is it seemly that such a mind—having no face and no speech—should be both father and mother to Itsil? I ought to be as fathers to her, I who speak aloud, and play with her and make her laugh and smile! Mother also she has—mothers, for you are Ard's twin—and she has a sister as well! When she grows tall, is she to become his bond, as Tasman was to the Sorud, who were first her protectors? As soon as Tasman became an adult she did run into their bed!"

○

Ah, most bitterly did I weep then, because I knew, this I did not want. And afterwards, over and over did I take Itsil from his breast and cared not so much how I took her, except that she be taken. Whenever she went to him and I could get her I took her, and he took her again—this, that he came, I began to await in anxious joy. Then did I touch those two arms a moment, when they reached down over my breasts to take her, and their springing hair grated across my bald palms as he lifted her. I began to love him.

Ah, it was not meant! but it was meant by my body, caring not whether the mind were careful and unsure! It was as if all my cells tightened and glowed. I wept often. It was not like that milk-play with the Sanev, that more than milk-play, when they did touch me and Ard in certain places, that secret pleasure. No, it was my whole body equally, even the inner skin of my nostrils, the very roots of my hair. It was more than me, it was the room also and the ordinary movements of the others around me, it was Itsil's bony limbs, the taste of fruit, the smooth white roots that twined in the passages, the great stems over ground, the World, the falling light, the brown water at flood that combed my naked skin. Ask Ur had said: *It was enough*, and now this was also enough—almost enough. It was Atwar, however he was, the rich dark of his light. Yet was I afraid.

O

Itsil and Atwar bonded! never would we then be a city, if he kept her; they would be speechless together—in those far days, if it should be so, would we perhaps remain a time, and speak words together, till we and our language and all our remembering faltered and fell away. If they and their children and children's children should inherit the forests of the Moon—naked, white-haired, a city of them, faceless, silent!

Ard

I cared not for Atwar, or for Itsil enough to make any courteous gesture towards him that would say, "Give me back my daughter." For she wanted me not. Even Ask who played with her, I could not see she loved, and Tared she suffered. Ah, she suffered Atwar also, I believed—for how could she love him, when he never stroked her, never laughed, never spoke to her with his mouth in words or with his face in kindness? She took that breast like a drinking-cloth that lies inert in a seep and no one has offered it.

Such a bulged, unseemly breast. It was no woman's breast either, for it stood low and small in the centre of his wide, flat pectoral—it was like a swelled-up bruise—that the other pectoral was level and proper, made it even more ugly to see.

When I suckled Tlin I held my breast in my hand and put the big nipple forward to her, and gladly felt her pull at it—she did ever squirm and laugh. Indeed, this one breast was at the time larger, for it had milk in it, but the difference between these breasts was not as with his!

Tared had said, once, "Do you put her to the twar breast again, Ard—if she can call milk out of the body of men, she can call it out of her mother's breast, where she has lain before." And my sister held Itsil over against me, beside Tlin. But Itsil refused.

Indeed I would have loved her, had she let me.

Yet was I glad when she spoke, when her mouth slowly rounded, with great concentration, to try out the simplest of sounds. And I went on again with my Tales, if the twins were with me and not Tared, and told them as I had done before about their fathers. Tlin repeated these stories happily, and called the Sanev *Fa* and said their names.

○

We went as far as the pool in the mornings, Tared leaving Itsil there when she climbed out into the farms. In those days was Atwar gone away early, and Itsil somewhat stiff and silent; yet given as long as the sweetest morning, which is a whole day, as it is counted in the World, she would play there comfortably enough with her sister.

Itsil had ordinary curiosity, though often she would not permit herself what she liked—if Tlin played with an interesting root, or a pretty stone, and offered it to her, Itsil must throw it aside, and she spent much time breaking the little piles, the dolls of dikes and houses, that Tlin raised by the stream.

Yet, Tlin made them for this purpose. I saw that if she would have something for herself, she kept it well away from her sister.

The running pool was very cold, and shallow, but Tlin got about in it willingly, to gather up what Itsil threw into it. I was glad to see her lay a stone, that Itsil had heaved in under the fall, carefully over on the other bank, and come back, her white hair streaming, and squat and watch Itsil expectantly; and Itsil did go after it, sometimes.

○

Here had I sat with them a year ago and thought, *So big they will be, that they can crawl up after Tared into the farms, and alas, I will not want to follow them.* And now they could not only roll and crawl about, but walk as well. And I wept, because it was not as I had foreseen: grown they were, and had I kept them both through all that time, it would have been the increase of happiness. I would have grown with them gradually, carelessly, perfectly as I did before. But only Tlin had I accompanied on that path; only she could I now recognize. Little Tsil was that memory, that black-haired babe who remained as she was, and was gone.

Tared would come down to us. She had not much pleasure of Itsil, either—ever it was she who went to Itsil and took her, and Itsil who allowed it.

○

Itsil did say *Fa*, though it sounded more like *Ba*, and for the names of Nevi and Nevar she said *Newi*, *Newar*. Sometimes Tlin, whose speech was very clear, said these unwords too. Tlin could call us all by name; indeed, she could say whatever she thought, and we all understood her. Itsil mouthed and mouthed as if she would—long and silently did she work at a new word, before she dared lend it any sound!

Then once at the fire she called Atwar *Newar*.

"Do not name him so! He is Atwar!" I shouted, and jumped to my feet.

Ask sprawling beside me said, "Ard, you throw earth into our eyes. Why are you angry? Itsil has called him that name for days. And so does Tlin—sometimes she says "Nevar," and that is about one of your Tales of Nevar-Nevi in the World, you can be sure. But Atwar has been Newar this last while, for them both. Have you not heard it, Tared? I have heard it. It is not such a bad name. Do not be so angry, it is a different name after all."

"You would have perhaps that Itsil calls Atwar *Fa* also? And Tlin hears it?"

"Ard, Ard, do not weep! he is as much *Fa* as she has."

○

Still did Tared bring Itsil away from Atwar whenever she could, and I saw how, if he took her again, Tared sought to keep him by her, leaning back into his belly when he reached over her, and holding his arms.

I said, when I had seen her do so, "Is this how you will tame him, Tared? Do you think he sees you, or does he think he is lifting up Itsil from among a pile of roots, or out of a yeast-pit? He does not love your smell."

Then I saw, for I watched, how she did clean herself, when she had been in the farms—she scoured herself in the course with a handful of furze, till she was scratched and shiny, and all her scars shone pink on her bald face. Her hair she combed the furze out of, too, and washed it of earth, though she bound it not, and it sprang wide and high around her head. I watched, and saw she ate no more yeast, only fruit, and this made me sure she loved him. Her face had a new open look, but at the corners of the eyes some pinching tenderness—I pitied her then, though I did not say it; and I stopped mocking her.

In this way, I said to myself, do I love the Sanev, and it is better for me, because they loved me and taught me to love them. They saw me very well!

Atwar sees her not, or any one. And it seems she cannot teach him, either, for he pushed her away in the passage, when our brother made her go after him, and walked across her where she sat crying in the rill.

Yet she will be his bond if she can.

And seeing her, I thought of that proverb: *For the snake in his season,/ is the whole World the lust of his eye.*

○

Atwar came in and, as was not usual for him, went directly to the seep and drank. Then he squatted back and raised his lip, and tilted his whole head back on his nape, towards the shadowy roof of the room. Then he scooped Itsil to him, and went over to the passage, and suckled her. Rank he smelled, of the heat over ground. He wore but the blue dress at his neck, and a short furze around his genitals—a pouch such as Ask now wore being newly adult and shy.

Ask said, "I will go to him again, as soon as Itsil sleeps."

"He stinks now more than he did," I said.

Tared was glad when I spoke so, and in pity perhaps I said more than I meant. There was in Atwar some restlessness— but I would not acknowledge it.

Tared said, "I will sit before him also, if he does not speak in these next hours. We must make some change." But Ask Ur would not let her.

"Take Itsil as soon as she sleeps; that is more useful," he said.

○

Ask had said, "Atwar is preparing, I am sure, to speak. Hour by hour I remained before him, and it seems now—he is like a strong wall that has a small crack, that is slowly extending. This is how it is, to look into his lightless eyes. There was at first some answer—my mind received it—but it was so slight I cannot even say, His eyes did narrow, or, His cheek did twitch. Then nothing. It was I who became as him, empty and still. So we swing a little to and fro like a slippery pool. I received his look and I suppose answered it."

"You do look as he looks, sometimes, Ask," I said. "You look stupid, sitting before him so. He has no words in his mouth."

"But now I think he has swung to me, a little—he will utter! It is as if he holds back by his will, what he must tell us—"

"He might not speak. He might strike you."

"I will strike him, if he does not speak to me soon." Ask took a big breath and blew the air out, loudly.

"The wall is in your own chest then as much as in his," I said.

"I feel it so. I am tired of this."

"You are very stubborn."

○

Atwar went over ground and rode the flood westward. He had not spoken.

"Ask Ur, go after him—you are strong enough to follow him now!"

Ask threw himself down. "I do not need to follow him yet. I know where he is going, and I will meet him coming back. Now, leave me, I am falling into sleep." He rolled over on his back in the furze and flung his arms above his head, and sighed aloud. "How is it he can stay waking so long? and swim so long without breathing? Even so, I am heavier than he, and lighter in the Moon's air. I am stronger."

Then he slept as he was, heavily, with his arms spread wide and his mouth open.

VII.
Atwar's Mansions

Ask Ur

It runs west from us now, this Tale; and Atwar's grove, that we called home, lies over the Moon's limb, to be sometimes visited. Then, if I come to the half-island at nightfall as the water is receding, I can still see the traces of our ruined pit: it is filled; the current has worn away the point and the polder and there is a smooth beach and no brim, there where white-haired Tlin and Itsil used to play. The mounds are smoothed almost flat, and the doors filled. Our two great trees are the same, and the World's light falling in its crescent over the half-island, at the edge of the shadow of the stone. The sound of the slow waters meeting is the same as it was.

Later, the trees brace themselves against the night. Crack! Crack! resounds far and near among the stems, and one tree or other suddenly shakes off its glassy shards so they drift down crackling.

If we did not come, no one would hear this. Yet does the hand of the night tighten around the stems; they do crack in the silence.

○

I stood at the height of Hadley, for I would see Chmedes if I could, before I set forth. I looked west over the wide, flooded plain. Tolcus was covered by dark waters, Stillus a flattened ragged ring of isles with an isle in its centre. At the limb I thought I could see Chmedes' brim—a low white blur against the stars. The last dirty cloths of rain swept outward past me, their hems not quite reaching the surface of the plain. Gray, they crossed the Half World hanging ever in his place in the high southwest. Out over the slope lay the stones in the World's light, and under far, invisible stones innumerable shadows lay on the water. A brilliant path of worldlight reached outward from the foot of the slope—it led toward Chmedes, if I would tread in it.

From there would Atwar come, for I had seen him before, and this time we would meet—not in any grove, where he would turn aside and hide and be silent, or in house among the others with their weave of pain, or in Four-island darkness under ground, and me still weak and small to resist him, but in the open, exactly—if I could reckon it—between our house and his mansions.

That would be Tolcus. I set off downhill, leaping.

○

We came towards each other over the *mare* in the crack of its tightening skin. It was as a marsh-lake, flooded still, but with the furze sticking out of the whitening surface in battered tufts and isles. I was dressed and gloved and went quickly forward—for I could still leap, though not as far—the shallow water burst in thin shards under my hands and feet, or held, and rocked; the air burned in my throat, but I was warm from my striving. I thought I could see him—then I saw him clear, coming ever nearer, walking low and dark with the white breaking of the water under his tread, so he walked in a little cloudy foam, but as yet far off, noiselessly.

We met over Tolcus. Its rim was an absence: the broken tufts ceasing around a clear, black lake, that rocked under us, but held. I was now tired, as I stepped forth on its shining surface—I would have rested if I could. Far over on the other side, Atwar stepped towards me.

Ask-Ur and Atwar—both adult, both twinless—perhaps it was as brothers we would meet. Yet was my knife in my pouch!

○

He was a little taller, but less light—and I knew this meant he was less strong.

We drew close—surely his body as well as mine did seek to align the rim, so that we met in the very centre. Ah, it bore us up, but its shard-cells clung as yet so precariously, that it swayed to the least step we took. When we were close together, and stood up on our feet, it did swing under us in a slow, gentle motion, and would not cease. I thought, if we struggle much, we may fall through it, to hold each other within the water—there could Atwar's lungs endure, twice as long as mine.

I put my two arms around him, clasping my hands together in the small of his back—I held his arms also against his body. So close is the face of the twin from birth to death, as his face was to mine! His lip lifted, his teeth clicked against mine as he turned his head, pulling himself away but I would not let him go.

So we wrestled over Tolcus, in the worldlight, the only sound the sharp intake of our breath, the skid of our gloved feet on the lake. We fell together and rolled, and the surface rose and dipped under us—I saw first his wild head against the swollen World, then I saw the World past his shoulder. When he lay under me its light glinted off the secret blackness of his eyes.

"You will speak to me," I said gasping, "You will tell me."

What was it he must tell me?

The surface held long though it groaned—then it split under him, and I sprang back: I was kneeling at a black lip and he was gone. I crept backwards. It rocked and oozed, rocked and swayed. After as long as I had ever counted for him and at some distance, he broke clear again, and climbed out—I crawled towards him, and he towards me—we fell down clasping each other—then I fell down into the breaking water but not holding him, and he was gone down. To come out was impossible, for every time I grasped at the water's lip it broke away.

Then Atwar was before me on his belly, and did pull me out carefully.

So we broke that surface and it laboured to heal itself, healing ever harder. And ever I returned to him, weeping I wrestled with him among the shards, and held him, for until he spoke I would not let him go.

○

Ask Ur has become as travellers in the World, who carry letters to and fro; travellers are not themselves at fault in what terrible thing the letters could say—they learn them and their mouths repeat them without shame. Ah, what is it Ask Ur must repeat of Atwar, or bring from him? He has no speech!

No men have milk in their breasts, yet he did increase his necessity, and the milk did spout! Even so will he speak, for he has again increased his necessity.

Tared

Ah, when Ask had made me follow Atwar into the house—I wanted to, I did not want to. I went down between the roots, our ordinary rounded walls, the pebbles in their familiar rills underfoot. I thought he would be crouched with Itsil near the entrance to our deepest room, as he was used. But as I came to the first bend in the passage, I nearly fell against him. He was coming up alone, lower than me on the slope so his face was level with mine.

His fingers went immediately to his throat and the tied dress, and I put my hands against my throat and dress also, I thought I was answering him. I saw that one woman-breast pushed out between his wrists, the black-red nipple on its mound, the thicket of hairs. I was in the heavy dark of his light, it was all around me.

His unlook—was it changed? I could see nothing in the shadows under his brow.

Then he put out one hand, and smote me—not hard, not hard but as if deliberate, careful. His face lifted past me towards the entrance and the light. I stepped back but I fell, and lay in the rill, and he stepped across me and went out.

Then I wept, angry at my brother for what he had made me do, angry and ashamed. There was Itsil looking upward in the passage, the mist of her hair and face-hair blurring her half away. Her lip lifted.

I touched not Atwar again, before we were bonded.

Ask Ur

Can I describe to you Chmedes so you will see it, the coolness, the sweetness, the great light? His mansions are not as anything we could have imagined, and if they were Outdead once, they were now so grown over with the Moon I could not have said, this they made, or, this was made by the water only.

And I came there living, he spoke, I had defeated him.

○

I knew he would attempt it, and so I released him—so long we had lain then, that his hair and garment were caught in the lake's clutch where it healed itself under him. My footglove too was caught where I lay. He coughed, and pain winced his face—for I had pressed on his ribs and torn their webs. A face that can tell pain can also tell joy.

Atwar spoke! His voice level and dark and very slow, without modulation, but surprisingly clear, as though each word whitened, making its own space around it. Words I would once have called crazed, but I had waited too long. I wanted to understand him!

His cheeks pulling back, his face close to me, his tongue tracing the edges of his lips. "This mouth, is angry. This word, and this word, and this word, broken teeth, in my mouth."

Again tracing his lips. He had many snows! His gaze sliding off, the unlook.

"You make, my eyes, uneasy."

He made no sign that I should reply, every word having the same texture, the same difficulty of utterance. Now he was so long silent I said, "Atwar, have we in some way harmed you?"

"How you move, your noise, harms me, you are many, it was better to cut you, into small pieces, one piece, one of you, one without words, in her mouth, one, was my intent."

"Do you mean, to make us separate from one another in your mind?"

THE TAMING ○ 241

"To see you, separately." He was saying, now even more slowly, "When you move, you are shards." Then he said, over and over, perhaps till he had numbered us, "That one, one, one, one, one. Separately."

He was also saying, with this word, his and Betwar's name, given by the namers, that was *Avskel*, which means the separate ones.

I stammered in my mind. How had we harmed him? So much I would ask him! "Would you have kept me with you then, at Four-island, if you could?"

"Kept. Kept." As if he pondered it. "That one, It-sil, was without words."

"But now she speaks! and now you come among us, and do not think we are so many—"

"I have quieted you."

Now he sat up, tearing his hair and garment free, and when he had done this, he stood and turned from me.

I said, "Why did you take the dolls?" but he called them another word, which is, *shard-shadow*, or *shadow*; he said "Such shadows, do not harm, my eyes."

"Are you blind?"

He did not know what I meant.

O

When he had spoken he took me through Tolcus; my footglove I left there, and there were pieces of his hair and furze caught in the surface, and the lake at the centre was all scuffed and scoured by our quarrel.

O

I have written already in book how his night-house kept him, with a taper, through the Moon's night. But in Chmedes is the lake so deep, and deeply so cold, it can never burn away, and deeper rises that heat the Moon keeps hidden, enough for us, so that here in caverns of shining green lie temperate lakes, long passages, round arching roofs as high as the canopy, shelf after shelf and stem after stem. With his taper he cuts them as he pleases, and they form as they please—here Itsil swam with him then, here was his furze-floor to greet her and the curve of the shelf where he slid with her into the water.

He burned a way in with his taper, so slow and far that we fell through a space of air into the water under us—it was within a great cave, lighted through that glassy roof by the Full World overhead. It led southwest all the way into Chmedes—we walked on a long shelf and swam between immense forests of glass, and I supported him; it became dark except for his taper, then light as we came through.

We played! And I taught him to laugh—perhaps it was that his ribs still hurt him so, and his face having broken had no way to mend itself; when he winced for his pain he could not but go on into grinning. I thought, He is very stiff in it, but they say he laughed much in the World.

He came into the Moon laughing.

O

Quickly we returned for the others, coming to them as the last water steamed from the course, in the growing heat of the day. We saw them from the far bank, a crowd, staring out of the south room; they had thrown out the stinking furze, and there they were all crowded together, and not underground despite the season.

What was wrong? The fire pit at the point was now a gaping hole, that widened outward into the course bed, and the other of the two trees leaned towards it strangely.

"The roof of the house fell in on us," shouted Ard, "in the night, and only because of Itsil did we live, for she would sleep near the passage, and so we lay there as well."

This she told speaking fast and eagerly with Tlin loudly chirping after her, and ended, "I would go with them under ground, I am sick, but we dare not—" and burst into tears.

"Ard, now Atwar will bring us where you will never be sick again."

"Have you seen his mansions?" they asked, and it seemed after my long absence their voices were indeed discordant, clamouring. Perhaps it was with Atwar's ears that I heard them.

"Be a little still—for I have assured him you are tamed, and when he hears your noise he will not believe me."

They were all very still then and Atwar came forward; and as we came I took the blue dress from his throat and soaked it in the course-bed, and gave it into his hands, and this water he did most courteously squeeze out over their upturned faces.

"Atwar is smiling!"

"No, that is from the pain in his ribs, for I hurt him. But he will smile, and speak—he spoke to me. He can laugh as well."

Tared, in tears, lifted toward him wan Itsil, and he wrapped her against him—he would suckle her, but she turned aside, and instead grasped after the dress. She and Itsil stuffed the wet cloth into their mouths, clambering over his knees, staring at each other gladly over its folds.

But the lowest room we could not enter; it was blocked from its door with dust and stone. That whole roof had tumbled in! So we crept as low as we could, and lay in among the roots, and brought furze for a bed, and after we had slept I told them, speaking soft and slow for Atwar's sake, about Chmedes, and everything that had happened.

○

"He speaks in such snows! It will be long, before we can understand each other. And he is harmed by our rapid speech and movement, that he calls shards. He would see us as dolls and birds, and hear the birds, (I have seen them!) and the unspeech of Itsil. It is, that we have been too many minds for him, each with all such great attention—"

That snow of shards—for his snows had great clarity, when we did consider them—it was as if he saw us, not as one blind, but as the newborn see, perhaps, before they begin to choose and set aside the numerous detail and flashing of the light, to cherish one part, and set aside another. To make separate, Atwar said. His unlook protected him from the sharding of the Moon, but we came in great movement, and clamour, and blue he had never seen close at hand! He must learn those turns gradually. He did not like to do so! Ah, how was it we looked to him in the Moon?

We were ourselves sickened, when we came here!

During all the whispering of this did Atwar sit among us, and beam, as do parents beam upon their children who think they are playing dangerously—such a look was his first

THE TAMING 245

human look, made by the forced smile of his pain.

Tared, before she slept, had drawn Itsil within her arm, and herself lay against Atwar's shoulder. And by chance did her head fall back listlessly in sleep, by chance did that beaming fall upon her face.

Ard whispered to me then, "Ask, she loves him."

"So she is happy now, I think. I think, also, you would do well to befriend Itsil, and let Tared care for that breast."

Ard grinned. "She does eye it most avidly!"

Tared

There is a grove past Chmedes, that stands to the lake's lip—great waters fall there in flood, they care not whether they come over in any channel or bed, but pour in a wide band through the stems, and then the fruit falls down also, more than we need. It is a high rim, but there are paths, and in the evening we lie there, and look eastward at low Hadley whitening at the end of the plain. Atwar has shown us how to fall, too, through that slow fall without harm. For we cannot leap any more as we once did, but we can fall as slow as the water, which is also a kind of soaring.

○

The Talus already climb, and leap, though they hardly walk. I am teaching them to walk upright, though they run on all fours with Ask Ur and their father—yet do Tlin and Itsil teach them also, and stand on their feet courteously, when they come with me into the farms.

Yes, I did for a second time salvage that yeast, for my shame—I had despite my scouring a little with me in my skin, when the house fell. And now we have our great farms past the grove.

There is a low lake in the morning, half under the trees, and near it the remnant of a pit-pool, and there did I bear the Talus with Atwar holding me, and his chattering teeth knocking against my cropped head. Our sons are black and strong, but I wonder, whether there is not some deficiency, for their hair becomes reddish as the hair of pregnant women in the World, who eat not at the bluffs. They were born in an eclipse, it is therefore, says Atwar.

There the birds play. Beautiful are his mansions and they go in as we do, when it is needful, but when the furze smokes and the mist rises, and again when the Moon's wind follows the flood with its rain, it is best over ground. And they are now many, a great flock, that throw themselves upward one-minded over Chmedes' rim, and turn and soar, as close and well-woven as a cloth of rain.

Atwar has shown us where they build, and how they bring in bits of furze to their beds, a myriad of small round dwellings over a ledge far in towards Tolcus—they can dig into that hardwater as into soil; but we have not shown these to the Talus, in case they should disturb them. Frail, frail are these small birds born, in a frailest case of light—then later they emerge—it is not good if they fall, before they are strong enough to fly.

And we are also many! Tlin and Itsil count us often enough, but not so it corresponds, for they count ever their *Fa* as well, as Ard teaches them: "With Nevi and Nevar, we are in the Moon," they say, and count the names off on the Talus toes, so Tlas and Talal must believe their toes have names as well.

○

The Selen grow. Ah, when I see them leaping though the slow brown foam, their white hair streaming upward, lost in it, their down-white bodies, I think these two are the true moon-children!

But the Talus with their tight curls—their faces are perfectly Lofot. And they are fearless—who knows whether, in their sturdy adulthood, in the days of conversation, they will not go as ambassadors into the World and swim on Lofot shores?

I see not any likeness in them to the ways of my brothers, when they were children. Perhaps because the Talus are my sons, and so unlike any other! But sometimes watching Itsil and Tlin I am remembering the sister-light around us, me and Ard, the same colour—

It is similar, as it must be for all twins born apart, be they female or male. But Itsil for all her imperious ways is not Tared in the World, nor is Itlin Ard. Tlin loves Itsil more than Ard loved me! for I was in the catch of the scholars, to become that rigid doll they were making of me. And I was harsh with Ard, who resisted them, and would not learn, and kept intact her stubborn being—ah, she was ready to receive the Sanev body, to love them!

I have changed much.

○

Saska would have loved these Selen, growing up in his city. Their generation is the visible sign of his prophesy: "It is all wiped clean!" Itsil he would have loved: she has a look of him sometimes, a downlook, a sadness. Because of what happened to her, perhaps she is kept for him in the Moon, the sign of the City that he prophecied.

And she goes sometimes away—I have seen her across the far caves, she steps out on a platform, and kneels combing her fingers through her wet hair. It is greenish when it is wet, cave-green is the hair of Ard's daughters.

And in the grove, she walks in the early morning of the day from stem to stem, as white as a stem, touching the roots as she goes, with the level strings of sunight banding the shadowy trees with light, as her body is combed and banded by the white down.

Ah, there is Tlin, following. Tlin does not scorn her sister, as Ard scorned me in the World. She delights in Itsil, whatever Itsil gives or withdraws!

Far over the cliffs I see their pale bodies, their hair like the corona of the occluded sun, transparent against the light. Now they are out on Chmedes: they slide, fall slowly to their knees, crouching and gliding. They stand; now Itsil walks a little farther on and stands, and Tlin stays where she is, desolate. She will wait till her sister turns.

Now the red-smoke is rising around Chmedes. I can hear, as across water, across the slick of the steaming lake, their clear faint voices, their laughter.

○

I think it will be that Tlin becomes our brother's bond. There was a slight path in my mind—I walked not on it, yet it was there—that both twins would go to him, as they became adult, as do twins in the World. Yet I see in Itsil's ways that she does not fear to be alone. Tlin's despair will turn her to him, and if this came about, it would not break Itsil's heart.

Ah, these paths are but play in my mind! Whose children are contracted to love the ones their parents delight in? Yet this is a small city. I cannot prevent myself, as I go about the farms, from looking down these many paths, and they are but soft snows, melting and re-forming.

And we are not closed by the ordinary ways of the World!

○

So the paths go out, glide and cross into one another unknowing. They are not as Ard's one path, for she walks forward resolutely, towards Nevi-Nevar, Sons of Snow. Would that it corresponded! would that their heart even half so well remembers! Would that they are not as untouchable as their name!

○

The Selen walk gracefully, and with their perfect legs it is easier so. Soon they will be the tallest among us, though they are yet children. Even Itsil has nearly ceased to walk like Atwar if she goes to him.

Ah, she has long forgot how he suckled her. She likes not to be stroked by any of us; yet there is between them a firm love and courtesy—if it were not so I would be jealous, perhaps!

As for his milkbreast, it has shrunk again into a man's despite my ardour. For this is still my secret delight, when we lie together in love, to part the pelt of his breast and make that nipple spring into hardness between my teeth, or at the click of my tongue!

So in the root-room did I find it, when they left us at our bonding, tight and painful and as my mouth touched, did my legs loosen across his body—he lay back, I was his house and well—I enclosed him. It does not correspond, as they maintain in the World, that the uncut can have no ease in entering the secret house of women! and in his slippery dress of childskin have I found more play than ever children find, more adult pleasures! Therefore have we whispered, as we roll the Talus in milkplay over our laps and laugh at their foolish baby ways: them will we never cut, or any other male children born in the Moon!

Ard

Not befriend—for I dreamed—as clear any dream of Tared's when she wakened terrified and would not tell. Clearer—for it came not when I slept, but in another kind of waking.

○

Not at first did the new-bonded come to Chmedes. So it was Ask Ur who showed us, in pride, the way to Atwar's mansions. And what he said, that I should befriend Itsil, came to pass.

○

First, when Itsil was taken, I housed great grief, but could find no finishing—ah, then I made that wall in my mind. I think it was her death I made, for I could not bear day after day that unfinishment.

But now there came to me, when we were over Tolcus and going forward, and I sat down to rest, a sudden clearing within me, that there was space for this dream, this journey! And my grief opened in me, as if I were again in the house, as if again, in this very moment, Atwar appeared and snatched her from me.

Ah, that wall I made—and I need not have—perhaps then, for I suffered great pain. But Itsil did not die, it did not correspond. Only ungood will come from the mind that refuses to correspond with what is!

Itsil suffered also then, and I would not think it or countenance it. She suffered as much as me—so much, that it was easier for my body to cruelly think her dead, than to be helpless to find her.

○

Ask Ur and Tared went before me with the twins over bright Tolcus but I stayed and dreamed, and in that dream did I stand in the old house, and Atwar took Itsil—and I swiftly followed him through the grove.

THE TAMING ◯ 251

And though I could not prevent him, or speak, I entered close after him into a place very like this place—but smaller, for Atwar's mansions I had not yet seen.

And when Itsil wept there, and knocked her head at his breast, I came close, I saw, and did weep greatly, and touch her and comfort her.

And I did touch that breast and encourage him, till it grew big, and I did not think it ugly more, but beautiful because there was milk in it.

And dreaming I watched her grow—quick it went past me, how she wept, and grew too tired to weep, and became white haired, and grew long, sucked and throve. Ah, that wall was a mind's-wall only. They do appear to us absolute and they are as wind. It is gone.

I got up, I was on Tolcus, I ceased squinting, I leaped after the others through the great light. I came to them, and my living daughter.

◯

Thus was Itsil unlost, and from that time we are healed and ordinary. This does not correspond, to say I befriended her. I recognized her.

◯

Now will the Sanev come!

Ask Ur says that when they come, they will leap as we did, and swim the air easily. But we who are used, were we to return to the World, would be crippled even worse than before, and carried from house to house, and so would our children. The World is not ours, it has become strange to us. And the Moon—till they come, am I even here a stranger. Only I will understand, when they sicken; I will comfort them, I will take them under Chmedes and into the good dwelling of my body. Impatiently do I wait!

Therefore I would say, Nevi-Nevar, come to us, leaping over the sward, even so, come quickly!

Tared

We came also at last to his mansions, but even in Four-island house we lay, our light kept us in joy. That worldshape—we swept it—it is an accurate doll of the Moon—this side which is seen from the World. Now Ask Ur writes on it, and he has learned it well.

○

Ard felt my belly when we came, and talked much—more than I needed—and told me how I would bear. Yet it was pleasant with her busy around me, to be the one who was given water, who waited for it and was given!

And Ask Ur began to rove much with Atwar. They laugh, they care not about the climate, they know how to wrestle with it. Their skin shines when they come in, blacker than black, but Atwar's hair grows more gray strands—I braid it in patterns across his head.

They have made great fires, greater than we had dreamed, when we conspired to make a fire on Hadley in those days. It was a careful undertaking, prepared over many days—ah, that was a great joy to Ard, when we stared with the children across the *mare* and first saw Hadley burn and all his hills!

Red, red light against the black sky! Then they burned the high islands two and two, to tell the generations. Soon must Atwar find two more isles to burn, till the furze is grown. But it has only good of the fire, and returns more thick and red than ever.

The sward they have visited, and there attempted to enter it, and the Outdead houses, but could not, even by digging deep into the ground. They saw the first-house tree we had burned hanging blackened as it did, but from higher on its stem there extended small roots downward, like white hair, and even Atwar is convinced that it lives, that these will eventually enter the earth. But of his other, inadvertant fires he will not speak, except to say he was ashamed. In the Sea of Vapours nothing lives now—that roof could not mend.

They were gone for four-or-eight days. They burned the furze around about the first grove to the width of a course, running and igniting it as the Moon hardened, so the fire would be contained. Thus they have said to the Watch, "You see us preparing for you." And this we are sure was seen in the World!

Atwar afterwards cleared the soil by dragging a plank, so it is marked in long lines outward as around his smaller fires. Then he and Ask Ur made a trench and dug furze deep into it, to burn a whole Moon's night, a thin circle of fire, visible from the World.

○

Then the World did answer us, not only from Fu-en, but also from Lofot, and from the South—and very lately, there have been fires across the sky, from limb to limb across the very Moon. A kind of darkened roof Ask Ur has made, to look closely at the World. He says that when such pricking occurs in the South, we must watch the sky as soon as three days later, as they are counted in the World.

And he has made much book, diligently. The children bring him leaf and prepare it; he has already taught the Selen to read. As for the Tales, we sing and sing them, and some are foolish, and some correspond. Atwar listens, he is courteous.

○

"Atwar, do you remember Betwar your brother?"

"In your smell I remembered him, and in Ask Ur's face."

"He is not like Ask Ur. Perhaps, if those fires are wise, you will see him again."

"These Sanev will push to be the first."

"Yet I think it will be the south-folk, for it is their pricking fires. In Fu-en, who is left who is wise?"

○

Atwar told us that Crisium was once seeded and that it is now closed off and dead. He does not know what happened there, but that was very long ago. He told us how, when he came, he had gone into the Outdead houses at the Sward. Chmedes was once like them, he said. Indeed, shadowy behind the smooth green walls, we can discern what might be Outdead shapes. Atwar does not want Ask Ur to burn them free.

"We know so little, Atwar! I am glad, there will be soon that conversation between the two worlds."

"On that day, I will hide," he said.

○

He has taught us the unlook, and we are I know more quiet than any family or city in the World. In those hours we turn back into our bodies, and our eyes open to receive the scape around us. Then can we see the flush of the flower creep over the furze, though it is so slow, and the gathering roll of the mists from hour to hour. We can see the World's air curling on the blue coasts, distant and yet very clear—Ard also, if she will look at it. The World's dawn can we see also, moving across his face, and follow the nudging sun and the steady slide of the stars. Ah, so did the downy Talus receive the unnamed light as soon as they were born, without learning; the children see so, they will not forget.

It is hard for us to stay in it, as Atwar can, for the mind leaps forward saying *This I recognize*! or *This I will name with a name*! yet in Atwar's unlook does the Moon rest as it is ever nameless; and so I have learned to turn my face to him also and receive him.

○

The End

Appendix

A note on the translation

The language *Riksprok* as spoken in the World has no word for "cold", "ice" or "snow", except the obsolete *Nev*, found in some ancient texts. Sorud Twel had explained it to the child Tasman as "congealed water" (*Moonfall*, p.77) but in modern speech it had come to mean a vivid verbal image. The children, coming from a climate where cool weather was rare and considered pleasant, called the extreme cold they experienced in the lunar night *Svalsval* and *Felsval* which (translated literally as "very cool" and "wrongly cool"); the sensation on their skin they called *Svalbrand* or "cool burning". The root *Sval-* occurs also in a word for frost (*Hevitsval*); ice they called *Hardwatar*. In translating their texts, I have used the literal terms at the beginning, when they must have been strongly imaged—later they would certainly be used straightforwardly and I have translated them more simply as, "chill", "whiteness", and "hardwater." *Hardwatar-raft* (floe) I have translated as "block", occasionally "raft". They called the melting of ice at first *in Hemwend watarlik Water* ("the return of water into its likeness"), later *Watarwend*, although the verb *smalt* (melt) was a more natural choice—its meaning however is confined to melting by heat (for example, the oozing of oil from burning leaves). Extreme lunar heat they called *Hedhedhed*, in the usual repetitive superlative.

"Atwar's mansions": The word for house or dwelling is *Wo*, which also means "place". When the children referred to the superior dwellings they believed Atwar to inhabit, they used the term *Glaywo*, literally, "houses of joy". I have translated this as "mansions" because it had that Biblical flavour of yearning and opulence. They called his grove *Atwarwo*—translated here as "domain."

Firs, translated "furze": the oxygen-generating lichen of the lunar barrens. A few more word-combinations, singular to the Moon, are listed below.

For the Tales referred to in *The Taming*, and for further

information about *Riksprok* and a dictionary, see the Appendix to *The Children of Atwar*.

For the Story of Tasman, and her sons Atwar and Betwar's childhoods, see *Moonfall*.

For the story of Betwar and his children Saska, Ask, Ard and Tared in the World, see *The Children of Atwar*.

○

cave: *Stenwo, Hardwatarwo*
cut into separate pieces: *hug in Skel*
"learn the turns": *ler Wendos*
lichen: (colloq.) *Glaygras* ("fields of joy")
mist: *Dundamp* (fog: *Dundundamp*)
Moon's (light) rain: *Stofmatar*
separately: *avskelik*
shard: *Tind, Watartind*
shelf, stair: *Fladpyt*
small of the back: *Inblindsid*
smoke (of lichen): *rotskoor*
"smoke and flower" (become bright and active): *skoor u fro*
waning Earth: *Twelwerd*
waxing Earth: *Twarwerd*

Poet and artist Heather Spears has won the Governor-General's Award once and the Pat Lowther Award twice. A Canadian living in Copenhagen, Denmark, she travels widely in Europe, Canada and the middle East, drawing, giving readings, teaching and studying. A graduate of the Vancouver School of Art, the University of British Columbia, and Central and St. Martin's School of Art (London, England), she has been the recipient of many other major awards including the Bronfmann Award, and Macmillan Awards for both writing and painting. Her book of poetry, *Human Acts,* won first prize in the 1991 CBC Literary Contest. Her writing and drawings have appeared in venues as diverse as *Canadian Forum*, *Medical Post* and *The Manchester Guardian*, and her work with children in hospitals and war zones has touched hearts in many countries.

other Tesseract books by
Heather Spears

...if all the normal people share one body with a twin...if you were the only one-headed freak in a world of these two-headed people...if the Moon were falling into the Earth and only a mutant could fit into the spaceships of the ancient Outdead who were, like you, mono-cephalic... what would your fate and the fate of your children be...?

Moonfall
ISBN 0-88878-306-X
$6.95 (mass market paperback)

In *Moonfall*, Tasman is born, the only one-headed person in a future Denmark where humanity has evolved into a race of tall, two-headed conjoined Twins. Only Tasman can fit into the ships of the high-tech ancestral—one-headed—Outdead. But finally it is Tasman's son Atwar who must save the Earth from the falling Moon, while his twin Betwar is left behind.

The Children of Atwar
ISBN 0-88878-335-3
$7.95 (mass market paperback)

The Children of Atwar tells of the third generation of separate Twins, Saska and Ask, Ard and Tared, and their cruelly-warped childhoods, as their bodies are deformed and their psyches are trained, in preparation to follow Atwar to the Moon in the ancient shuttlecraft.

Order from: Tesseract Books, 214-21 10405 Jasper Avenue, Edmonton, Alberta, Canada T5J 3S2. Send cheque or money order (US customers pay in US funds, Canadians add 7%GST) Include name, address, postal code/zip code, telephone number. Add $3 postage per book. Buy a subscription to Tesseract Books and we'll ship and invoice all new titles hot off the presses at 30% off (subscribers can also order backlist titles at 30% off) Write for details and our catalogue. (*Turn the page for more great Tesseract titles...*)

if you enjoyed this book...
try these other Tesseract Books:

Blue Apes
by Phyllis Gotlieb
ISBN: 1-895836-13-1 (pb) 1-895836-14-X (hc)
Price: $8.95 (pb) $21.95 (collectors' edition hardcover)
A long-awaited collection of the short stories of SF great Phyllis Gotlieb. From "Blue Apes", a story of discovery, loss, and betrayal on a distant planet, to "Sunday's Child", an account of an alien born to human colonists, Gotlieb explores issues and passions that are deeply human, even when her characters are not. Gotlieb brings a uniquely Canadian viewpoint to the American-style SF tradition.

Jackal Bird
byMichael Barley
ISBN: 1-895836-07-7 (pb) 1-895836-11-5 (hc)
Price: $8.95 (pb) $21.95 (collectors' edition hardcover)
The children of the colony world Isurus play a complex and dangerous game -- but their childhood games are good preparation for adult life in a climate of revolution and political/cultural upheaval. Intrigue, conflict, intricate manoeuvring are the stuff of life to the colonists on this strict, rigidly controlled, almost uninhabitable planet. *"A stunning debut, full of psychological as well as technological insights."* – *Douglas Barbour*

ON SPEC: the first five years
ISBN: 1-895836-08-5 (pb) 1-895836-12-3 (hc)
Price: $7.95 (pb) $21.95 (collectors' edition hardcover)
The best short fiction from the first five years of the Aurora-Award-winning magazine of Canadian speculative fiction. Includes the Aurora-winning short story "Muffin Explains Teleology to the World at Large" and many others. Edited by the ON SPEC Editorial Collective.

Mail-order information on previous page. Stores: Tesseract Books are distributed in Canada by H.B.Fenn &Co.: ph. 1-800-267-FENN.